THE GIFT

ALSO BY SCOTT TERRY

Cowboys, Armageddon, and The Truth

The Gift

the Gift

Scott Terry

 Torchflame Books

Vista, CA

ISBN: 978-1-61153-591-4 (paperback)

ISBN: 978-1-61153-592-1 (ebook)

ISBN: 978-1-61153-650-8 (large print)

Library of Congress Control Number: 2024922002

The Gift is published by: Torchflame Books, an imprint of Top Reads Publishing, LLC, 1035 E. Vista Way, Suite 205, Vista, CA 92084, USA

Cover Illustration: Ben Baldwin

Interior layout: Jori Hanna

The publisher is not responsible for websites or social media accounts (or their content) that are not owned by the publisher.

The Gift is a work of fiction. While much of this story matches the real experiences of people who struggled with religion or sexuality, the people/places/events in this story are entirely fictional.

THE FIVE POINTS
NEIGHBORHOOD, DENVER,
COLORADO. SEPTEMBER 13, 1958

A MAN COULD BE WHITE IN FIVE POINTS. FEW WERE. At the slow corner where Broadway comes out of its narrow bend from the other side of the railroad tracks and crosses over Blake Street, a person could sit alone in the dim light of any room in a certain red-brick apartment building, on any floor, maybe in hopes for a cease-fire of solitude, minding one's own business over the outdoor clamor of other people's struggles—which could tell you much, or tell you nothing.

When a drunk man staggers out the first floor to Blake, slobbering in pursuit of an unknown party and shrieking, "You crazy muthafucker!" one doesn't really need to know why that man is chasing another. One only needs to know that the person being chased is almost certainly a muthafucker. When Mr. Herkelrath's boots pound each wooden stair tread late at night in a quick succession of thuds to the outdoor prowl of urban darkness—one, two, three, four, five—as Mrs. Herkelrath leans out the front window of Apartment 202 and wails, "I hate you, you goddamn sonofabitch!" one doesn't really need to know the precise facts for why she hates him so. It is sufficient to only know that he is a goddamn sonofabitch.

In her bedroom on the third floor, Pansy Blackwell sorted books alphabetically by title, all spines pressed into a flat façade of neatness. The windows on that side of the building had been bricked shut. Unwanted details of other people's drama often slipped under Pansy's closed door, infecting her dark sanctuary like dirty smoke from the coal fires that gave comfort to some but polluted the homes of others. A White girl, tall and heavy-bosomed over a thick torso with the square facial features of her father, Pansy found refuge in books and clothing, which, unprompted, she repetitively folded and unfolded, stacked and hung, obsessing over imagined untidiness that no one had ever accused her of.

That morning, a Saturday and well after the breakfast hour, Pansy was coaxed to join her mother, Loretta, in the front room.

Loretta pushed hair back from Pansy's temples—thick and unbrushed as Pansy had yet to wash for the morning. Hair like her mother, like her grandmother. Soft to the touch, nearly the hue of dark walnut with a very gentle ripple.

"Father O'Shea will be coming from St. Bartholomew's today," Loretta said.

"Why?" Pansy asked.

"He has a gift for you," Loretta answered.

"A gift? From a priest?"

Loretta pulled her daughter into a soft embrace. "They made room for you at St. Bartholomew's. They gonna put you in the school, there."

Pansy gasped.

"On Monday. Fer free," Loretta added.

"My birthday!"

"Yes, it is. They'll feed you lunch," Loretta added.

"Lunch? What kind of lunch?" Pansy wanted to know.

"Oh, what a silly question. I don't know what kinda lunch." Loretta paused, then said, "It's the same food the sisters eat, more'n likely. They ain't no reason to cook separate lunches. You'll find out, on Monday. Maybe they'll do sumpin' special fer you at lunch. Fer yer birthday."

The short Irish priest from St. Bartholomew's, not yet thirty, cleanly shaven, pale but relatively handsome to some tastes, knocked twice. Loretta knew who stood opposite her door before she rose to answer. Firstly, because she had requested that the father might visit, but secondly, because she had never before invited anyone to knock there. Requests for social visits didn't happen in that building, except on the second floor, where men paid visits to Rosie Paulette, who allowed men to fondle her breasts for money.

But the priest had arrived, so Loretta rose to perform a ritual of graciousness, intending to invite Father O'Shea to sit at her table where she wished to offer him tea. She wiped both hands sideways across her dress and cracked the door halfway to her waist.

Her husband, Lick, wasn't home, she told him, but Father O'Shea did not feel he needed to know this. He grasped Loretta's hand. His thumb stroked the web of flesh between her thumb and forefinger—an odd habit people had spoken of.

"'Tis perfectly fine," he replied. His eyes rolled upwards with an exaggerated air of kindness, as if God himself was unconcerned by this detail. It really did please her to have this priest come all the way to her home, she said, and he believed her, he said, because it wasn't common for him to make house calls. The stench of boiled cabbage hung in the air from the previous night's dinner. Loretta apologized for not offering him tea, then allowed him inside. Her jaw tensed; her eyes darted sideways in both directions. She hesitated before stating simply, "As you can see."

Plaster walls, unpainted, were cracked and crumbled, pine lath exposed where previous tenants had been derelict. The priest looked to Pansy, who was seated at the table. Two chairs were strewn away. He took it upon himself to gather one and bring it near so they might embark on the conversation he had traveled for. There had once been a fourth chair, but Lick had sold it to a neighboring tenant for a dollar when he came to the conclusion that a family of three would never have need to seat four. At one time, in a moment of whimsy, Loretta had torn three pages from the 1952 Union Pacific calendar and tacked them to her front wall, and just recently had added a printed platitude from the Catholics, reminding parishioners to remain loyal to Christ.

Pansy stayed quiet. Loretta stumbled through a few sentences of inconsequential things. The weather was beautiful for a walk from St. Bartholomew's, yes? Yes, it was certainly a fine morning for a walk, he acknowledged. There's a big storm coming, he mentioned. Yes, that's what they say, Loretta replied. She joined him at the table, sitting near. Had he moved to Denver directly from Ireland, she asked. Yes, he certainly had. The church had sent him here from Ireland, and yes, Denver was certainly very different, nothing like Ireland at all.

"We're s'posed to see some snow soon," Loretta repeated.

"Yes, it's a little early for snow, isn't it? Which brings us to ta matter at hand, which is a discussion of yer daughter . . . 'tis ta reason I have come." He turned and addressed Pansy. "You've been boptized, yes?"

"Oh yes, of course," Loretta responded hastily—and a lie.

"You've learned the rosary?" he asked.

Pansy looked to her mother.

"No, she hasn't," Loretta replied. Pansy did not yet know the rosary, nor did she spend time in prayer.

"Ta rosary is important," Father O'Shea stated. "Ta rosary is vital to participatin' in ta life o' Mary and finding ta way ta Christ." He reached a thin hand, soft from a life of religious devotion, to Loretta's thigh—resting it there in what she felt to be intimacy. "We are reminded tr'out sacred Scripture t'at God our Father is lovin' and merciful. Glory to ta Father, and to ta Son, and to ta Holy Spirit. Ahmen."

Loretta rose and strode to the bricked-off windowsill, then lifted a porcelain figurine from the makeshift altar. "These were my momma's. She's dead now, sumpin' like fifteen years ago. When I was a little girl, I called 'em God dolls. My momma said that was okay." She returned to the table and handed it to the priest. "This un was 'er favorite. I don't know why."

His lips parted in what may have been humor. "Do you know t'eir names?" he asked.

Loretta shook her head. "Oh, no, I don't know no names. Maybe she once told me, but I surely don't remember."

"T'is one may be St. Cat'rine. Her feast day is celebrated on September 15t', which is ta day she died."

"September 15th! That's Pansy's birthday! On Monday!" Loretta's hands flew to her cheeks. "Oh, my! Well, ain't that just sumpin'?"

"St. Cat'rine devoted her life to caring for ta poor. She converted her husband ta God as well, I might add."

"Well, that is just sumpin'." Loretta leaned over and retrieved the God doll from where he had set it. "She cared fer the poor. Maybe that's why my momma chose her. As her favorite."

A flicker of superiority illuminated the priest's face. He crossed one leg over the other. "Perhaps St. Cat'rine chose yer mother. All t'ese saints who came before you are part of yer family. She won't leave you if ye're fait'ful to ta Church."

Loretta nodded. "My momma was faithful. St. Nicholas Church, until it got sold to the Baptists." She looked to him in the manner of sharing secrets. "My momma said there wasn't no way in hell she was a turnin' Baptist."

The priest drummed his fingers on the table. "Well," he said casually, "ta get back to ta topic at hand, by ta generosity of ta church, we do have room for Pansy at St. Bart'olomew's. It's a gift, from ta church." He nodded at the package he had brought with him, now lying on the table. "Ta uniform." He pushed it across to Pansy. "I believe it should fit. You will pay for ta uniform, of course."

"Pay fer the uniform? How much?" Loretta asked.

"Ten dollars," he said matter-of-factly.

"Ten dollars?" Loretta slumped hard against the back of her chair. "Father, we ain't got no ten dollars fer nothin'."

"Should I speak ta yer husband?"

"Oh, no! Lick is not a man of God. He's a man of lust. He's bound for hell as soon as the devil takes him, that's what he is." She twisted her hands in frustration, then tucked them tightly into her lap.

"My child, we don't determine who God sends ta hell."

"He don't pray," Loretta whined.

"Then pray for 'im. God will hear yer prayers. St. Cat'rine helped 'er husband ta God. Perhaps you will do ta same for Lick. You were married by ta Church, yes?" he asked.

"In the back room of Spanky's Bar in Lynch, Kentucky, before we gave up on coal and moved out here. To Denver." Lost in her own reflections for a short moment, sobered by remembrances of that distant day, Loretta looked out to Blake Street. "I don't know if thangs are really any better here." She turned back to the priest, her eyes darkened by a cloud of loneliness. "Father

McDonnell came all the way from St. Stephens to marry us. He was a good man to come all that way, but Lick only did it 'cause I told him he had to. To make Momma happy." She again paused, then cast a vacant look at the God doll in her lap, slowly stroking her thumb over its garment. "It was the last time Lick ever made anyone happy."

The priest had returned to silence.

"The floors were sticky. In the bar. The whole place stank o' spilled beer, even in back."

Father nodded.

"Father McDonnell only came 'cause the weddin' wasn't in the bar, up front. It was in back, in the room that wasn't a bar." Loretta paused in memory—her lips tightened. "There wasn't no other choice. We couldn't afford the church."

"So, you weren't married in ta Church," he stated.

"No. But my husband . . . Lick . . . " her words trailed off, a few soft shakes of her head. "I don't know what to do with him, Father," she lamented. Consoled by the warmth of his manner, she felt comfort, as if he poured divine salve over despair and longing.

"I see. Well, we mustn't forget God," he murmured, then leaned close. Father O'Shea was a disobedient priest in that way, straying from the rigid practices of Catholicism.

He eyed her makeshift altar at the near wall, three wax stubs blackened by fire. "Ton't burn yer buildin' wit' offerins to ta saints," he warned. "You could light ta buildin' on fire."

Loretta's gaze turned dark. "That's what Lick says. He don't believe in saints, but he's durned sure afraid o' fires. That's kinda funny, ain't it, given where . . . oh, I'm sorry. Please forgive me, Father."

Loretta laid the skirt flat in her lap, running her hand over its pleats. The hemline would fall modestly below the crook of Pansy's knee, denying accusations of a girl being sexually flagrant. An extra-large, short-sleeved blouse—not crisp but rinsed and wrinkled—previously owned long enough by other Catholic girls to have been aged thin but bleached white enough so the wrinkles could be overlooked.

She leaned to Pansy, her thin line of lip held nearly closed to soften the ugliness of neglected teeth, and whispered, "Lick don't need to know nothin' o' this. You cain't tell yer father. Promise," she demanded.

"Promise," Pansy mouthed in return. She pulled the knit sweater to herself. Faded blue, intended to only be worn when one was chilled, but she assumed it to be a daily requirement of the Catholic school uniform, even on warm September days.

Loretta held the blouse up to Pansy's chest, as both were then standing to inspect the uniform in the light from the single, small bulb in the ceiling. "They could put flowers on their clothes," Pansy added.

"You don't need no flowers. Life ain't always 'bout no flowers."

The late-summer morning sun rose bright on Monday morning. Doors slammed inside the Blake Street apartments. Laundry hung suspended over back porch railings, strung out to dry over the shadows of a narrow alley below. Garments flapped in the breeze as the city trolley, F-line, screamed to a stop out front. Small flats bustled with the makings of breakfasts and arguments and anxieties over missed trolley rides. In her Catholic uniform, Pansy slipped out the front door. Setting off for her first walk to St. Bartholomew's, she expected the day to be magnificent.

As the sharp crosses of St. Bartholomew's Church broke the horizon, three spires stabbed godly shadows into the sun's rising glare, and Pansy contemplated skipping, replicating the spontaneity of other girls on joyous occasions, imagining their hearts had been inspired, as was hers, with the anticipation of school and nuns and God. And the promise of lunch. One mustn't forget lunch. A butterfly, at that moment, ready to soar on a liberating breeze, alighting at a destination where one might be rescued from everything that seemed wrong. *Perhaps I should skip,* Pansy nudged several times. "Skipping could be magnificent," she said to herself, out loud this time. "Skipping will get me to school sooner. Better to be early instead of late. One should never be late."

She pondered how the skipping should be, the mechanics of an unfamiliar joy, then launched into the crosswalk, three ungainly hippety-hops across the Larimer Street intersection. Her breasts nearly burst the confines of their Catholic sweater as traffic slowed for her crossing, leaving her to conclude that skipping was most definitely only for other girls. *I am fifteen. Almost a woman. I won't skip.* She continued with a determined pace until she passed beneath the school portico. A slight shade cast itself over her entrance.

Inside the protective embrace of the westerly church court-yard, she smiled broadly and caressed the folds of her skirt, basking in the authority it granted. It was a fine thing, she felt, to own a uniform—a Catholic uniform—a costume to mask the imperfections of her genuine life, a costume to meet God.

Engaged by a heavy stream of his morning piss but enticed to the sounds of urban bustle through the toilet window, Lick saw Pansy's rush to get out. Not knowing specifically what he had seen but knowing what he had learned, Loretta first cowered in the bedroom, then ran to their back door. Lick pursued her to the wooden balcony.

Eager to make himself useful, Jester pointed to the third level, where broken remnants of railing dangled over the alley. "Poor thing just fell down there and split her goddamn brains out!" Breathless with enthusiasm, he rose on the balls of his feet, peering over the squad car that had stopped sideways on Blake Street, aiming to catch another glimpse of the gore. "Never seen anything like that in all my life," he added.

Blood seeped from Loretta's skull, bright crimson in its freshness. Men in pressed trousers and skinny ties hovered over the gelatinous puddle, smoking cigarettes, taking notes, and sharing quiet discussions of what had happened that morning, along with tales of things that had filled their hours the previous day and the week before. Out front, passersby stopped to speculate on the significance of police cruisers blocking traffic, knowing that something of great consequence must have taken place. Wild explanations emerged, and people spoke at length of the situation, and most who hadn't even made their way to the back side of the apartment building soon knew of the dead body laid out below the third-floor balcony.

The crowd swelled. Two men in black ties and white short-sleeved shirts heaved Loretta's body, not yet stiffened in death, into the dark confines of a canvas sack. Jester, relishing the attention, volunteered to be the only witness. "I seen everything," he told the investigative team. "Everything. He threw her right off them goddamn stairs. That's what he did."

Bystanders lingered, milling near the scene but not in the middle of it. Some details shared weren't true, but the things people say in response to drama aren't always factual, nor do some care whether that is so. Sometimes, people just want to hear stories and are willing to sort through them later, determining if anything they heard had any basis in truth.

2

GETTING OFF THE BUS BEFORE REACHING HER
destination was bad behavior, a policeman insisted the next
morning. Uncle Luther would be expecting Pansy in Salt Lake,
but an officer would escort her to Uncle Luther's home. Her
uncle would not greet her at the bus station. No, the officer did
not know why this was so. In response to further questioning
from Pansy, he did not know anything about what Uncle Luther
looked like.

"You don't know what your own uncle looks like?" he asked.
No, she'd never met him. "Well, in the meantime, do not get off
this bus for any reason. Do you understand me? Do not get off
the bus until it gets to Utah, or you might get stuck in some
hellhole in Wyoming. We're not responsible for young girls who
get stuck in Wyoming."

This same policeman had searched Lick's pockets and turned
up a dollar and forty-three cents. Inside the Blackwell's flat, he
had scoured the place for anything that might jump out to him
as evidence. Little looked to have value, save for three porcelain
God dolls he removed from the windowsill, the clothing in

Pansy's closet, and a small address book he pulled from under Loretta's delicates at the bottom of a cardboard box.

"Here you go," he said and tucked the change into Pansy's hand. "I counted it when I took it out of your dad's pocket. A dollar and forty-three cents. There were some books in your room, but you can't really expect to haul a bunch of old books on the bus now, can you? You can buy new books when you get to Utah." He set a worn, tweed suitcase in front of Pansy. "This came from someone at the station, an extra he had at home."

She lifted it to her lap.

"You can keep it," the officer said.

Pansy fingered the leather bindings—much having disintegrated into wispy flaps of cowhide, the stitching rotted. The two metal hasps, intended to hold the lid closed, were only doing so on one side. One hasp had broken clean off.

"We packed it with your clothes. There wasn't much else worth keeping, if you ask me," he said.

The valise wasn't heavy. Pansy ran a quick mental inventory of what, if the policeman was honest, was inside. Still costumed in her Catholic uniform, she thought of her four cotton dresses, the blue one festooned with flowers. Precisely eight pairs of underwear, making her wonder who had lifted them from her closet floor. An embarrassed flush crept to her cheeks. Three cotton slips, four pairs of socks, and a tight overcoat that she most often left at home as its snugness had become confining. Her only shoes were on her feet. She could have looked down to verify this but was certain they were where she had last put them, which meant they could not be in the suitcase.

The officer handed two paper sacks to Pansy, each sealed with a very precise crease at its top. "My wife packed you a lunch. She said it wouldn't be right to send a girl off without something to eat, especially after her mother's been killed. There's an egg salad sandwich with chopped onions in there. My wife makes the best egg salad. Oh, and happy birthday, by the way. Yesterday."

She unfolded the first for a quick glimpse at a magnificent apple, which made her question the generous mind of the woman who had given it. A fat sandwich leaned on its side. The second sack, stuffed with molasses cookies, threw off a warm fragrance of clove and cinnamon.

"My wife baked those cookies just yesterday. There should be enough in there to last you for the whole ride," he said.

Pansy imagined they might last her a week, but didn't say so.

She chose an aisle seat, midway down the bus, her teeth clenched in resolve not to cry in public. The gray skies encased travelers in a windstorm of whiteness, and Pansy then contemplated how cookies might soften her troubles but didn't feel good manners would allow for such behavior, this being her first time on a bus.

Sedated by its crowded warmth, she slept.

Seated on the aisle about three-quarters back, a pencil-thin Black man was the most magnificent human Pansy had ever gazed upon, even driven to dream of. His wool pinstripe suit of dark gray, striped in bold vertical lines of ivory, impeccably pressed, hugged his body so firmly as to be noticeable, highlighting his slender frame and accenting the tightness of his youth. About twenty years old, she estimated. His dark skin was the enticing hue of a dark chocolate candy bar. His suit must have cost a fortune, she imagined, and then asked herself what, exactly, would comprise a fortune—certainly, more than a dollar and forty-three cents. Two rows ahead and across the aisle, she often turned to gaze at his magnificent self, contemplating how it would be to speak of his beauty. Can a White girl compliment a Black man? Of course, she can, Pansy decided. A young woman, fifteen, was of the age where social propriety was not completely required.

Pansy inhaled, not realizing the act of doing so, thinking of her predicament—she was certainly in a predicament—and fantasized about a discussion of this man's magnificence. She might then confess to him that she was alone, her mother dead, just yesterday. She turned again to admire him. His jacket, folded neatly across his lap, draped just over the knob of his knees. He had folded his thin, lithe hands, black as ebony and shiny with the vigor of youth, overtop. Seemingly, he had settled into a quiet meditation, biding time in a relaxed but upright position. His eyes were closed, a peaceful demeanor to his countenance. She imagined he only knew pleasant thoughts, unencumbered by trials.

3

The sun rose behind a thick cloud of winter gray. The previous day's snowfall lay in a wet and sloshy soup, undisturbed about the perimeter of Uncle Luther's house, seeping east to Emigration Creek. Officer Art Walton had retrieved Pansy from the bus terminal and then driven her to Uncle Luther's. It required precisely six minutes to get her to her uncle's front door—except Uncle Luther hadn't one. Walton parked in the slush out front, grimaced in puzzlement, growled loudly, "Where's the fuckin' door?" and then strode off to investigate. Returning to the street moments later, his path blocked by thick stands of cottonwoods on the side he had chosen, he grunted, "This is a helluva thing."

He made his way to the rear, where Uncle Luther responded to Walton's knock, wearing only a long cotton bed shirt of the type that was no longer in style for men. Draped above his kneecaps and stained at his chest, Luther was indifferent to his presentability. "Well, I think I know who you are," he said.

"Luther Blackwell?" Officer Walton asked.

"You expectin' someone else?" Uncle Luther answered.

"Maybe you oughta put a door on the front of your house, like normal."

"It's my fuckin' house. I'll leave the door where I damn well please," Uncle Luther retorted.

Pansy brought her suitcase inside and set it on the floor, but don't put that there, Luther complained. "You might as well take the bedroom. I'll be dead soon. Maybe tomorrow. As long as you're gonna be lookin' after me, you might as well have the bedroom."

Uncle Luther retreated to the dirty bedding where, just the night before, he had dragged his mattress and an iron frame out to the front room to sit squarely under the picture window. The St. Vincent de Paul store would deliver a bed for Pansy later in the week, he promised. He'd just called them today, he said. Pansy was mostly silent, but he eventually ran out of words, and by morning, his surliness had evolved into kindness. She decided Luther resembled his brother, her father, Lick, in no way. "Why don't you call me 'Uncle'," he said.

Uncle's shack had the barrenness of poverty, its occupant having little desire for things, or scant money for what he wished. Piles of newspapers, most old, a few recent, some read, many just collected or forgotten. The front room—tiny, intimate. A tall, red oak, straight-backed chair that he had pushed over to the wall rested in disuse opposite the door. It was the only one. Uncle hadn't put any thought into maintaining a tidy living space in perhaps twenty years. Being so near death for the last few may have contributed to his foulness, but his lack of house-cleaning was most likely the moral defect of one who was content to live in filth.

Pansy closed the bedroom door, absorbing the peace of its

darkness. Before falling asleep on the floor, she unfolded her dresses and hung them in his empty closet. Her four dresses stretched across the shoulders of wood hangers, buttoned halfway up, sorted by hue. Her bone white dress always on the left; the robin-egg blue dress always on the far right.

The next day, she asked Uncle how to operate the 1941 electric Speedy King washer machine outside. Then, she organized his kitchen and laundered his bed sheets for their first visit to the Speedy King in six months.

On October 1st, a Social Security check in the amount of $53.47 showed up in the mail. Pansy had collected everything from the wooden box nailed to a post out near the street that afternoon, as she had been asked to do every day previous except Sundays, stacking what little had been delivered, without inspection, on the near side of Uncle's bedside table. He slit envelopes on their short sides with a double-bladed pocketknife. Just the previous Friday, he had received an electricity bill for a dollar and seventy-three cents. Then several days when the postman didn't walk the long gravel road to the shack, having nothing to deliver. When a green envelope arrived from the Social Security Administration, Uncle slid a disability check from its enclosure and handed it across his bedside to her.

Pansy held it aloft.

Laughter broke from Uncle. "Never seen that much money before?" He rolled sideways. His coughing softened to a rumble.

Pansy gasped. "Where did it come from?"

"It's my Social Security. I git it every month," he explained.

"Without getting out of bed?"

"Well, sure, the government sends it to me, just waitin' for me to die." A great smile crossed his face. "Hah!" he shouted.

"I'll bet the Social Security never thought I was gonna last this long. Guess I fooled them!"

Pansy lowered the check to her belly, clutched against the folds of her dress, and again gasped, this time in horror. "What if you get caught? Fooling them?"

"Get caught?" Uncle Luther snorted. "I'm not stealin' it, fer Chrissakes. It's my money, from the government. They pay me on account of I'm about dead. They pay me 'til I die. That's how it works."

"It just shows up, without asking for it?"

"On the first of the month. Every month. Until I die. How else you think I pay the bills?"

"I didn't know." Pansy began a count of little black dots that resembled numbers. The paper was lime green.

Uncle Luther pointed his index finger in her direction. "Now, this is what you got to do. You take that check to the bank and put it in my account. Take twenty dollars out fer spending."

Pansy thought of what could be done with twenty dollars—a veritable fortune. "What do I do with the twenty dollars?"

"You bring it back to me, o' course." His brow tightened, and a slight frown settled on his face. "You're not gonna run off with my money, are you?"

Pansy shook her head in denial.

"Okay, then. You bring it back to me, and I'll write you another grocery list, and then you'll go shoppin' again. You can do that?" he asked.

She nodded. She'd been shopping for groceries already. Strict instruction on how to get there—no dawdling while you're away. The previous week's groceries: $3.16. Eggs, bread, rolled oats, cream, and toilet paper. A bit of ground beef and potatoes that, from his bedside, Uncle had instructed her to fry in a heavy cast-iron skillet.

Luther raised himself upright.

"So you'll head over to the Zion Community Savings and Loan at 900 South Street. It's a good walk from here, sixteen blocks after you turn up the road there on Foothill. I counted 'em once. I cain't walk no sixteen blocks no more. That's why you're here." He paused in remembrance of previous difficulties. "I done it last month. I had to stop and rest so many goddamn times I thought I'd be dead b'fore I ever got back."

Pansy turned for the door.

"Where you goin'?" Luther asked.

She looked back, the check clasped firmly in her hand. "To the bank?"

"Jeezuzz Christ. You ain't never seen a check before?"

Pansy shook her head, no.

"Christ." Uncle slid his legs from under their swaddle of blankets. His knees went wobbly, but he made his way to her, his left fist clawed around a ball-point pen. "Well, I guess that ain't so unusual. I didn't know what to do with a check when I was fifteen, either. But a bank ain't gonna give you no money if I ain't signed it."

He laid it flat against the wall, scrawling his endorsement on the back, then handed it back to Pansy, who turned it over to see his simple but illegible signature—a large and loopy L, leaning to the left, followed by a multitude of up-and-down motions of the pen.

"Now put that somewheres so you won't drop it. You cain't just carry it in your hand out there in public. You lose that check, and someone else is gonna git my money. You should git yourself a purse someday, but anyway, just go up the road to Foothill, as I said. Then turn left on 900 South. When you git there, ask fer Phyllis. You tell her you're gonna visit every month to deposit this fer me, and if she don't believe you, she can call me. She has my phone number. EL 5-3481." He again jabbed his finger in Pansy's direction. "You might wanna remember that. Might come in handy someday."

Pansy looked to the phone at Uncle's bedside. In two weeks, it had not once made a sound. She had never lived in a house with a telephone and wondered why one needed it. Who would you talk to? Phyllis, at Zion Community Savings and Loan. That's who you could talk to.

In January, the Social Security Administration raised his monthly check by $3.71. Uncle added a box of raspberry gelatin and a container of frozen whipped topping in celebration.

Pansy scoured the instructions on the gelatin box more than once. "Do you have a measuring cup?"

"Why would I have a measuring cup?" Uncle asked.

She shrugged, emptied the contents into a bowl with a coffee cup of boiling water, then blended it until smooth with a fork, per what the box had indicated should be done to achieve what a bowl of gelatin dessert was supposed to be, captivated to see printed instructions for preparation—something she had not known her mother to be aware of. *Dump in bowl. Add water. Stir.* Voilà!

She slid the finished product into an appliance they referred to as the icebox, then leaned over to give it a slight jiggle, testing its temper in impatience.

A fleeting smile came over Uncle. He patted his bedside. "Come over here. I have somethin' to show you."

She closed the icebox door.

"I got a present for you," he said.

She drew near, uncertain of the potential for his humor. "Go over there," he said, motioning to the near corner, "and git that folder, the brown one, fer me. It's under the newspapers."

Pansy had moved this folder before but had not seen its contents. She wasn't nosy in that way. She had lifted it more than once in her zeal to clean but would not have invaded Uncle's privacy by sorting through his personal effects. She brought it to his lap. He motioned to the chair to his right, then slid some papers from the envelope and across his blanket. A photo. Weathered, ragged at each corner. He pointed to himself as a young man, in the middle of the image, on the front step of a Kentucky derelict. Brothers Leroy and Lick framed the edge of the scene, their mother standing in the doorway, all in demeanor with the dullness of poverty. None smiled.

"It's the only one I got. It's not like we were rollin' in money to throw away on pictures," which he pronounced as pitchers. "You can have it. That's your grandmomma, right there in back. And me, o' course. And then that's your daddy—he's the little one—and Uncle Leroy." Uncle rubbed his finger near its top, at the corner where the eave pitched steep above the cabin door. "That's the old house. The mine's right out there in front. You could hit it with a rock, if you wanted, but you cain't see that from the pitcher."

"So that's my grandmomma," Pansy murmured, looking into the face of a woman who appeared grim, but perhaps wasn't. She lifted the photo for inspection and pondered the possibility that the old woman may have passed her personality traits to her children. Was Uncle Luther most like his mother? Or Lick? A hint of a smile softened her gaze. "She has a necklace?" She brought the photo closer. "Are those pearls?"

Uncle shrugged. "Beats me. Don't know where she woulda gotten pearls. We didn't have no money for pearls."

"What happened to them?" Pansy asked.

"The pearls? Hell, I don't know. Maybe they got buried with her. When she died, no one asked me if I wanted any pearls." He huffed in thought. "Maybe they went to yer daddy."

Pansy shook her head no, certain the pearls hadn't gone to her daddy.

"Well, it looks like the only thing you're gonna inherit from your grandmomma is a pitcher of her pearls," he stated.

Pansy mused in uncertainty. "They probably weren't real."

"Well, no, o' course not. Goes without sayin', they weren't real. But the last thing you need to be thinkin' about is pearls. There ain't never gonna be no pearls hangin' 'round yer neck." Uncle's face pinched into the stiffness of a man with memories of mistrust. He turned to Pansy. "Your daddy never bought no pearls fer yer momma, I wouldn't think?"

"No." Images of Loretta, the Denver apartment, returned. "No. She had nothing."

Uncle paused. "No, I s'pose not," then drew a slow breath, again aiming a bent finger in her direction. "You know, you could learn from that."

"Learn what?" Pansy asked.

"How some people don't ever find no get-up-and-go. Some just cain't find it in themselves to go after somethin' better."

Pansy raised her head in offense.

"Just sayin', maybe yer momma coulda gone out and done somethin'."

"Done what?"

"Gottin' herself a job, maybe," Uncle said.

Pansy's back stiffened.

"I'm just sayin'." Uncle raised his arms into the air. "Look at me. I did somethin'. I got outta them damn coal fields and got me a house. Yer momma coulda done somethin' instead of wallowin' like a pig in mud."

Pansy turned the photo upside down in her lap.

"You brung clothes with you, but that's all you got? You didn't have nothin' else?" he asked.

"I brought my momma's God dolls, too! They came from her momma. That's something!"

Uncle sniffed. "Well, those'll do you a lot of good."

Pansy rose, then walked to her room. She looked back to Uncle, through the open door. "I left all my books in Denver."

"Yer books?"

"I had books, but I left them behind," she said.

"What'd you go and do that for?"

"The police told me I could buy new ones when I got here," she answered.

Uncle scowled. "Well, they were damn sure wrong about that. I ain't got no money to throw away on books." He softened at an additional thought. "But you could go up to the libary and git some there." A brightness came over him. "They got all the books you want over there. Fer free. It's not like you got much else to do, other than take care o' me, of course. But I'll be dead soon."

Pansy glanced often to the wind-up clock hung high on the front wall, and when the long hand eventually snapped to 9 a.m., she abruptly rose from her chair.

"I'll return soooon," she said, "unless I get lost." She stepped out into the cold sunshine.

Uncle rose, fully upright from bed. "Don't you be doin' that! Don't need you gettin' lost on me." He came to the doorway. "And don't be goin' into that Mormon temple across the street. I don't need you turnin' Mormon on me, neither."

Pansy nodded, having no intentions of turning Mormon.

"And don't be jumpin' off the third floor when you get there," he warned.

She snapped to his direction. "Jump off?"

"People jump off when they're wantin' to die. That's what I've heard."

"Why would they do that?" she asked in horror.

"Because it's a long way down. If you're wantin' to end it all, that's an easy way to do it. So I've heard. People go to the libary, just to die." Uncle chuckled at his humor.

Pansy grimaced. "I don't want to die!" She then pushed her way out into the cold, feeling a rise of urgency as she made her way up the gravel road to Foothill. Strong waves of satisfaction took her thoughts when she turned north on State Street. A great snow had fallen the previous week and still lay splattered where it wished and to where people had pushed it into piles.

Pansy only entered the library on the heels of another who hadn't lacked the confidence to do so, then went to the third floor to view the Mormon temple through a rear window. *Don't turn Mormon, either.* A block to the east, the Cathedral of the Madeleine—the church of her mother—also reached for the glory of God.

She returned to the first floor and settled in to a long exploration. An earnest librarian, a thin woman, Mrs. Chalker leaned into Pansy's path. She had pulled all wisps of hair to the rear of her head in a tight restriction, as if in tedious desire to never see them again. The pencil line of Mrs. Chalker's mouth parted. "What sort of work would you like to read?" she asked, in the welcoming tone of a professional who lives under the placid spell of organization.

"It's my first time, in a grown-up library," Pansy answered.

"Welcome to the library. How may I help you?" Mrs. Chalker asked.

"I'd like some new books to read," Pansy replied.

"Of what topics?"

"Adult books. Not books for children."

"I presume your preference is fiction?" Mrs. Chalker's lips, still so very thin, offended Pansy little, now.

"Yes, ma'am," Pansy said.

"Perhaps you should start with the classics," Mrs. Chalker suggested.

"Why?"

"Well, that would certainly be a fair question, I suppose. Why, indeed. Would the work of Mark Twain appeal to you?"

"Tom Sawyer," Pansy stated. "No. I've already read it."

During the short and cold days of winter, Pansy succumbed to complete submergence in the written word.

"What would you do if you knew this was the last night of the world?"
  "I don't know. I hadn't thought."

Ray Bradbury, *The Martian Chronicles*

The warmer days of spring rolled in.

Uncle declared it was time Pansy got some new clothes, as if he had wakened with the stunning observation that spring mornings were meant for change.

"If I die tomorrow, I don't want no one sayin' I didn't have enough sense to put some clothes on you. Three dollars should git you plenty at St. Vincent's. They got clothes there. From the church people. Good clothes, but cheap," he said.

Pansy folded the currency into the tiniest square, clasped hard in her fist, then walked there with the intent to find nothing more than a pretty dress. Inside, elderly nuns paced the aisles, unhurried, as essential tasks were accomplished by volunteers and believers in the cause of charity. A short man, Father McCombie often traveled to the store to offer his superior skills in supervision, but only when free of religious obligations. Rarely was he found there, which hadn't anything to do with his height, but he took great pleasure in being known as the man in charge, which had everything to do with it.

Pansy laid two dresses and a pair of brown leather shoes, low in heel, across the counter. "My momma was Catholic," she volunteered. "And my grandmomma, too."

"And you?" Father asked. "How about you?" Was she Catholic? She'd not ever been or thought of it, she answered.

"Well, if your mother was Catholic, and her mother before, then you are certainly Catholic as well. You've been baptized, yes?" he asked.

Yes, she nodded. Her mother had once said so.

Three nuns hung nearby, wishing to stretch over his shoulder and participate in the conversation without the insubordination of pretending to be in charge.

"Have you been to confession?"

"I've not been," Pansy replied. "But my momma used to go, back in Denver."

"Well, that won't do *you* any good," one nun erupted, the same who had shoved a bra into Pansy's selection of clothing. "You'll need to go to confession yourself, to confess your sins."

"Sins?" Pansy pulled her head erect. "I don't have any sins! I'm a good girl."

A smirk of holiness crept across the father's lips. He rose, making an act of folding his hands together in devout seriousness. "Well, of course you do. All men are sinners, but the sacrament of penance will give you a new beginning. Anything you have done can be forgiven, no matter what, and you can find mercy and healing. It is important that you attend confession. When you leave the confessional, you are new again in the eyes of God, free of sin."

"I might visit the church this afternoon," Pansy said to Uncle.

"The church? You're not turnin' Mormon on me, are you?"

"No, no! Not Mormon. But I've been to the Cathedral of the Madeleine." She rose, carrying two plates, both hers, to the sink. "It's the most magnificent church. I went in once, last week."

"Don't know why you would get wrapped up in that foolishness," he said.

"My momma was Catholic." She paused in deliberation of a religious doctrine she had only recently claimed as her own. "The father at St. Vincent's says God will forgive you of anything if you confess."

"What do you got to be forgiven for?"

"We're all sinners. That's what the father said," Pansy answered.

"We never took part in any of that church nonsense, not in our family," Uncle said.

"My momma did," Pansy corrected. "She was Catholic. So was her momma."

"Well, good for her. Maybe that was her problem."

"I have my grandmomma's God dolls."

"Surprised your daddy didn't throw 'em in the trash. He wouldn't take any stock in that foolishness. Your Uncle Leroy, neither . . . 'course, he's dead now." Uncle chuckled. "Leroy knows if God is mad for him not goin' to church, now that he's dead and all. I'll be sure to ask when I see him. After I'm dead. I'll tell him you said hello."

"Yes, you can tell him I said hello." Pansy looked vacantly out the front window, musing in thought of her dead uncle. "How long ago did Uncle Leroy die?"

"Leroy? Hell, I don't know. Five years? I don't remember. He can tell me how long he's been dead when I get there. Hah, hah!" Uncle Luther hacked in frustration. "Goddamnit," he muttered, spitting a thick phlegm into a coffee cup. "I shouldn't be laughin' like that." He launched into another diatribe about medical incompetence. "The doc told me I don't have nothin' to be laughin' about, since I'll be dead soon."

Pansy went to his bedside and retrieved the spit cup from his table, certain he would again knock it to the floor.

"I quit him after that. The doc said I wouldn't make it more'n a couple months after I last seen him. Sometimes them damn doctors don't know what they're talkin' about!" Uncle groused.

"You should eat your breakfast," Pansy nudged, pushing a bowl in his direction, still warm as it was early; the morning sun had only begun its travel over the mountains. He'd finish it later, lukewarm and clotted. *Get me some more cream for my breakfast*, he might instruct, at 3 p.m.

Pansy went to the sink, rinsed dishes, then returned to the chair at his side. She ran a hand across each of her forearms, extinguishing the dishwater droplets that had stranded themselves in colonies there. They sat for a time, in silence.

Eventually, breaking the stillness, Pansy asked, "How did Uncle Leroy die?"

Uncle spat a sharp stream of air through his lips. "Hell, if I know. I sent him a letter once, but it came back 'deceased.' The post office don't send those letters back with the words, 'Dead. Got run over by a truck,' scribbled on front. Christ, someone mighta shot him in the head, just fer bein' an asshole." He leaned to Pansy. "He was an asshole. In case you didn't know."

Uncle returned to a hard stare at the Wasatch Mountains. "Leroy said he was gonna get rich once he got to California. I don't think he did, though. People who get rich usually let everyone know about it."

California is where people made their fortunes. This is what Pansy had heard. She wondered how it would be in California. The Sunshine State, people had called it. Nearly everyone had orange trees in their yards.

"I almost got rich," Uncle said, "after I got out here from Kentucky." His grin widened in memory of what had once been his. "There was plenty o' money to be made. Got me enough to buy a house. I gave six hundred and forty-seven dollars fer this house back in 1942."

Pansy pulled herself upright, sitting straight and rigid as if granting undivided attention.

"The guy I bought it from was a railroad man and just about dead, like me. Said he didn't want to die in the place, so he sold it to me and left town."

Pansy rose slightly, inclined forward. "Left town? Where did he go?"

"Hell, if I know. Didn't think it was any o' my business where he was goin'." He took a slow glance around the room. "His old house might be a shit hole now, but it's a sight better than that one we had back in Kentucky. You ain't never seen that one. We didn't even have no toilet to crap in. Everyone had to do their business outside."

Pansy nodded.

"There was one well for all the houses. No wires outside fer 'lectricity. Some people didn't even have no windows. Just fuckin' holes in their walls, lookin' out to the mine." Uncle rolled onto his back in search of elusive comfort, a vacant gaze at the ceiling above. "The coal companies built new houses for miners, and some people got things better—'cept all the miners who got the new places got up to their eyeballs in hock to the mines. Some fellas couldn't ever git out, even if they wanted to. Didn't have a pot to piss in. Owed their souls to the mines by then. Your daddy was one of the smart ones, o' course. Got outta Kentucky b'fore coal took everything."

"My daddy killed my momma," Pansy snapped, her eyes flared wide to hear that her father had ever been in possession of an admirable attribute.

Uncle Luther drew a long inhalation into his chest. "Yes, that's what I heard. Threw her right off them goddamn stairs, is what I heard. You'll have to own that fer the rest o' your life, I s'pose."

Pansy said nothing.

"Well, your daddy's gonna rot in prison." Uncle sighed. "Sometimes you just gotta let things go."

4

AT THE RED BUTTE CREEK BRIDGE, WHERE THE stream crossed under East Sunnyside Avenue on its descent from the canyon, Ace Sharkey stood on the bridge abutment. One Saturday, Pansy smiled in his direction. The next, she boldly spoke, introducing herself to the thin man who fumbled in reply.

Of delicate build, Ace was tall, perhaps an inch more than Pansy. Noticeably graceful. By the time Pansy stopped to converse with him on the bridge, she hoped that he might be hers. "Good morning. My name is Pansy," she said.

Charmed by her pursuit, Ace failed at first to appreciate Pansy's most notable attributes: curvaceous, hair below her shoulders, the fullness of her hips. What he grasped was the way she looked at him, with longing and ownership, as if coveting companionship.

Hung on the rack of new arrivals at St. Vincent's, a simple, white cotton dress adorned with dime-sized specks of blue flowers sprinkled across the fabric caught Pansy's eye. She pulled it to her shoulders and giggled with excitement.

Myrtle Green gushed when Pansy laid it across the counter. "Oooh, you're buying the pansy dress! I would have bought it myself if it had fit." She pulled it over to her side of the till. "It's waaay too big for me, though."

"The what dress? What did you call it?" Pansy asked.

"The pansy dress . . . see?" Myrtle laid it back on the counter. "Those flowers, right there. Those are pansies. Blue pansies."

Pansy inhaled. "Oooh . . . I didn't know. Pansies . . . " She ran her hand over the fabric, gently pressing its flower petals. "This dress is perfect for me!"

Pansy emerged from her bedroom, casting her skirt in an airy flourish. Uncle Luther turned sideways in acknowledgment.

"That's a fine dress you got on, there," he said.

"It was fifty cents." She turned at the hip, then again whirled in a semi-circle. "It's the prettiest dress I've ever had. It has pansy flowers."

Uncle Luther squinted. "Looks like polka dots."

"Well, you're not looking at it up close. It's a pansy dress." She curtsied, dipping its hem to the floor. "I'm going to keep this forever."

"Tryin' to catch someone's eye, are you?" Uncle asked.

A hint of a smile crept to her lips. "Ace will like it."

Uncle eased back under the embrace of his blankets. His muscles stiffened in discontent, and he pushed his chin in her direction. "Are you goin' over to see yer friend today?" He asked this because she had bathed—the pansy dress washed the previous evening, just pulled from the clothesline this morning. On this day, a Friday, Pansy had pulled her hair to the back, taming its exuberance into a heavy ponytail.

Yes, she nodded. This is the day she travels to the bridge at Red Butte Creek to see Ace. In a shady hollow of cottonwoods carved by a shallow circle of fallen trees, they would ponder the bare necessities of life. The arrival of winter.

"Well, hell, you better git him to marry you. You're a grown woman now—seventeen you are. Back in Kentucky, you coulda already been married and pregnant. Hell, you coulda already been pregnant a couple times in Kentucky. And fer that matter, fer Chrissakes, it's good to see you do somethin' other than stickin' your nose in a goddamn book all day. Maybe that man'll get your head out of them damn books."

Giggling, Pansy imagined having babies with Ace. She had determined that they would have two children and hoped to name them Whitlow and Violet.

"I'm going to surprise him today. I'm going early to his house. I've not been there yet, but it's time, I think," she said.

"Well, I s'pose that's one way to find out if he's a man who likes surprises. You might want to hope so." He waved a finger in her direction. "That man will marry you as soon as I'm dead."

Pansy was standing now, looking to the mountains as if searching for hope and direction. "We only met last month," she said to Uncle. The Wasatch range had been visited by an early snow; their peaks capped in a thin cloak of white. "But I'll marry him, if he asks. But not until after you're dead."

She pulled a deep gulp of air into her lungs, willing the nerve to broach a private subject, then turned and knelt beside his bed.

"I have something to ask you." She looked to him, cautious. "What will happen to this house? When you're dead?"

He raised a hand from under his cocoon, frail, thinly shrouded in the luminosity of aged skin, then waved it across his bedside as if to shoo unwelcome spirits that were prematurely knocking at his door. "Go take a look outside."

Pansy made her way to the exit, sticking her head outside into the early autumn frost. Emigration Creek ran at the back end of the property, sometimes fast and cool but currently cold and slow with its willow thickets and deep, shaded pools. She took a step outdoors, then leaned back to the shack, her head thrust inside for clues to the meaning of Uncle's command. Uncle's grin cast no illumination on the quandary, so she turned back to the creek and scanned its far shadows, the forest of weeds that had emerged the previous spring as it did every spring, waist-high but dry and dead now, and her walking trail amongst it, weaving a narrow path to the water's edge.

She stepped back inside, her question still unanswered. "I don't know what I'm looking for," she said.

"You see anyone out there?" he asked.

Pansy shook her head; no, there wasn't anyone outside. She had just looked.

"That's right." His voice nearing a whisper, now. "There ain't no one standin' in line to git my house. There ain't no one out there, so I don't see no reason why you won't have it when I'm gone."

Pansy clasped her hands together, then returned to the dimness of the front room.

Uncle squinted and stabbed his forefinger in her direction. "As soon as you git this house, that man'll marry you. Mark my words."

She frowned at the prediction and scanned the room as if it had come into focus for the first time. The shack would eventually be hers. When Uncle was dead. There wasn't no one else standing in line to get it.

Just a stone's throw from the bridge abutment, Pansy could see Ace's front door, painted the dull color of white paste. Minutes later, standing out front, she debated the number of times she would knock.

"Surprise!" she screamed when he came to the door.

A steep flight of stairs led to the depths of the lower floor. Two small windows. A thin coat of sunlight trickled through. Semi-circles of corrugated sheet metal outside kept each window from suffocating in snow. The basement had been split into two units, one accessible from an exterior entrance that led to Ace's apartment and the other via an interior door inside the kitchen of the first-floor flat.

Ace leaned close and whispered, "My neighbor doesn't need to know you're here."

Pansy glanced across the narrow length of his apartment: a kitchen, a bed, and a bathroom. Spare and undecorated, his tidiness was perfection to her.

Ace helped her from the last step. "The bishop split the basement into two apartments. He did it without permits."

"How do you know?"

He nodded to the wall where a short counter held dishes. "Because my sink and the one in the other unit share a drain, so I can't use mine unless he's not using his." Still speaking under his breath, he added, "Not unless either of us wants to overflow the sink. It's a pain in the ass, really."

"Why do you whisper?" she whispered.

Ace turned directly to the wall in question, speaking loudly. "Hey, Jimmy . . . you over there?"

A pitched voice traveled back, unmuffled. "Yup. Whaddya need?"

"Not a thing. Just wanted to see if you were home." Ace

grasped Pansy's hand and led her back outdoors. "That's Jimmy. He's the bishop's nephew." Pulling her out to the furthest corner of the property, he stopped in front of a wooden barn and laughed out loud. "Jimmy has issues. And luckily, I have none, because he would run to the bishop and tell him, if I did. He's that kind of guy." He opened a wide door and walked inside the barn.

Built of cedar planks in a board and batten style, hay bales lay intact, dry, stacked into random layers of one, two, and three high, still bound in old baling wire. Ace led her there, and they spent the remainder of the day, nearly 'til dark, conversing of life and literature. There, in the barn, Pansy moved into his arms.

It was now the second day of November, and the days had turned short and cold. Emigration Creek was already tinkling in glassy splinters of winter ice. Uncle had turned the dull color of tallow. In two weeks, the cottonwood leaves would begin a slow flutter—a graceful descent when the winds came from across the Great Salt Flats of Utah, forcing summer foliage to crackle in defeat, leaves pushed across the landscape, dry and spent.

Phyllis Hester, Zion Community Savings and Loan employee, cashed Uncle Luther's Social Security check in its entirety for Pansy, leaving a balance of one dollar and forty-seven cents in his account. Pansy had scrawled his endorsement on this check after practicing it six times on the inside of an empty saltine cracker box. A big loopy L, followed by up and down squiggles on a stretch of cardboard that she had torn open and spread across the table, inside out. The ease with which she forged his signature surprised her.

"You might not see me next month," she said to Phyllis. "The end is very near."

Phyllis clutched her chest in sympathy. "Oh, that poor man," she gasped. "I will pray for him."

Back home, Pansy turned each bill right-side up and placed them in order by denomination. She riffled through the stack, then again checked the shack's thermostat, ensuring it was turned off. Before dawn, she slid the bathroom window open to its full extent, letting the interior flood with the bitter cold of winter. She boiled water for a cup of tea, and when the winter sun first glanced through the window, she again unfolded the letter that had arrived the previous Friday. For the second time, she read its contents, paced her way through the shack, then eventually walked out to Emigration Creek. The brittle weeds crumbled under her advance to the water's edge. The stream licked at sharp edges of ice. The creek failed to lift her spirits, as so often before, so she sobbed and cursed the letter that had been sent from the Salt Lake County Assessor's office.

Mr. Luther Blackwell,

The Salt Lake County Assessor's office wishes to send one final notice that you have not made payment of the total amount of property tax that is due on your property located at 37 South Railway Avenue, Salt Lake City, Utah. Three years ago, you requested an extension of two years for the payment of property tax, but after repeated reminders, you have not paid any amount thus far. This is the last warning for payment of total property tax, due within fifteen days of receipt of this letter.

If you are unable to pay the full tax due, which now totals $172.17, we will be forced to foreclose on your property. The property will then be sold at public auction to settle the tax delinquency.

Yours truly,
Vincent Matheson
Salt Lake County Assessor

Not until the sun had descended just past its zenith, a few hours yet from dipping below the western horizon, did Pansy stumble back to the shack. She lit a match and turned the letter to ash over the bathroom toilet.

Before darkness came, she made her way to Ace's basement. Pansy grasped his hand and led him to the hay bales in the barn. Ace returned to his apartment for a heavy wool blanket.

She pulled it across her thighs, laying its edge over to him. In subdued stillness, they gazed up to the rafters. "Is there anything to eat in your kitchen?" Pansy asked. She offered to bring him something from Uncle Luther's house, if he was hungry. No, there was no reason for Ace to see Uncle Luther, she explained. Uncle would die soon. Very soon, she assured Ace. "What will I do when Uncle dies? Probably leave Salt Lake, don't you think?"

"Do you ever think of leaving Utah?" she asked him.

"And go where?" Ace replied.

"To where opportunities might be better."

"I was born here. Born in this house, back when we lived upstairs," he explained.

"You lived upstairs? Why don't you live there now?"

"I can't afford that!" Ace said. "The bishop didn't give a crap that my dad was dead. Business was business, he said, so I moved down here when he asked me to pay that rent."

"But you don't think of leaving?" Pansy asked.

"Of course not. I've lived here, in the same ward, for my entire life. The Yale Ward, that's our church."

"You go to church?" Pansy asked, surprised.

"Almost never," Ace replied. "I don't like church, and they don't like me."

"Now, why wouldn't they like you?" Pansy rolled to her side. Her skirt twisted around her legs, binding them in tight constraint. "I like you," she whispered.

"It's like one day, a long time ago, someone decided that the Sharkeys were pieces of shit," Ace explained. "That philosophy got passed down through the church, all the way to me. My dad tried hard to be what they wanted, but he didn't fit what he was supposed to be. I don't even know what was so bastardly about him, but it seems that I inherited it. Whatever it was."

"Then why do you go at all?"

"I don't. The last time I went was for Pioneer Day, three months ago, and I only went to the picnic, without all the church preaching."

"I've not been to Pioneer Day," Pansy said.

"Well, of course not. You're not Mormon." He raised himself to one arm in curiosity. "Are you?"

"I'm Catholic."

"Catholic?" Ace's eyes widened.

"But I've never been. My mother used to go," Pansy said.

"You've never been to church?"

"No." A contented gaze softened her thoughts. "I've been inside St. Madeleine's twice, but not for services. It's simply magnificent. I'm going to go to confession. Soon, I think."

"Why would you go now, if you've never gone before?" Ace asked.

"Well, why wouldn't I? My family, on my mom's side, were all Catholic, back in Italy," she replied.

"So, you understand my problem. I was *born* into the LDS Church. Being Mormon is part of me," Ace stated.

"That's different. My mother belonged to the first church, and her mother before her, and her mother before that."

Ace poked her shoulder. "But you've never once gone. Your problem is the same as mine. You think you belong to a church simply because your ancestors did." He rose, casting the blanket across to her, then sat cross-legged on the straw bales. "All of my forefathers, aunts, uncles, all of them before me, were

Mormon. They came across the country, some in wagons, but most just walked in the great trek to Utah. The pioneers. Pioneer Day celebrates them. Practically everything closes for the holiday, as you know. So, I went to the picnic at Liberty Park, but I didn't go to the services."

"Do you feel guilty?" Pansy asked.

"Sometimes. The church seems to think it's my responsibility to carry on what is part of me. It's similar to what you think about the Catholics. I'm supposed to get excited about Pioneer Day, but I don't. It doesn't speak to me like I think it's supposed to when God wants you to be part of things," he said.

Pansy sat upright, grasping his hand. "They say you won't really understand the love of God until you get to heaven. I'll ask the priests to pray for you when I go to confession."

"Heaven? Fat chance for that. The bishop told my dad he'd never receive the Celestial Glory. The implication was that I'd never receive it either," Ace said matter-of-factly.

"The bishop said you won't make it to heaven? That is the most horrible thing I have ever heard!" Pansy protested.

"No, he didn't say it to me; he said it to my dad, but if my dad couldn't receive Celestial Glory, I won't either."

"Celestial Glory is a strange way to describe heaven," Pansy noted. "Why not just call it heaven, like everyone else?"

"Because we don't have an ordinary version of heaven like everyone else," Ace replied. "Celestial Glory is the highest stage of Mormon heaven. It's the best part of heaven. People who were married in the temple go there. If you weren't married in the temple, you won't ever find your way to Celestial Glory."

"That's not true!" Pansy retorted. "God doesn't say you have to be married to go to heaven."

"*Your* God might not," Ace replied, "but mine does. You can't enter the best part of heaven unless you were married in the temple. And White. And rich. If you're a run-of-the-mill average man, such as me, you won't ever get into that part of heaven."

"And White?"

"Of course. Mormons don't want Black men dirtying up the best part of heaven. Blacks are bound for the lower section, which is more like hell. 'The sewer of heaven,' my dad called it. It might as well be hell. We don't believe in hell, but the part of heaven my dad went to could just as well be it. When my dad died, he expected to wake up in the sewer of heaven," Ace said.

"But it's still heaven? Then how bad can it be?" Pansy asked.

"A Mormon spends his life in shame if he believes that's where he's headed. The 'Telestial Glory,' it's called. It's the lowest part of heaven where liars and whores and non-believers go. It's like hell in heaven, and once you're there, you can't ever get out. That's where my dad thought he was going. To spend eternity with the Blacks. And liars and whores. He would have been fine with the whores."

Pansy shook her head in disbelief, then stretched out beside him, nearly atop in embrace. Her hair, bound at the top in red ribbon, fell across his chest. "That's just awful," she murmured. "Downright awful. Black people should get into heaven just as easy as anyone else. And whores don't go to heaven, just so you know. Whores go to hell."

Ace shook his head. "We don't believe in hell. Not the way you do. The Telestial Glory, in heaven, is as close as we can get to hell."

"How could you *not* believe in hell?" Pansy asked.

"How could you believe in hell? You've never been to church."

"True." She sighed. "I feel bad for your dad, though. The poor man probably spent his life in shame."

Ace exhaled pensively. "Most likely. Funny, I've never

thought about it in those terms, but I think he spent his entire life knowing he was a lower-class Mormon."

"And you? Ashamed?"

Ace didn't reply.

"Sorry, don't mean to pry." She again ran her fingers down his chest, resting her hand above the waist of his pants.

"I'm not ashamed." A bitterness took his thoughts. "The whole religion is a crock of shit if you ask me. Being Mormon is like having a hand-me-down that was given by my ancestors, but it doesn't comfort me when I need comfort. I don't fit the Mormon life. You have to be married to be Mormon. I'm twenty-five and not married. That's not usual around here." He gave her a concerned glance. "Never thought to ask. How old are you?"

"Nineteen," Pansy lied.

"Hmmm. I thought you were older," Ace said.

Pansy sat upright, then asked, "Then we're back to my original question. Why don't you leave?"

"Leave for where? You can't really leave the LDS Church whenever you feel like it. Even today, 1959 and the modern civilized world, the Church—my church, not yours—still rules everything that happens here. There's a price to pay for leaving," Ace said.

"Mrs. Chalker is Mormon, and she's always been very kind to me. Mormons don't treat me badly," Pansy mused.

"Well, of course not. You were never Mormon, and they likely don't know you're Catholic, which, by the way, is viewed by Mormons as the least godly religion on the planet. If you tell them you're Catholic, they'll think you're a piece of shit in God's eyes, too, but they wouldn't tell you so to your face. You won't ever have Celestial Glory, either. But me? I'm a descendant of Mormon pioneers. All the people who give me work are Mormon. They would poison every square inch of my life if I told them what I think of their religion," Ace said.

"What about family?"

"I don't have family. My mom died when I was born, then Dad two years ago, but if my parents were alive, they'd be Mormon. Mormons shun people who leave."

"Even parents?" Pansy asked.

"Especially parents," Ace confirmed.

"That's terrible. I can't imagine a mother abandoning her child." All was quiet for several minutes. Eventually, a solution occurred to her. "You could leave then, not having family and all."

"Mormons don't just up and leave the Church and become Catholic," he said.

"No, I suppose not."

"In Mormon-land, the only option is to sneak out of church early. Just hang out on the sidelines. The Church prefers that you not make a big deal of it. Just pretend. Keep your mouth shut. So that's what I do." He exhaled in disgust. "You know, damnit, I don't really like thinking about it so much. Let's talk about something else."

"Sorry." In silence, Pansy's thoughts became emboldened to take the conversation in a direction she had only recently imagined.

"What if you marry a Catholic girl?" she asked.

Ace laughed aloud. "Then I'd be sure to end up in the sewer of heaven. A Catholic girl can't enter the LDS temple for any reason."

"That's sad," Pansy pondered. "They want you to be part of them, but only if they can remind you that they are better than you."

"Yes, that's what we just talked about. I thought we had changed the subject," Ace retorted sharply.

"Sorry."

Silence again engulfed the barn, each absorbed in independent thoughts of what the evening should become. As the cold wind of nightfall continued to blow, the sun nearly asleep and faded through the single window over the hayloft, Pansy's feelings for the man who didn't want to be Mormon warmed to the point of desire. She tugged at his shirt, pulling him over to recline beside her. She felt his breath on her cheek. They lay this way for some time. Pansy let the pleasure of this delicate intimacy fill her soul, then, with purpose, she unlatched his first button, spreading his collar wide. She gently brushed her lips against his, then leaned heavy atop, pushing him into the straw. Ace opened his mouth to her insistence.

"What would your church think of this?" she murmured.

"They'd say we're both headed to the sewer of heaven," Ace replied.

Pansy giggled. "There's no such thing as a sewer section in heaven."

"Say the Catholics." He slid out from under her, partially. "Making out with Mormon boys is gonna get you in trouble."

Pansy flung her left leg across his hip. "No, that's the difference between your religion and mine. Catholics don't care a bit about your religion. God isn't going to deny me heaven for kissing a Mormon. The fathers would, however, care about this." Abruptly, she rose to her knees and yanked her blouse overhead, tossing her thick hair to the side. She leaned forward. Her breasts bulged as she tugged her left bra strap impatiently. She shrugged, her bra fell to the straw, and then she fondled herself, aroused by her boldness.

"Touch me," she demanded.

"They'll kick us out of church if we get caught," he protested.

"Oh, shut up. Catholics don't kick people out of church."

"You sure?"

"You're silly," Pansy said. "I'm certain I couldn't possibly get kicked out of the Catholic Church, certainly not for making love. But I'll confess next week."

Moments later, stretched across the straw, she burrowed into the vacant space below his shoulder. He was cold, there. She could warm him, she thought. "I love you for caring," she whispered.

The Wasatch winds howled as the sun sank over the horizon, and the darkness took the barn into its grip. "You love me too, don't you?" she asked.

"Sure, I do," Ace murmured.

Pansy sighed contentedly, then rolled over to face him.

"Marry me," she said.

Ace looked for her eyes in the blackness. "Marry you?"

"Yes. Marry me. You love me. You just said it. We can leave Salt Lake. We can go to California. I have an uncle in Fresno. They say he's rich! We can go there. Yes?" She rose on one arm to face him, euphoric at the thought. "People get rich in California!"

On Monday, Pansy knelt in submission inside the church confessional. In a gush of words, she confessed to her intimacy with Ace. But it was only because she loved him, she confided. They would marry soon.

The priest leaned forward in curt rebuke. "You cannot ask for a blessing of your desire to marry, child, while confessing to carnal sin. The church cannot marry you until you have shown that your marriage is not born from lust."

A somber silence engulfed the confessional. In disinterest, the father leaned back to the seclusion of the far corner. Pansy brought both hands to her mouth, smothering the heaviness of her breath.

"Is there anything else you wish to tell me, my child?"

"No, that is all."

On her way out, still inside the sanctity of the church, an abrupt foulness entered her thoughts.

"Fuck you," she muttered.

Leaning far over the Red Butte Creek Bridge at the northern abutment where canyon water pooled in deep grottos, the trout congregating in its protection, Ace Sharkey again peered into its depths as he had done countless times before. The stream was slow now, withered in the autumn dryness. The cool springs from higher canyon altitudes had disgorged most of what they had to give. Nature was settling in dormancy. The winter months were normally a time of complacency for Ace, as people with odd jobs were few. Come back and see me in the spring, is how people responded when he asked for work at this time of year. In his wallet was a stack of folded currency totaling twenty-seven dollars.

The weight of Pansy's proposal wasn't burdensome. No cravings had pushed him to seek romance, nor had he sought the comforts of women in the city's red-light district on Commercial Street. But one week ago, Pansy had pushed him to consider something unthinkable—the abandonment of Utah.

"My Uncle Leroy lives in Fresno," she had reminded him just the night before. She opened her mother's red address book and pointed to the penciled scrawl. "See, that's where he lives. Uncle Leroy Blackwell. Right there in Fresno. He told everyone he was going to get rich."

Ace took it from her and read the address aloud. "One forty-seven, Tulare Street." He paused, then repeated the street name. "How do you pronounce that?"

Pansy plucked the booklet from his hands and tucked it into the confines of her breasts. "I haven't any idea. I've not been there, but we'll ask when we get to Fresno."

"Have you called?" he asked.

"No. We'll just knock on his door when we get to town." She reached for his hand. "I have a photo of him, when he was a child back in Kentucky. He'll be pleased to see us."

Ace nodded in acceptance.

"Uncle Luther gave us fifty-seven dollars to get married," she said.

"Fifty-seven dollars! Tell him thank you for me," Ace responded.

"No need for that. Uncle will pass soon. He went to the hospital this morning. I don't expect him to leave." She squeezed his hand. "It's a perfect opportunity to be married."

"I'm sorry I didn't meet him."

Pansy bowed her forehead to his. "It's okay. I have you," she whispered.

"Yes. You have me." He pulled away from her embrace, then rose. "You won't be allowed in the church, you know."

"The church?"

"To be married," he said.

"Well, silly, I have no interest in the church." She stood and gathered him back to her embrace. "That doesn't bother you, does it?" Without waiting for his reply, "We'll marry in Fresno. It will be a whole new start in California. We'll get married in Fresno, and certainly not in a church. We could leave tomorrow!"

Pansy pulled a heavy winter coat from Ace's suitcase the next morning and rubbed the thickness of its lining through her fingers. It would be unnecessary in California, she said. California is a land of sunshine. She tossed it into the pile of discards, then gazed in long satisfaction at what she had done.

Ace retrieved his jacket from where it lay on the floor. "We're not in California yet." He turned to his neighbor's wall. "Hey, Jimmy!"

Pansy opened her mouth wide in horror. "What are you doing?"

Jimmy's shrill voice returned. "What's up, Ace?"

Ace whispered to Pansy, "He could probably use the clothes."

Her eyes contracted; her brow crumpled in annoyance. "No, he can't," she hissed. "It's no one's business where we're going!"

Ace turned and spoke to the wall. "Never mind, Jimmy. False alarm."

"False alarm, nothing," Jimmy replied. "I know you got a girl over there."

"See?" she mouthed.

Pansy walked to St. Vincent's that afternoon and paid twenty cents for a used handbag. Returning to the shack, she filled it with personal mementos. The faded Kentucky photo. Her mother's tattered address book. Accumulated cash. That evening, she pulled Ace to the barn. Inside, with the door closed under a full moon, her lovely pansy dress slipped to the straw. She drew him to her embrace.

"We're not married yet," he murmured.

"We will be, very soon."

The single ceiling bulb illuminated her bedroom in the early hours the next morning, Sunday, but only momentarily. Pansy had returned the evening before, just after the last train had blown by at ten—the warmth of a sated lust lay heavy in her thoughts, a soft smile on her lips. Her bedroom was the only room in which she turned on lights, preferring the rest of Uncle's shack to remain dark.

Pansy pushed lines and depressions from her pillows, pulled the sheet corners tight, erasing evidence of the fabric ever having been defiled, then walked from her bedroom with resolve.

At the front door, she looked north for one last memory of Emigration Creek, vowing to forever remember its deepest pools, then east to the dark grandeur of the Wasatch Range. She turned back to the interior shadows, debating if anything inside should be taken to Fresno. Uncle's clock struck time. Six a.m. No, there was nothing of value. The long wail of the first morning train blew to her back. To her right, the bright glimmer of moonlight came through the window. Her gaze fixed on the dark shadow of Uncle Luther who lay rigid in his bed. Uncle: the good man who had shared some simple kindness after her mother had been killed. *Thrown right off the goddamn stairs,* she reminded herself. Sometimes, it's best to let things go, Uncle had said.

"Goodbye, Uncle Luther," she whispered. He had gone cold and stiff nearly three weeks ago.

5

PASSING THROUGH THE VAST TRACT OF UTAH
wasteland, the bus crossed into Nevada just before lunch. Ace
appeared to be deep in sleep. A long stop in Elko. Another in
Winnemucca, two hours of boredom around a short lunch in the
station. During long hours of darkness across the barren desert,
Pansy drifted into fantasies of Fresno. A large two-story house
surrounded by a placid sea of orange groves. California had
miles and miles of orange groves, she had heard. Soft, sweet
peaches. Apricots, too. All glowing in the golden California sun.
They would rent a house just outside of town but close enough
to walk to its center.

When they turned from the banks of the Truckee River and
drew within sight of the rugged city of Reno, the sun broke due
east. Pansy hadn't slept, but she had often reached out to Ace,
laying her hand on his thigh in ownership.

They would have a long layover in Reno and then commence
their journey to Fresno, arriving that evening before the California sun had set. She coaxed him into the diner outside the
terminal, where Ace declined to eat. "Toast," Pansy insisted,

ordering for him. He grumbled when their waitress set a plate on the table, the bread's corners dark.

"We shouldn't be spending money," he muttered.

"Toast is only fifteen cents," Pansy replied, pushing it nearer, which he then took and ate.

She sipped hot tea. "Reno is an interesting place."

"It's not California," Ace replied. He raked his hand across the table, collecting breadcrumbs into a loose pile, drawing a precise line down its center. Half to the left. Half to the right.

"I love you," she whispered.

He pushed the crumbs over the table's edge, then rose and returned to the waiting room. Pansy claimed a spot where reading choices were splayed out over an end table and sorted through what had been discarded by previous visitors.

She shoved a *Reader's Digest* in his direction. "This is sure a funny magazine. Never seen one before. Have you ever seen one of these?"

Ace shook his head, no.

She turned pages in ponderance, or rejection. "How to Make a Killing in the Stock Market" did not prompt her to read further. "How to Live without Laxatives" was only compelling from the standpoint that she had never before imagined that people did, in fact, live *with* laxatives. She turned the page in disinterest after the second paragraph clarified that the essay was directed at people who had succumbed to the ills of laxative addiction, which she had certainly not.

Ace could be a laxative addict, she wondered. No, he would have told her. Ace was an honest man.

And on this day, when she wasn't married but told herself she nearly was, she turned to page 129 for an essay titled "What the Marriage Manuals Don't Say."

Women are slower than men to reach sexual climax, she read in the first paragraph. If a man would just take his time, everything would be hunky dory. *Such an odd description,* Pansy thought. It was something her mother would have said but appeared out of place in this discussion. This was something she must share.

"Ace . . . " Pansy whispered. "Look at this." She held the magazine aloft and pointed to its center. "Right here, it says that women are slower to reach climax than men. And it says that if you just take your time, everything will be hunky dory."

"It says *what?*" he asked.

"It's a story about what marriage manuals don't say. See, right there." She pointed to it. "That's the title. You should read this." She again pushed the magazine in his direction.

"Right now?" he snapped. "I don't want to read that." Snarly, Ace had become distant well before seeing the lights of Reno. She chalked it up to a distaste for bus travel.

"Well then, I'll take it with me. You can read it on the bus." She nodded firmly in declaration of what he must do, then resumed her enlightenment, wishing to become further educated on the subject of sexual gratification. Most newly married women, she read, entered their marriages with inhibitions and mistaken expectations that marriage would make them deliciously lewd. Pansy re-read that sentence five times. Deliciously lewd. Language of that sort had caused her to fall in love with words. Not once in her life had she expected to become such . . . but the thought was tantalizing. Provocative. *Deliciously lewd.*

But not much of anything in the written word, to the best of her recollection, had ever taken hold of her imagination as the column "It Pays to Increase Your Word Power," which provided a short vocabulary list of words one should know, sorted alphabetically, and in this issue was devoted only to words beginning with the letter "V."

A vernacular version of speech was defined as a language of a locality, and Pansy immediately recognized that her dear mother had been prone to speaking in the vernacular. *Good to know,* Pansy thought. She inspected the front cover: thirty-five cents. Thirty-five cents seemed a fair price to pay for a vocabulary list that would increase her word power. This was something to break the boredom of the bus ride as she embarked on the rest of her journey to the golden sunshine of California.

The electric wall clock, mounted over the cigarette machine, turned to eight o'clock. Ace was staring at the long hand as it clicked to the top of the hour. Their connecting bus to Fresno would board in one hour.

Locked in exploration of her *Reader's Digest,* Pansy scarcely moved when Ace returned from the washroom.

"How much money do you have?" he asked.

"Eighty dollars and thirteen cents. It's enough to get us started in Fresno." Pansy had done this math already. A rental house could be found within their budget, which she had estimated to match what Ace had previously paid to the bishop. Twenty-five dollars a month, he paid. Maybe a house would cost less in California.

Ace leaned over and whispered. "It's not safe for you to have all that money. What if you get robbed? Or lose it."

"I won't lose it," she said.

"But you might. We should split it," he insisted.

Pansy pondered the suggestion. Eighty dollars was the most money she had ever carried.

"You should give half to me. It's safer that way," Ace prodded.

"Okay, I'll give you half." She reached into her purse, counted the bills, and handed a portion to Ace.

He thumbed through the stack, then gave thirteen dollars back to her. "That's too much. You didn't count the money I already have."

"Oh, yes, I didn't think about that," Pansy said.

"It's safer this way," Ace whispered. "You have half, and I have half."

"Yes," she agreed. She returned to her vocabulary list.

The wall clock read 8:25 p.m.

"'Vicious,'" Pansy quoted from the *Reader's Digest*. "That's a word I'm going to start using."

Abruptly, Ace stood, lifting his suitcase from under the bench.

"Where are you going?" she demanded.

"To the bathroom." He looked at the opposite wall when answering.

"You were just there! Twice!"

"I need to change shirts. This one stinks."

6

PANSY PACED THE STATION, EVEN TRAVELED OUTSIDE
to the parking lot. She invaded the privacy of the men's
bathroom.

"Ace?" she called, thrusting her head into its vestibule.

A big cowboy exited, prompting her profuse apology. "I'm so
sorry," she said. "Was anyone else in there?"

"No," he replied.

For just a moment, Pansy considered reporting Ace to the
police as missing—but that couldn't be done. How many years
could she spend in prison for the theft of Uncle's Social Security
check? She chose a seat in the lobby and pondered her circumstances. The bus to Fresno would depart in fifteen minutes. Ace
had gone, taking his suitcase with him. He had half of her
money. The man who would be her husband had stolen from
her. *I hardly knew that man,* she eventually said to herself.

7

THE CALIFORNIA SKY HAD TURNED TO A THICK, GRAY porridge. Mountains of rice straw were burning across vast lengths of farmland after harvest, sending thick clouds of pestilence into the wet soup of Central Valley fog. Trapped in its gloom, Fresno strangled in the murkiness. Pansy walked the circumference of the Greyhound lobby, then sat to rest when her single bag became heavy. The companionship of another, now gone, had made the fantasy of Fresno seem possible. Reachable. Travelers brushed by in harried purpose, even sat next to her. One might inquire into her well-being, she hoped. She couldn't tell them, of course. One couldn't expect strangers to grasp her hand in comfort. The gloom outside grew darker, and Pansy looked to the wall clock. Night was near. She rose and thrust her hands deep into her coat pockets, fingering her red ribbon. She made her way to the main entrance but paused in uncertainty. She was quickly pushed outside and cowered against the exterior wall. Sister Alice White, a Jehovah's Witness, called out to her. "Hon?"

Pansy looked to the Black woman, who had stepped

forward, thrusting both hands out in greeting. "So pleased to make your acquaintance," she said, encasing Pansy's hand in her own.

Pansy pulled back.

"Hon," Sister White said. "You look lost."

Pansy shook her head in denial. "I just arrived." She looked at the table of literature, which Sister White seemed to be proffering. A White man sat behind the table.

Pansy stepped closer to the table and lifted a thin piece of literature in curiosity. "This is free?"

Sister White brightened. "You can have both copies of the *Watchtower* and *Awake!* for a contribution of ten cents." She joined Brother Fred Leach on the far side of the table.

Pansy returned the magazine to its place.

Sister White gathered several more from her canvas bookbag, then thrust them forward to Pansy, splayed out in the shape of a fan. "Hon, these are back-issues, which are free. You can choose one."

Pansy pulled a magazine from the fan.

"Hon, have you ever wondered why there's so much pain and tragedy in the world?" Sister White asked.

Pansy shook her head, no.

"Well, God's Word tells us that we are in the last days. He will soon bring all the wickedness of this system to an end, but there is hope for some to escape," Sister White explained.

"Escape to where?" Pansy asked.

"So glad you asked!" Brother Leach replied. He stood, but he balled his fists and rested them heavily against the table. He leaned towards Pansy. "It's all part of Jehovah's plan, as laid out in His word, the Bible. He intends to destroy the wicked, and the righteous will then live on his Earth. Everlasting life in God's new world, right here on Earth, is what *we* will have. All part of God's plan." He tapped his fingers in certainty on the green cover of his Bible. "Have you ever read the Bible?" he asked.

"My mother was Catholic," Pansy said.

"So, you didn't read the Bible," he said smugly.

"We didn't have one to read," Pansy conceded.

"No, of course not. Catholics don't read the Bible. That proves they aren't the true religion." Fred crossed his arms over his chest. "As true Christians, Jehovah's Witnesses believe in God's Word. We study the Bible, and we help people understand how it can impact our lives today. Jehovah has a plan for your happiness."

"Hon," Sister White stepped from around the table and thrust a hardcover book, mustard in color, into Pansy's hands. "You are welcome to this. *You May Survive Armageddon into God's New World* was put out by the brothers several years ago. It will be of great help in understanding the promises of Jehovah." Sister White grasped Pansy's hand. "Hon, we are here almost every day. If you wish to learn more, you can come back and see us."

Pansy pushed the literature into her purse. "Thank you," she said, then turned to the street. It was now dark.

"This wicked system is near its end!" Brother Leach repeated. "The Bible's prophecies are coming true as we speak!"

The Venture Hotel, opposite the bus station, wanted seventy-five cents for a single night's stay, advertised out front. Visitors could pay less, if they thought to ask.

On the third floor, Pansy curled up on a single bed, crumpling her pansy dress. Her room had two windows, one of which had been bricked up. The shared toilet was further down the hall.

She woke the next morning but remained face down on the bed, frozen in uncertainty. Eventually, she rose and retrieved the gift from Sister White. Scrawled in pencil, inside the mustard-yellow cover, was the inscription "Evelyn Lee—1955." Pansy read its introduction—a blathering of evil and wicked systems and the plight of those who continued to grope in the world's darkness. Her pulse rose. By midnight, she had reached the final page, having absorbed the horrors of bloodshed at Armageddon, the salvation offered by Jehovah's people—described as the one and only true religion.

Beyond her window, the Southern Pacific Railroad Depot spanned a full block. At dawn, gnawing hunger sent her thoughts to the café inside.

She acknowledged Sister White and Brother Leach out front by smiling in their direction, then made her way to the cafeteria.

Sister White was waiting for Pansy's return. A Bible study was free, the woman guaranteed. There was no obligation whatsoever, short of accepting the love of Jehovah, courtesy of a religion that she referred to as "The Truth."

"Are you in need of help?" Sister White asked.

Brother Leach had retreated behind his table. "You're not in trouble, are you?"

"No, no," Pansy insisted vehemently. She was in a predicament, she would have said if pressed, a relentless predicament ever since her mother had been killed. But not trouble. "I'm staying across the street." She pointed back to the hotel.

"At the Venture Hotel? Oh, honey," Sister White said. "How old are you, sweetie?"

Pansy lied. "Eighteen."

"Where do you live?" Sister White asked.

"I don't know, yet. I just arrived . . . but my uncle is dead."

❖

Sister White climbed the stairs to the third floor of the Venture Hotel, confident in her purpose.

She opened their Bible study with a prayer. After uttering "Amen," she looked at Pansy and said, "Jehovah is a God of mercy and wants you to live forever in his paradise on Earth." She then laid her Bible on the bed. Pansy lifted it to her lap and opened to the middle, caressing the pages with both hands.

"I've never opened a Bible," Pansy confessed.

"Most people haven't if they don't know The Truth," Sister White asserted.

Pansy turned the pages randomly.

Sister White reached over and retrieved it, then opened to Revelation, Chapter 21. She turned the book away from herself so that Pansy might read a passage that the sister recited from memory. "And I saw a new heaven and a new earth, for the former earth had passed away . . . and he will wipe out every tear from their eyes, and death will be no more." She grasped Pansy's hands. "All things are possible with Jehovah. The end of this system is so near. All of the pain and suffering will be no more. You will be made perfect, as Jehovah intended, if you survive Armageddon."

Sister White turned the conversation to more pedestrian questions, but Pansy wasn't to answer most. She had come to Fresno to see her favorite uncle, she replied. The uncle had died, unbeknownst to her, she said.

Sister White grasped Pansy tightly at the door, a warm embrace that made Pansy think of her mother. "Just imagine," the sister promised. "Living forever in Jehovah's perfect world, right here on Earth. And by the way," she added, "Brother Leach owns a cleaning business in town. He is always looking for help. He asked me to relay that message to you. You could start tomorrow, he says."

A heavy gust of sage and sandalwood swept through the entry of Frederick Middleton's home when Brother Leach unlocked its double door. A short stack of currency lay on Fred's bedroom bureau. A tin coffee can in the double closet was heavy with a daily unloading of pocket pennies. *His lack of concern could tempt one to steal,* Pansy thought. A temptation came to her. Perhaps she would put things elsewhere, for safekeeping, which she said out loud to Brother Leach.

"Move nothing," he scolded. "Our task is only to clean, not to make decoration decisions for him."

The need to control cleanliness was a compulsion, Pansy realized. She simply wouldn't be satisfied, she said to Brother Leach at the end of the day, until a home was spotless.

Within three weeks, Pansy was feeling the effects. She was fatigued. More so than she had reason for, she thought.

The response from Jehovah's Witnesses to unwed mothers who show interest in The Truth is a bombardment of affection. Pansy fell into their embrace, unaware that some concluded she was most likely a victim of rape.

She would not succumb to questioning. Some wished she could be coerced into sharing the details of her past. Others argued she wasn't required. She wasn't a Witness when whatever had happened to her—this *thing*—that had pushed her to The Truth.

A week before going into labor, Sister White attempted to lull Pansy into relaxed preparation. They prayed often. Much justification could be found in the Bible for compassion to an unwed mother.

"Have you chosen a name yet?" Sister White asked.

No, Pansy hadn't.

"Well, you will have to give the name of the child's father to the hospital for the birth certificate. Would you like me to start that for you?"

Pansy shook her head, no.

William Whitlow Blackwell arrived on August 17th. A big baby, he popped out on time and in a manner that seemed urgent to embrace life. Pansy pulled him to her chest, swaddled in a blanket, and the scent of a new life reached her nose. She inhaled deeply and thanked Jehovah for this magnificent gift. On William's birth certificate, she listed his father as "unknown."

Pansy returned to work a week after William's birth. Not fussy, he slept when she hoped him to, but eventually, he went to the care of Sister White at her daily bus terminal post. The sister pushed him in his stroller on weekends while walking the streets as a pioneer for Jehovah, and when she laid William out to nap, careful in the way she positioned him, Pansy could see her love for a child who was not hers.

One week from Christmas, Pansy was welcomed to accompany Sister White in proselytizing. They walked a small downtown territory encompassing three residential blocks. Not yet allowed to verbalize her thoughts of what may or may not be The Truth, Pansy was encouraged to smile often and carry a Witness Bible. At every apartment complex on their route, Sister White turned to search-party mode, hunting down laundry rooms and unloading *Watchtower* back-issues for discovery by tenants. One never knew how Jehovah might find his way into people's hearts, she said.

Unable to corner anyone into a lengthy discussion of God,

Sister White invited Pansy to the Sears' coffee shop. Pansy ordered tea and a baked Danish. To their waiter, Sister White handed a pamphlet announcing the local Kingdom Hall worship schedule and an offer for a free Bible study. "We're out in service to Jehovah today, sharing the good news of the kingdom with our neighbors."

He laid the invite on their table, then turned away. Sister White said to Pansy, "It's important to witness to whoever we can."

"Whomever," Pansy corrected.

"Yes, that's what I said."

"How much time should I include on my timecard this week?" Pansy asked.

"Oh, you can put down two hours. Or you might add a little more, if you want. I like to think that I am always out in service to Jehovah. It would be difficult to count the hours, exactly," Sister White answered.

"Okay," Pansy said.

Both agreed it to have been a fine afternoon. "Just lovely," Pansy said. William hadn't been a burden.

"Not in the least," Sister White replied. "He's a good baby. We'll do this again, soon."

They rose and walked across Fulton Street to catch a bus to the south end of town. Pansy had moved there to be closer to Sister White, just one floor above, in a four-story apartment building.

Sister White again inquired into Pansy's past.

"Oh, I can't imagine why anyone would want to know where I moved from. That was an earlier time, before I found Jehovah, and there is no need to dwell on the past," Pansy replied. It was not her first time responding to intrusive questions in that way.

"Well, people talk, you know. People say things, and perhaps I could set them straight."

8

ACE SHARKEY CALLED THE TELEPHONE OPERATOR ON September 15th, 1965, asking if there was a public listing for a woman named Pansy Blackwell in Fresno. William had just entered kindergarten.

Pansy had been on Ace's mind often. Their relationship had been so quick. So short. So distant. So easy for Pansy to classify as an evilness from Satan.

Ace wanted to apologize. Pansy had most certainly met a new husband, perhaps a man to heal his cruelty. Yes, he was cruel, Ace knew. He had been a terrible coward. When she answered the phone, he'd tell her how pretty she looked on that day before they were to be married. *She'll be pleased to know that,* he thought. All women wish to hear they are pretty, yes? Yes, they certainly do, and she'd be pleased that he had remembered it with such detail.

He'd talk about the weather in Reno as if it were the most beautiful thing he had ever felt or could remember, and he'd discuss the gravity of that day, now that five years had passed, because both had moved on, each having found their places in life. Ace would tell her why he had abandoned her. She would forgive him, and they would agree to let the past remain there, moving on in peace. But most importantly, she would be ever so pleased to know that she had not been forgotten by her first love, because the only thing more painful than being abandoned is being forgotten.

The next morning, after their short phone conversation, Pansy wallowed in sorrow, then anger. She regretted telling Ace that he had a son. She wished she could retract that from the phone call. The explanation he had given for abandoning her in Reno weighed heavily. Eventually, it gave her the words to assuage her pain. "That man was a queer," she said to herself. By the end of the day, her regret had soured. It had turned to vindictiveness. "He will never see his son," she uttered aloud and felt peace at the decision.

9

In the northern California town of Farnsworth, where most thought themselves appreciative of good humor but wouldn't have been consumed in thought by how to make it, the most hysterical thing in the whole wide world that Richard "Dick" Stinchfield had ever done was to tie a string of firecrackers to a cat's tail and hold a lit match to the fuse. Dick laughed himself so hard that he cried at the telling of what he had once done and would share it with all who were willing to listen. It did not bother him, neither what he had done nor the telling of it, lacking the self-awareness to recognize evilness.

Dick Stinchfield was very short and very round. His attention span mimicked rubber balls bounced hard off rigid surfaces. His silhouette was globular, his face a beach ball, but there was an anxiousness to him, a demeanor that often darkened with dread, as if in fear of punishment for his secrets. Men who suspected his weaknesses were emboldened to taunt him. His habit was to dress in worn, cotton work pants, long and baggy, then yank them halfway up to his neck—strapping them in place with an old canvas belt that once belonged to his father. Someone had once told him that, should he pull his pants any higher, he might choke to death. Overweight but not in pendulous softness, his fat didn't cascade like globs of melting paraffin but collected under his diaphragm, pressing his gut into a hard protrusion. Limpid arms and legs mimicked the sogginess of overcooked string beans, flopping aimlessly when in motion. "Damnit, that man looks like a frog," someone had said. A thick-necked but weak-jawed creature, his lips were wide and fat, always wet, but he had deep pools of cornflower blue eyes and blindingly beautiful teeth.

Dick had inherited the small campground on the north side of Yreka—a business he routinely shut down for four days each summer for the annual District Assembly of the Jehovah's Witnesses. On July 12th, 1968, he traveled to the assembly in Sacramento, California. "The End is Near!" was the theme. Hughes Stadium was stuffed to capacity by twenty thousand who had traveled hundreds of miles for the three-day event.

The current issue of *Awake!*, titled "Is It Later Than You Think?," laid out in dramatic prose the primary hope and anxiety of the faith, which was that Jehovah would soon bring an end to the world—a prediction that hadn't changed since the religion had first come into existence in the 1880s. Tightening the calendar on their expectations, the Witnesses had published another call to urgency for followers: Was time running out for this generation? What would the 1970s bring? Very few years remain! This corrupt system of things is soon to be destroyed by God!

An earnest follower, Brother Stinchfield had been chosen to lead two theatrical reenactments of biblical events. He would first play the role of an ancient Israelite, Abraham, who was instructed by God to murder his young son Isaac. A reluctant second-grade boy, Bobby Sullivan, had been asked to play the part of Isaac. Bobby had no lines to learn. He was only required to recline on the altar and pretend to let Brother Stinchfield murder him for Jehovah.

Brother Walter Hess, a thick and authoritative mountain of masculinity from Fresno, was asked to play the part of Jehovah by concealing his presence behind a wall of cardboard. He couldn't be seen on stage, of course, as everyone knew that Jehovah could not actually be seen.

Dick had stuffed a foldout bed from camp into the back seat of his Town and Country Chrysler wagon; then he rolled it out as a pretend sacrificial altar for their first rehearsal at the back end of the convention parking lot. He wrapped himself in an old, white sheet to resemble what he imagined the wayward Israelites wore many centuries ago.

Bobby, barefoot, laid out on the pretend altar to rehearse his impending murder. Dick insisted, "We should tie him up for reals, dontcha think?" But when the first rope bound Bobby's ankles to the cot, the kid screamed, "I don't wanna get sacrificed for Jehovah!"

On stage, Dick followed the script to the letter, as required. The murder of Isaac aborted by heavenly intervention, Dick made his way to the other side of a cardboard barrier, then returned as the Apostle Paul in a new sheet of green stripes. He waved his arms about as if sweeping away the ills of sin, then fell to his knees and looked to the heavens in feigned blindness, proclaiming his undying allegiance to Jehovah, who promptly granted the return of his eyesight in compensation. While the audience again broke into applause, Pansy Blackwell, seated in Section F, Row 27, Seat J, felt the flush of the Holy Spirit move through her soul.

The crowd broke for lunch—some pulled coolers from under their chairs, others formed long lines for burgers. Tanika Duncan stood with Pansy and William, deep in the burger counter queue. Tanika had recently moved out from Mississippi —Pansy had met her at the Fourth Street Laundromat but turned the Bible study over to Sister White. That morning, on Pansy's recommendation, Tanika had purchased two dollars of ten-cent meal ticket scrip, pale blue in color.

Pansy, yet to receive lunch, was still gushing over Dick Stinchfield's presentation. "That was the most magnificent presentation I have ever seen. That man is a true gift from Jehovah."

Tanika lifted the top bun from her burger, searching for condiments. "They should put onions on these."

"I look forward to these burgers every year," Pansy said.

"Pickles would be nice," Tanika suggested.

"Yes, well, the spiritual food is certainly plentiful at the convention, don't you think?" replied Pansy, changing the subject.

Tanika shrugged. "What do I do with the leftover tickets?"

"You can use them tomorrow."

"I'm not coming tomorrow," Tanika reminded Pansy.

"You might, perhaps?"

"Can I get my money back?" Tanika asked.

"No, they don't give refunds," Pansy said.

Tanika shuffled the fake currency from one hand to another, having separated each stub from its perforated sheet of ten. "Can I use them at the next assembly?"

"Well, no, of course not. The next assembly will change the color. You wouldn't expect the organization to take tickets from an old assembly, would you? I have a whole collection back home. All different colors," Pansy boasted.

Tanika stuffed the meal tickets into her purse.

Brother Dick Stinchfield, a single man, stood a distance away. Pansy took three bold steps to meet him.

"Your presentation was truly magnificent," she gushed. "A real blessing from Jehovah."

Dick ran his tongue over his lips. "Well, I appreciate that. Thank you very much." He rose to his toes, peering at the name badge on Pansy's left breast. "Is that Fresno I see on your badge?" He tapped the plastic badge on his lapel. "Brother Stinchfield. I'm from Siskiyou County, way up in the northern end of the state. I own a campground." He reached a stubby hand out to Pansy for a handshake she eagerly accepted. "How long have you been in The Truth?" he asked.

"Eight years. I count my blessings every day for being part of Jehovah's true organization." She pushed William out to meet him. "This is my son, William."

"Ahh, he looks like a fine young man," Dick said. "Is your husband in The Truth?"

"William and I are alone," Pansy replied. "I am not married."

Her breasts drew his attention, but Dick recognized that others could be stumbled by inappropriate staring. Sister White, an observant woman, took notice.

"And what do you do in Fresno?" he inquired.

"I work for Brother Leach, cleaning houses. You must know him? He's our circuit overseer," Pansy said.

Dick's head snapped erect. "Cleaning houses? Ah, yes. Brother Leach. Well, that sounds like a wonderful opportunity to work in the companionship of other Witnesses." He placed his hand on William's shoulder. "And does this fine young man help you?"

"Well, he's usually in school, of course," Pansy answered.

Dick smiled. "Ahh, yes." He wrapped his fingers around the collar of William's shirt. "How do you enjoy Fresno? I hear it gets hot there."

"Fresno isn't an ideal place to live," Pansy replied. "But the new system will be here soon."

"Yes, this wicked system is going to be over very soon," Dick agreed.

Dick made conversation, grasping William's collar as if laying claim. William didn't say a word in complaint as his mother appeared flushed in the presence of the man who had been cured of blindness by Jehovah. Dick suggested that the cleaning business was a good career in these last days. "By the way, I am looking for a cleaning person at my campground," he said. "It's a good job. Comes with free housing. Our congregation is very small. Would be great if we could get a sister to move up to help us out. Maybe you're interested? Well, I'd sure be happy to talk with you about it more. It comes with free housing; did I mention that?"

10

On Monday, July 22nd, 1968, Dick Stinchfield loaded Pansy and William Blackwell into his 1948 Chrysler Town and Country station wagon and drove them away from Fresno. By the end of the day, Pansy and William had become Farnsworth residents, numbers 744 and 745.

Just a week prior, William had eavesdropped on telephone calls his mother had made to Dick—a one-sided eavesdrop, hearing Pansy's commentary on her understanding of how the need was great for more of Jehovah's servants at the northern end of the state. Most of her words seemed to focus on kitchen utensils, bedding, and furniture. She ruminated over what was needed and what would be provided, or what could be sold and what could be given away, but most often, she gloated over the fact that leaving Fresno meant leaving people who wanted to get in her business.

By telephone with the Fresno congregation secretary, Dick had already requested Pansy's publisher file to be sent to him. Pansy was not aware that the congregation kept records of the behaviors and personal histories of its members, but Dick had received it in the mail a week before. He had pondered its contents. Wondered about the condition of her arrival to The Truth as an unwed mother. That scandal aside, the file assured him that Pansy had been a fine servant of Jehovah.

The night before they departed for Farnsworth, he had spent the night at the Fresno Comfort Motel on the west side of town, breakfasted alone the next morning, and then pulled up to Pansy's apartment. Idling in front, Dick stacked the seven cardboard boxes of possessions that Pansy had carried out to the sidewalk inside his car, then slapped his hand on the hood in the vulgar manner of gluttony. "You wouldn't believe what my dad used to shove inside this car!" He leaned in to Pansy. "Runs like a champ. Just like the day my dad bought it." The paint, bleached by two decades in the sun, was still reminiscent of its original avocado color, perhaps similar to the inside of the fruit now, near the pit where the flesh is most pale, almost yellow. The front hubcaps were missing; black rims peered out like sightless eyeballs.

"Well, might as well head on up to paradise," he said.

Pansy had packed lunches for their journey, and she settled into the green vinyl of the front seat, preparing herself for a welcome exit. The night before, she had thought of how she would bid Fresno farewell. The previous Thursday evening, just outside the Kingdom Hall, she had embraced Sister White in a tight grip of affection, promising to call soon.

The Central Valley peach trees, then almond, flew by in a vast blur of orchards. English walnuts with gnarled, grafted stumps of black walnut grew right up to the edges of Highway 99, and then miles of flat grazing land burned brown by the summer sun pulled the horizon into clear view. Dick nearly hyperventilated at his good fortune to have found an employee to clean camp. His congregation would increase by two new members. An accomplishment in the eyes of The Truth. Siskiyou was a magnificent place to live, he assured Pansy. She concurred that she could see his descriptions in her imagination, the majestic beauty of the northern state, and then Dick didn't shut his mouth for precisely two hours and fifteen minutes, at which time he simply ran out of things to say. Dick's blathering gave William reason to like him. Or hate him. He wasn't sure.

Farnsworth was paradise, Dick again stated. "It's the perfect place to see an end to this wicked system."

Pansy nodded. "The new system could come tomorrow. We only have to wait on Jehovah to fulfill his promises."

"Exactly: 1975. The End will be here by then," Dick stated.

"How do we know?" William asked from the rear seat.

Dick looked at William in his rearview mirror. "It marks six thousand years since Jehovah created Adam and Eve. It's the perfect opportunity for him to destroy the wicked. At the end of the sixth day."

"Figuratively," Pansy added. "The Bible says a thousand years is like a day to Jehovah."

"The Bible tells us we are in the last days. All we have to do is look at the wickedness in this world. It will all come to an end. Soon," Dick said confidently.

"Stay alive to '75," Pansy said.

They were now traveling past the poor farming town of Orland. Dick pointed to a thick hedge of pink shrubs in the median. "Last summer, a family stopped right there and cut some branches off those oleander bushes to roast hot dogs. Killed every single one of them."

Pansy gasped. "Killed them?"

"Yup. Oleanders are poisonous as all get-out. Will kill you dead," he explained.

She turned to William, her eyebrows arched. "Killed them," she repeated.

The enormity of Mount Shasta, still blanketed in its thick embrace of winter snow, rose from the valley floor. An hour later, on the north side of its slope, they entered the Shasta Valley, which bucked and rolled like bareback horses at the Farnsworth Rodeo. On the western side of the valley, over by the county seat of Yreka, the land had been swept clean by men from China who had toiled for decades to stack lava rubble into short walls, defining property lines and grazing rights.

In spring, torrents of snowmelt first rushed and then meandered through the valley. Fed and starved by ice and snow from peaks above, the rivers drew fishermen from afar who paid good sums to catch wild, cold-water fish, greatly favored over the artificially stocked reservoirs in other parts of the state. The fishermen—invaders, men of wealth—came to Siskiyou with deep buckets of cash and spent it on cheap motels and expensive gear in pursuit of the elusive rainbow trout, only to release them unharmed. Men who had lived their entire lives in Siskiyou County grumbled about the wealth that some men expended to fish purely for sport.

Dick had never caught a fish. Couldn't stand the taste of them, he said, but earned his living from the passions of those who did. "That's Boles Creek, over there," he said, pointing off to the left. "They catch some big fish out of that creek, I've heard."

Polled red Hereford cattle picked their way through valley hillsides, fattening on native grasses and sometimes constrained by remnants of old stone walls. Long stretches of rusted barbed wire and rotting fence posts were strung across the landscape, confining livestock to land on which they were intended to graze, but it wasn't unusual for telephone calls to crisscross the county, informing others of cattle wandering places in which they should not be. During months of cold and rain, the Siskiyou landscape had hues of green, but on this day, well into summer, the lower hills were burned to a golden brown. Off to the right, Gregory Mountain had turned the ragged and dull hue of dust, not golden at all.

Dick left the freeway and drove through a vast swath of irrigated hay field. He stated that they were within spitting distance of their destination.

A street sign said they were now traveling up Farnsworth Road. Two miles later, where it crossed into the city boundary on the south side of town, Farnsworth Road became Eleventh Street for four blocks before again becoming Farnsworth Road, where it then ran through more alfalfa pastures. It then took a little dogleg to the right and ran straight for many more miles before turning back to the freeway and landing in the little town of Hornbrook, population ninety-seven, seventeen miles away. It would be two years before Pansy walked the sidewalk of Hornbrook. There simply wasn't any reason for the people of Farnsworth to visit there, or vice versa, unless they were trading cattle from one ranch to another. Or if there were a good horse you'd decided you must have. Or if you had been assigned the Hornbrook territory card on a Saturday morning and would walk its four short streets in service to Jehovah.

At Eleventh Street, Dick turned the Chrysler east, traveling slowly down Scobie Street, where four little square houses stood lonely on wide lots with full views of the southern pasture. A caramel-brown, dented Ford pickup, loaded with hay bales stacked three higher than the cab, was going west. Two blocks further, at the rodeo arena where two cowboys on horseback were roping calves for fun and where Scobie Street dead-ended, Dick turned left onto South Eighth. "Those are the Smidts," he said, pointing out the window. Jack and Sam Smidt often ran calves into the arena from their backyards next door—for private calf roping practice on land they didn't own. No one would ever tell them they couldn't do this.

"This'll be the only official tour of Farnsworth you're gonna get," Dick declared without looking over in Pansy's direction. "There's not much to see, but I might as well drive you around before it gets dark." Two blocks later, where South Eighth Street crossed Webb, he read the street sign aloud. "Now we're on North Eighth." Dick stopped in front of a sterile, single-story building. An upright concrete block announced itself as Farnsworth Elementary School.

Dick then cruised up and down four residential blocks, stopping to read the street signs out loud. "We're on North Seventh Street," he said. "Now South Seventh." Each, only one block long.

There were fourteen blocks laid out in short rectangles on the west side of the railroad tracks. Half as many on the east. All were split down their middles by wide alleys of dirt. Some blocks were vacant pastures of weeds. Others were doomed to eternal emptiness, save for one or two homes where there might have been room for a dozen more. Prather Street was partially paved with irregular scabs of gray asphalt for one of its blocks, then turned to gravel for three more until dead-ending at a field where a vast and brittle stand of oats waved in the wind, yellowed with maturity, and too late to be cut.

For reasons no one remembered, Farnsworth was deposited in the northern shadow of Gregory Mountain. There was no reasonable explanation for how this came to be. Mt. Shasta hulked over the entire valley, but if you lived in Farnsworth and wanted to see if Shasta was still around, you'd have to walk to the western edge of town, over to Thirteenth Street, and lean over to catch a glimpse beyond the slope of Gregory Mountain.

Merely a hill, Gregory was three simple humps of dirt, one taller than the others, all a dull and dead hue of brown.

There was one single, solitary sidewalk in Farnsworth, on the main drag of Eleventh Street, where the business district had been in a long state of rest. Each store was shuttered tight and had been for years. The sidewalk traveled two blocks of Eleventh, but only on the west side. The opposite side, where the railroad tracks ran from north to south and split the town in half, had no use for a sidewalk. That was where the railroad tracks were. The power had intentionally been turned off, and retail storefronts gave few hints as to previous identities.

Across the street, a hundred yards from the tracks, Clark's Grocery was stuffed into the first floor of a two-story cinderblock structure. The building may never have been intended to be a grocery at all. A warehouse it had wanted to be, maybe.

Dick stopped in front. "This's where you'll do your shopping." He pointed to the shell of a second floor. "The whole place almost burnt down, can't remember how long ago."

People lived in Farnsworth. Pansy could see this. Cars were parked in driveways, though some may have died and been sitting for eternity. Pickup trucks vastly outnumbered sedans. Children's toys and old living room furniture were strewn behind chain-link fences in front yards that hadn't any hints of intentional landscaping. She heard a dog bark—just once—and was struck by the discovery of two lush and manicured lawns at the corner of Fifteenth and Prather. This stood out to her as admirable, being the only homes in town to seed and maintain grass in their front yards. Pansy had not glimpsed a living soul, except for the two cowboys and the barking dog, which Pansy hadn't seen but heard.

Dick continued down three blocks of West Spiers and turned into the ruts of an old driving path. He eased the car down a long tunnel of overgrown lilacs. That was where he ended their long drive, at his parent's home: a little house painted in more than one shade of green. Dick killed the engine where the tunnel had led them, opened his door, then raised his arms in a great stretch. Pansy hadn't yet exited, but when Dick made his way to the front door of the cottage, she scraped her damp palms against her skirt, then leaned into the cushion of the vinyl seat and gave a great sigh. Farnsworth was everything she had prayed for.

It wasn't yet dark, and the sky was clear. Bereft of streetlights, Farnsworth would vanish into darkness when the sun went down. Dick had closed his car door hard, out of habit. "And here we are," he almost yelled, stretching his arms wide. "Of course, the place might need a little scrubbing."

Pansy pulled herself from the front seat and joined Dick at the front door. She noticed that it was another shade of green. "A pretty shade of green," she said to him.

Dick turned the handle, which wasn't locked. "You're not paying rent and all, but I would expect you to not cause any wear and tear on my property. This is my parents' home, you understand."

She ushered William inside. Dick stopped to take a long look at a room he hadn't visited in months. "This is the living room, obviously." A tired couch in fuzzy gold cotton sat against one wall.

Her eyes flicked across the green walls; the cottage seeped in an imperceptible fog, like the tone of soft moss at a water's edge. Gold carpet in the living room. Wooden floors elsewhere, except the kitchen. Lime-green linoleum there. A wooden bookshelf stood opposite the front door, stacked several feet high with three decades of JW literature. Three art prints of places she did not recognize were secured to the wall above the couch with thumbtacks.

Dick tugged the pull-chain hanging from the ceiling, illuminating the bare bulb.

"As I told you, this house is a one-bedroom, but my father built a little addition on the back of the kitchen, which you could use for the big guy." He pointed to William. "It gets a little cold out there in winter, but I think you'll be just fine." He crouched in a failed attempt to look William in the eye. "Just think how much fun it will be to have your own room."

"I had my own room in Fresno," William replied, wondering why the frog-man had squatted.

"Oh. Yes, you did. Well, you'll get your own room here, like where you came from," Dick stated.

Dick turned back to Pansy. "I pulled the valuables out before Mom died, but much of my parents' things—sheets, beds, kitchen stuff—are still in the house. It's probably more'n you'll ever need. Who knows, you might find that you got too much stuff. You might have a yard sale someday."

Pansy nodded.

"But if your stuff turns out to be extra, be sure you're sellin' your own things and not mine."

Pansy's jaw tightened. She looked to the fuzzy couch, inspecting its wear. It was no worse than the couch she had abandoned in Fresno—sold to the Graham sisters for thirty-five dollars. More specifically, thirty-five dollars was for the rest of her furniture—two twin beds, two dressers, and one knotty pine dining table for four. The Graham sisters weren't willing to pay anything for the couch but agreed to take it for free if Pansy wished to leave it behind.

In the furthest corner, near the single window that looked out to the lilac tunnel, Dick brushed the upholstery on a green wingback chair. A small side table was stacked high with empty shoe boxes. "I found my mother dead, right here in this chair."

The thought that Cora would soon be resurrected by Jehovah came to Pansy. The woman would rise from the dirt, and Pansy would say hello. Would you like your house back? That's what she would say.

Brother Stinchfield pushed the bedroom door open. Two twin beds were dismantled—wooden headboards and iron rails stacked against the wall. Mattresses lay on the floor, one piled crooked on top of the other.

"Thought I was gonna sell them," Dick said. "But I changed my mind. One was Mom's, the other was Dad's. Figure you can move one out to the back porch for the kid," nodding his head in the direction of the kitchen where William was investigating.

Pansy scanned the room, not wanting to relay her opinions. Then, both returned through the hallway, entering the kitchen, where a great window opened to the outdoors. A grassy, green pasture stretched across the northern horizon.

"It's a magnificent view, isn't it?" Dick pointed to the near corner of his property. "That's the garage, over there." He walked the few steps to the laundry room. "This should make a bedroom for your kid." To his left, a worn washing machine. Next to it, a handmade table, at one time painted a clean shade of white. To the right, the roofline sloped low to a single window. He stepped out through the back door, down narrow wooden steps. "Careful. That step's a little rotten. Been meaning to replace it, someday," which was not to say that he intended to replace it soon. Soon is not synonymous with someday, despite some wishing that it was.

William had joined them out back. The three briefly stood together, drawn to the expanse of pasture, but Dick and Pansy soon returned to the kitchen. Dick wiped a stubby finger across the tiled counter, laying a thick line in its dust. He raised his hand to inspect what he had done, then ground the dirt between his thumb and forefinger. "You'll probably want to do some cleaning. Things get dusty. Especially in summer, what with the dirt roads out front. It'll get better when the rains come." He wiped his fingers on his belly. "Well, you'll know how to take care of that, but, as I said, you're welcome to use most anything in the house. Except for what's in the garage. I put my mother's things in there for storage. Some of it might be worth something, someday."

He walked to the front door. "My mother's soap is still layin' there in the bathtub. You can keep it. I'll pick you up at 7 a.m. sharp on Monday morning." He raised his forefinger and shook it at her, as if holding a stick. "You know, there are some days in winter when we don't have guests, so we might cut your hours a bit."

Pansy raised her head in alarm. "Seven a.m.? That's a little early and well before William will leave for school."

"School is closed for the summer," Dick stated.

"Yes, but when it reopens in fall, would it be possible for us to mutually agree on a later time? Perhaps 7:45?" Pansy asked. "That should give me ample time to walk him to school. School probably starts at eight."

"Walk him to school?" Dick raised his arms in mock indignation. "This is Farnsworth. I don't know how things were in Fresno, but kids can walk to school just fine in this town." He looked across the doorway to William, who had returned through the back porch. "Can you do that? I'll bet you can! You're a responsible boy and can get to school on your own. In fact, once we're done here, you might want to test that out." He turned back to Pansy and pointed in the direction of town. "Everything you need is just a block or two away. You can walk the whole town in about ten minutes. You might want to give that a try once you get settled. Nothin' bad happens out here, so you can walk all you like." He made his way to the front door. "Think of all the exercise you'll get."

Pansy turned in at midnight, having flopped a mattress in a corner, chosen after inspections revealed nothing to indicate which one had been Cora's. She wouldn't knowingly sleep on Fred's mattress. In the blackness of her room, she faced the door, which was closed, focusing on faint light through the window opposite. There was that—a small window, which wasn't bothersome as the house was small. *Why not be small,* Pansy said to herself. It looked out to a thick stand of cherry plums that had gone rogue just beyond—limbs twisting themselves into a tight bramble, branches bent low with yellow fruits the size of cherry tomatoes, blocking sight of the vacant field next door. Sharp angles of moonlight drifted through the window, then danced gently across her wall.

The home of the closest neighbor, across the open field, was entirely darkened. She reflected briefly on William, asleep in the next room, sprawled across the gold couch, and thought to check on him, but didn't. A pleasantness took her thoughts while she thought of her boy. He was not prone to idleness or mischievous trouble. William did not require overbearing supervision. Sheltered by the familiarity of her own blanket that she had unpacked, she slid in and out of awareness that she was drifting backwards and forwards—at one moment a lucid spectator of the moonlight waltz, another visiting the realm of her imaginings, but she decided the imaginings couldn't be dreams at all. She wasn't sleeping. *I am dreaming,* she said to herself, *but I am not asleep,* she confirmed and again slid inside the dream with hopes of extending its enjoyment. Visions of the soft caresses of her mother, Loretta, so remote, languished in the distant past.

Wonderment and gratitude for the Great Jehovah who had brought her to this place, where solitude caressed the little green house into a soft lullaby and the intrusiveness of others could not be found.

She woke early and rose before the sun reached over the Cascades into the Shasta Valley. She tiptoed across the kitchen floor, fumbling for the only light switch, contemplating how she would lay claim to what had previously belonged to someone else. William was still asleep on the fuzzy couch. The early Siskiyou air had a morning sharpness that tasted clean on her tongue. The thick paste of Fresno tule fog was absent here. The punishing heat that unfailingly suffocated the Central Valley each summer would not pursue them to Farnsworth, Dick had promised. She wondered if she would ever see it, feel it, again. The daily blaze of a Fresno summer had grown on her, become part of her, but she would not miss it.

The rising sun eventually touched the far edge of the great pasture, bathing it in a pink glow. Pansy leaned on the sink and basked in its beauty. It was the first time she had ever noticed how the first light of morning could tinge an entire thin and wispy stretch of cirrus clouds in pastels of color. Pink, then orange; the sky a baby blue in contrast. It was an omen, perhaps, of things to come.

Convinced that Jehovah had shown himself in the beauty of this landscape, tinged a hue of pink roses as if in pleasure at what she had done, Pansy sipped hot tea, cradling the warm teacup in both hands. It was a simple tea, black. A generic brand. She had turned it thick with sugar. The kitchen cabinets were far from empty. Salt, pepper, a few cans of tuna. More noodle soup than one could eat in a year, to her approximation. Four tin storage containers, staggered in size, flour in one, sugar in another, the other two empty. A sticky bottle of pancake syrup, half empty. She turned away from the pasture and took a seat at the table with Cora's teacup in hand, contemplating the great things she would do. She was here, in a new home. William would be fine here. They would build a new life here. Armageddon would certainly arrive soon, while they were here. Perhaps she would can peaches before summer slipped away.

William rolled off the couch when Pansy dropped a can of SPAM on the floor. She had quietly laid the contents of all the cupboards in methodical lines and groupings across the counters. The cabinet doors hung open. She fried thin slices of SPAM for breakfast and then took a quick walk to Clark's for the bare minimum of groceries to feed them for a few days. By late afternoon, when the sun was still hours from ducking behind the western ridge, the little green house was nearly scrubbed to death, and William then hadn't a thing to do. Having seen everything within Farnsworth's limits and encountering no one to say hello to, he found the invisible line drawn around the town's sixteen blocks. Precisely fifty feet behind his bedroom lay its boundary. The edge of town was quite definitive in this way. Stand on the south side of the back fence behind Dick Stinchfield's little rental house, and you were in the town of Farnsworth. Climb over to the rolling pasture, and you would be in the wild, cattle-grazing, unincorporated wilderness of Siskiyou County.

On its northeasterly side, barren hillsides shot diagonal lines of shallow ravines downhill, each succumbing to a soft roll at the pasture's edge. The swales of grass rippled in the breeze. The vast meadow created a desire to experience it up close, to feel the brush of the blades. The swales buckled, and tufts of slough sedge erupted high from stream banks, commanding one to investigate. The magic was powerful there and called to everyone possessed of an inner explorer.

There was a time, thirty years prior, when cattle were driven from the pasture and run straight down Farnsworth Road to the center of town, then loaded on rail cars, right there on Eleventh Street, where people could enjoy the parade, but that didn't happen anymore.

The immense playground drew William's gaze—the only barrier to exploration being a simple barbed-wire fence—originally strung tight but now limp with age. He found a weak spot and climbed over, leaving the little green house behind. The grass rose higher than his waist at the mudline of the Oregon Slough, where the drainage ran slow and murky in its travel north. In the distance, above the lower river bottom, a small shed stood as lonely sentry at the next rise, lodged in black lava rock. A mile west of the vast pasture, the slough eventually rolled into the Shasta River, which twisted westerly for nine miles to the great Klamath, then roared with foam and tipped itself into the sea. The ancient Weaver barn, two-story and built of old-growth redwood, soared five hundred yards away, tilting slightly to the east, a fifty-foot perimeter of soil tamped to a smooth finish by spring rains and the pacing of men. A tall man in a cowboy hat periodically entered and exited the structure, doing nothing specific that William could identify and too distant to give any thought to.

Investigating the bottom grassland where the stream wove in and out of concealment, William jumped the soggy tufts of mud colonies along the Oregon Slough. He slipped to his knees and then crawled out to the other bank but soon waded back in as if intending to bathe, thinking Pansy would be really angry if he drowned.

A loud voice shattered the quiet.

"Hey, you! Youngster!"

William turned. The big man at the barn was looking his way.

"Come over here," the man thundered, motioning with his arm.

A boy to not yet think he might question authority, William walked the long distance to the man who had entered the grassland. William had seen men of this nature before but never spoken to one. Wearing a striped Western shirt and straw cowboy hat stained by sweat, he was followed by a dog of many colors. The man asked a question. "Are you lost?"

"No," William answered.

"What are you doin'?" the man asked.

William shrugged. "Just walking around."

"I don't believe I've seen you before. Have we met?"

"No."

"I didn't think so. I could call the sheriff on you, you know, for trespassing." The cowboy frowned. "Are you the kinda man who trespasses on someone else's property?" he asked.

The question made no sense. A seven-year-old should not be referred to as a man. William squinted in puzzlement. "I didn't know this belonged to anyone." He looked around. "There's no house."

"That doesn't mean anything. Someone still owns the property, don't you think?"

William didn't respond.

"Well, don't you?" the man pressed. "Don't you think someone probably owns this, and that someone ain't you?"

"Sorry," William replied. "Are you going to call the police?"

"Well, why don't you tell me who you are first." The cowboy thrust his big hand out in greeting. "My name is Steve. Who are you?"

"William."

"Pleasure to meet you, William. How old are you?"

"Seven. Almost eight."

"You wanna tell me what you're doin' out here?"

"I wasn't doing anything." William turned back to face town. "We just moved into that house over there, the green one, and I was just walking around. I wasn't going to take anything."

Steve looked at the house near the southern edge of the pasture. "That house belongs to Dick Stinchfield."

William nodded. "Brother Stinchfield goes to our Kingdom Hall."

"Ah, yes, the Kingdom Hall in Yreka. He goes there. I know that already. And . . . so do you?" Steve inquired.

"We haven't been to Yreka yet. Where's Yreka?"

Steve pointed to the western slope. "About six miles, that way. So, you're not from here. But I know Dick Stinchfield. Dick let you live in his house?"

William replied with what made the most sense to him. "Well, we live there now, so I guess he let us do it."

Steve broke into laughter. "Good answer."

"Are you going to call the police?" William asked.

Steve shook his head. "There's no police out here. The sheriff takes care of things when we need it, but no, I'm not gonna call them."

"Okay," William said.

"But if you're wondering, I own this land," Steve explained.

"Oh. I'm sorry," William replied.

"You're sorry I own it?"

It was not in William's nature to assume an adult would joke about property ownership. "No, I'm just sorry for trespassing."

"Ahh . . . it's okay. I'm just foolin' with you. I'm not used to seeing kids I don't know wanderin' around my pasture, but you weren't hurtin' anything, so we'll just let that go. Deal?" Steve again shoved his hand out, which William took for the second time. Steve pumped it firmly, a quick but solid grasp. "Good handshake! I'm impressed."

Unsure of what to make of the need for handshakes and uncertain what, specifically, impressed the cowboy, William turned his attention to the dog that had trailed behind. "Is that your dog?"

"Yup," Steve answered.

"What's his name?"

"Booger."

"*Booger?*" William's mouth opened wide in astonishment. "You named your dog *Booger?*"

"Well, no, I didn't. Someone else did, before I got 'im."

William looked hard at the animal, searching for an explanation. "Why didn't you give him a new name?"

Steve laughed. "Well, that wouldn't be very nice, expecting your dog to come runnin' when you call him by something he doesn't know. There's nothin' wrong with his name. Booger is just fine, by him and me."

William squinted. "He's a funny-looking dog. How come he doesn't have a tail? Shouldn't he have a tail?"

"Someone cut it off when he was a pup."

"Cut it off?" William's eyes opened wide as saucers.

"Cow dogs don't have tails, except kelpies. They need tails, but most others have their tails docked," Steve explained.

William wasn't sure what to make of that; it didn't sound believable, but the cowboy seemed honest. He moved toward Booger, who didn't seem offended by the scrutiny. "He's got too many colors." William peered closer. "And he's got one blue eye. And one brown eye!"

"He's a mixture, like Heinz 57. Maybe Queensland heeler. I think he's got some Australian shepherd in there, too," Steve said.

"I don't know what Heinz 57 is." William squatted next to Booger. "Does he bite?"

"I'm sure he will if he doesn't like someone, but I don't know that he's ever bit anyone before. He won't bite you, if that's what you're wondering. He's my best pal, so as long as I'm here, he'll think you're my pal too, and we'll all git along just fine."

William stroked the top of Booger's head, moving to his ears, at their base where they flopped over.

Steve smiled. "Well, I guess we're good now, huh? Booger will be your pal, too."

William stood and brushed mud from the knees of his pants. Water dripped, then seeped into the dust.

"Looks like you got yourself in a little trouble back there," Steve said.

"I fell in."

"Damn straight, you did. All the way in, it looks to me."

Steve nodded in the direction of the green house in the distance. "So, now that you live there, I'll assume you're gonna wander over here again. Is that right?"

Again, William didn't answer. No need to answer questions with obvious answers.

Steve folded his arms over his chest. "Okay, let's assume the answer is yes. If you're gonna be spendin' time out here, I want you to promise me a few things."

"Okay," William replied. "What?"

"Well, now that you know I own this pasture, you should mind your manners. That's the right way to do things. You show some respect for your neighbor's property. Act like it belongs to you, even if it don't. Can you do that?" Steve asked.

"Yes," William replied, nodding.

"So that means when we run cows out here, you gotta be

respectful," Steve explained. "Don't be doin' somethin' that puts them in danger. Got it?"

"Like what?" *What could possibly put cows in danger, and why would anyone do so?* Steve asked odd questions, William decided.

"Don't be chasin' 'em around the pasture. If we got calves out here, you don't need to be runnin' 'em all over the property. And no shootin', either. Don't be huntin' without my permission. Got it?"

"Shooting?" William repeated.

"Yeah, shooting. Do you have a gun?" Steve asked.

"A gun? We don't have any."

"That'll change, now that you live here. Where'd you come from?"

"Fresno," William answered.

"Fresno? Don't people have guns in Fresno?"

"I don't know!" There was apparently no end to the silly questions this cowboy would ask.

"Well, I've never been to Fresno," Steve replied. "It's a lot bigger than Farnsworth, though. I know that for a fact." His gaze briefly roamed the pasture. "Might as well be a big city, compared to here. Did you live in town? With neighbors right next door?"

"We had lots of neighbors in our apartment building. And big trees on the side where people parked their cars. And there was a Safeway next door," William said.

"You had an apartment building? As in, you owned one?"

William grimaced in denial. "No, Mr. Weisner owned it. We just had an apartment with lots of trees outside. One fell on the apartment building once, and some people had to move out. Their windows got broken."

"Well, that's good to know," Steve replied. "Is that why you left Fresno?"

"No. My mom said everyone was getting in her business. She said people shouldn't be in her business."

Steve nodded. "Well, I can see that. I think that's how apartments in the city are. You live right on top of everyone else." He rubbed his forehead in thought, tilting his hat above his hairline. "I don't know that for a fact, though. Haven't never been in an apartment. But I've seen 'em on TV."

"Our apartment had rules. Rules about where you could play and where you could sit. Mr. Weisner said I couldn't sit on the stairs and watch people go up and down, since that was against the rules. And rules about how we had to pay him and how my mom couldn't put *Watchtowers* in the laundry room anymore," William explained.

"Sounds like a lot of rules."

William nodded. "People didn't shoot guns, so I think it was against the rules."

"Well, that was probably a good rule, I reckon. And now you live over there in Dick Stinchfield's house. Or his parents' house. His mom and dad used to live there."

"I don't know them," William said.

"No, they're dead."

That was not something William could talk about. He'd not ever seen anyone dead. But he didn't know them, and he had already decided that he liked this big cowboy, so something should be said to continue their introduction.

"Brother Stinchfield said his dad used to burn stuff in the can out back, but now it's against the rules, and we're not supposed to burn anything. He doesn't have insurance, but he told my mom not to tell anyone about that. He said people don't need to know his business."

"Good to know," Steve replied. "People in Farnsworth don't usually want to know anyone else's business. So, if you're a city kid, why don't we make things simple and just say that if you're wanderin' my pasture, you'll treat the place like it belongs to you. That means you'll take care of things, because I'm your neighbor, and we'll be friends. Sound good?"

William marveled at the gift that had just been bestowed: the right to trespass and the ease with which the big cowboy announced that they were friends.

"Is your dad home?" Steve asked.

"I don't have a dad. My mom says some kids don't have dads."

"Oh, she does, does she?" Steve again folded his arms over his chest, spreading his legs wide. "Well, I guess that tells us something. Okay then, is your mom home?"

"She's scrubbing the house to death."

"Good to know. Why don't you take me over so I can say howdy?"

Steve herded William in the direction from which he had come, weaving through a path in the tall grass that William had carved. At the slough, being unwilling to jump across, Steve continued to a footbridge. William raced across to the barbed-wire fence behind his house, then flopped on the ground where the fence had leaned over.

Steve showed up minutes later. "How are you gettin' across that fence?"

"I climbed it last time," William answered.

"Yeah, I imagine you did." Steve pointed to where it was nearly to the ground. "Someone's been climbing over there . . . might have been you?"

William eyed the spot. "I don't remember." This was not a lie nor an attempt to avoid trouble. That not the way William behaved.

"Well, let's just say it was." Steve shook a post that wished to fall over. "Need to replace this. Not a problem, but I'm gonna get plumb sick of watching my fence get all beat to shit by you climbin' over top, right there in the middle." Steve walked twenty feet to the nearest corner post—a tall, stout railroad tie turned on its end and impaled three feet into the soil. "Come over here. If you're gonna climb a fence, do it at a post. Like this." He thrust his size thirteen cowboy boot between the wire strands, then swung his right leg over as if mounting a horse.

"See how that works?" Steve shook the wire where his boot had rested. "And look at this," he said. "This is the strongest part of the fence. If you're gonna climb a fence, this is the place to do it."

William, very much impressed, repeated the process. He looked back at Booger, who had sprawled out in the shade of a heavy-limbed sycamore on the other side. "Is Booger coming?"

"Nope. He'll stay right where he is and wait for me. He's not goin' anywhere," Steve said. He grabbed the crown of his hat, a straw Resistol, and removed it to run some fingers through his hair, hoping to be more presentable. "All righty," he said. "Let's go meet your momma."

Steve Bultemeyer had a solid, slow-natured doggedness that oozed from his rugged self, like a balmy summer morning when you know the day is just going to be what it intends to be and there isn't a doggone thing to be done about it. Wide of hip and not narrow in waist, never in a hurry or a braggart, friends knew him as a man who did what he set out to do, without fanfare.

Pansy did not have the talent for the judgment of strangers at first glance and only saw Steve's knock as an unwelcome interruption. His eyes widened in surprise. A young woman, he saw. Too young to have a kid as old as William, he thought. Must have gotten herself in trouble somewhere, he decided. Trouble can find people, Steve knew. He did wonder, for just a moment, what kind of business she had going on that gave people reason to put their noses in it.

Steve turned his hat in hand. "My name is Steve," he said. "You're the owner of this boy?"

Pansy scowled and looked at William's apparent immersion in mud. "What did you do?" she asked him.

"He didn't do anything he shouldn't," Steve replied. "But we had a little pow-wow out there in the pasture, and we're buddies now, so I just wanted to meet his mother. That's you, I believe."

"Yes, that's me." Pansy came closer, then took Steve's outstretched hand in her own. "Pansy Blackwell." The roughness of his palm, weathered like sandpaper, caught her by surprise.

His eyebrows and mustache bristled—long, coarse as wire, relaying an age beyond hers. He sometimes smacked at the mustache with his razor, but only when the thought came to him, which was irregularly and not recently. It drooped so low as to make him look affected by persistent sorrow.

"You're renting from Dick Stinchfield, I understand," Steve said.

"We arrived yesterday. And you are . . . ?" Her eyebrows rose.

"My name is Steve, as I said. Steve Bultemeyer."

"Yes, you already introduced yourself as Steve. I'm just perplexed as to why you're here, in my laundry room. Do you live next door, or . . . ?" Pansy queried.

"Well, I just met your boy, and I thought it polite to introduce myself. I do own that barn and the entire 257-acre pasture you're looking out in back of your house, so I suppose that does make me your neighbor," Steve explained.

"Oh." Pansy nodded. "You *are* my neighbor. Okay." She

fumbled with a rag, then laid it flat on the clothes washer, folding it.

"Mom!" William interrupted. He pointed at Steve. "His dog's name is Booger. Booger!" He broke into giggles.

Wide pancakes of mud, plastered across his pant legs, had cracked in irregular lines of spackle. Its rubble now lay on Pansy's clean floor.

Pansy erupted. "Why are you wet? And filthy?"

"I fell in the river, over there." William pointed to the pasture behind him.

"The river?" Her nostrils flared, and she looked to Steve for an explanation. The big man felt the accusation—as though a river running across his land had bestowed some responsibility to prevent trespassing.

"The slough," Steve clarified. "It's not very deep. It's mostly just a lot of mud, but I think he's gonna need a pair of boots sometime soon." He nodded at the canvas sneakers on William's feet. "Those aren't gonna do him much good in cowboy country."

"Well," Pansy said, moving to the door. "Thank you for introducing yourself." Steve tipped his head in her direction, his hat still in hand. He turned to William. "Nice to meet you, buddy. I'll see you again soon, I'm sure."

Pansy could add up, nearly to the Lincoln penny, the cost of breakfast the next morning—William's favorite morning meal—small mounds of salted corn mush, pressed into flat cakes and fried in butter until the edges turned brown and crisp, then doused with syrup. The cornmeal was purchased at Clark's the previous afternoon. Thirteen cents. The syrup, free, from the Stinchfield's cupboard. William had once announced it to be his most favorite breakfast of all, which Pansy had then declared to be a special treat for her boy. In time, learning that fried mush wasn't known by his classmates in Fresno, he questioned why he was the only one to eat it.

"It wouldn't be special if everyone else ate it," Pansy had said.

William believed her explanation because she was his mother, after all, and when the day comes that you no longer believe your mother's words to be the truth, you might as well pack your things and head for the hills.

Breakfast finished, she pushed him out of the house. Go outside. Go play. I don't need you under my feet and all the other mumblings that mothers do when wishing for their children to be anywhere but here. Setting beds into their proper place didn't take long—she moved her own to another corner of her bedroom, then dragged the second mattress out to the back room and laid it in the darkest corner, which William had already taken command of.

Back at the Weaver barn, more than one bored ranch horse was chewing the splinters off fence rails in placid relief of monotony. A dry northeast wind had come up that morning, and the relentless drone of blowflies sang overhead. On the north side of the pasture where a dirt road came in from Farnsworth Road, an old loading chute sank its posts deep into the soil. A temporary jigsaw collection of steel corrals had been put in place for separating cow and calf pairs.

Using the footbridge this time, William wandered back across the great pasture to where his new friend, Cowboy Steve, was filling water troughs.

"Well, good morning. You're back. Already," Steve said.

"Already," William parroted.

"What are you up to?" Steve asked.

"We just had breakfast." A quizzical thought swept across his eyes. "Do you eat corn mush?"

"Can't say I have," Steve admitted.

"It's special. My mom says that's why people don't eat it."

"Good to know." Steve bent to tighten the screws on a water float overlapping the side of a galvanized water trough. "So, tell me somethin'. Are you plannin' to come over every day?"

William stood passively, unblinking, not intending to answer another silly question that hung in the air, waiting to be answered while the blowflies droned and the horses paced. The air was thick with the expectation that a question had been asked and an answer should be given. Steve pushed his hat back on his head, and William concluded that perhaps this question did require an answer. Of course, he intended to visit every day.

"Yeah, I can come over every day," he answered cheerily.

"That's not what I asked. I asked if you *intend* to. Do you intend to come over every day?"

"Well, yeah. I live right over there." William pointed back to the little green house, then glanced to all corners of the pasture. "Where do you live?"

"Maybe I live right here in the barn with the cows," Steve said.

"No, you don't!" William laughed so loudly that Booger took notice.

"No, you're right. I don't live with the cows. I have a real house out on the other side of Gregory Mountain."

"Then what are you doin' out here?"

"This is my pasture. Sometimes we move cattle out here, and then I come out to check on things," Steve said.

William liked this explanation. "So, I'm right over there," he pointed behind him. "I can see you out my window, and I can come help you. I can be your helper."

The right side of Steve's lip curled up. "Oh, you can? What can you do?"

"I don't know yet. You haven't shown me anything." William jumped a rock for no reason other than it was there and then made his way over to the far side of the corrals. Thirty-four head of red Hereford cow and calf pairs, just unloaded that morning and now pressed into long square pens in back, bawled in frustration. Another ten pairs would be driven out tomorrow. "Come on, Booger!" he called loudly to the dog. "Let's go feed the cows."

Steve laughed, a great bellow of sound. "So, you're ready to be a cowboy, are you?"

"Are we doing cowboy work?" William asked.

"Damn. You are a demandin' little bugger. Yup, that's what we do out here. I'm a cowboy. This here's a ranch, and I spend every day doin' cowboy work."

"Then we should feed the cows," William suggested.

"The cows don't need to be fed. I already did that," Steve said.

William turned, waiting for direction. Steve shoved his hands into his back pockets. "All righty," he grunted. "We'll find something else to do." He went to his truck and pulled a pair of fence pliers from under the front seat. "Follow me," he instructed, then made his way into the northern side of the pasture.

"Where we goin'?" William asked.

"We're gonna walk the fence. Don't want the cows gettin' through it."

"Why would the cows get through it?"

"Because that's what's in a cow's head," Steve explained. "Put some cows next to a fence, and one of 'em is gonna stand there all day wonderin' how it can get to the other side. And once it gets to the other side, all the others are gonna think it was a fine idea, and then your cows are gonna be where you don't want 'em. So, we need to walk the fence and be sure it's all standin' up straight. Don't want no holes where the cows can get through." Steve looked down at William as he said this. "Can you do that?"

William agreed he could absolutely do that.

"Remember that fence outside your house?" Steve asked. "All bent over the way it was? That piece is near to needing some work, too. Not unless you want my cows in your backyard."

William failed to understand how cows in his backyard would be a problem but recognized that the big cowboy was likely an expert. The ease with which Steve stalked the acreage, looking for random things that needed tending, always with something to do but without a list to tell him so, was impressive. William's life had been flooded by lists. Long lists of homes that Pansy would clean for Brother Leach each week. Well-organized pages of cleaning chores that must be done on Saturdays. The elementary school had a written schedule for when math problems must be solved, which took place after a scheduled lunch and after a written list of spelling skills had been tested. The Jehovah's Witnesses had lists for when people would give talks, when they would sing, and when they would pray. They had lists of neighborhoods for every town on the planet and the order in which each should be walked to peddle literature. Steve had nothing to guide him in what needed to be done nor the order in which such things should be addressed, but he patrolled the property with authority while cows bawled in frustration in the back pen.

William peppered him with questions: Why are they so noisy? Can you get rid of the flies? Can you clean up the mud? Can I walk the fence tomorrow to look for holes?

"We won't need to walk the fence tomorrow," Steve replied. "The cows aren't gonna push a hole in the fence between now and then, given that they're still penned up in back."

"Then what will we do tomorrow?" William asked.

"We'll do whatever needs to be done. The work don't go away, no matter how bad you want it to."

They were nearing the barn now, having completed their inspection of the pasture. Steve scuffed his way inside, scraping hay out of the entrance with the side of his boot, then entered a corner he referred to as the tack room. A half-dozen wooden saddle racks pushed out from the wall at waist height. One saddle, its leather worn smooth wherever it had been in contact with men in its seat, mounted a single rack. Its stirrups reached long to the floor. An entire collection of bits and bridles hung the length of one wall; a few nylon ropes lay coiled on the floor. Saddles—especially those unmarked for ownership—were worth a few bucks and wouldn't be left in the barn for winter. No reason to be stupid about it, Steve sometimes said, when loading them in his truck to take home.

William had followed, still unsatisfied.

"But how do you know what to do when you get here?" he asked.

Steve rustled around a shallow shelf. "You do whatever needs to be done first."

William frowned. "But how do you know what needs to be done first? Shouldn't you have a list?"

"A list?" Steve snorted, then leaned against the door frame. "A cowboy doesn't have a list. He has a brain." He tapped his temple. "If you want to be a cowboy, you gotta learn to think for yourself. No one's gonna hand you a list of chores. Follow me." He walked back to the sunshine, squinting toward the east. He pointed to the cows. "See them? When I first come out here in the morning, there's probably a whole bunch of things that need to be done, but what do you think is the most important? The thing that needs to get done first?"

Precisely, William thought. How do you know what to do first? That's the question.

"It's easy to figure out, if you use your brain. The most important thing is to take care of the animals. They come first. Always. So, do you think the cows are hungry first thing in the morning?" Steve asked.

A slow acceptance of this dilemma spread across William's face. "Oh, yeah!" he said. "Feed the cows!"

"Exactly," Steve affirmed. "So, if I drive out here again around lunchtime, what do you think I would do? Probably not feed the cows, right? They only get fed twice a day, morning and evening."

William liked this answer. "So, tomorrow morning, I can help you feed the cows."

"Not tomorrow. We're markin' calves tomorrow, then we'll turn 'em out to the pasture. That's why we just walked the fence, to make sure they can't get out. We'll feed 'em in a few weeks when they get all that pasture grazed down, or we might move 'em out to the other side of Gregory Mountain. But if you're itchin' to be a cowboy, you can help us mark calves."

"What are we markin' them for?" William asked.

"Just makin' sure everyone knows they're mine," Steve answered. He turned for the far corral, where two horses stood in the corner. They had sidled up nose to tail, ears twitching and tails swatting, keeping flies at bay. Steve slipped a halter on the big sorrel gelding, Mac, then walked him out to where William had climbed the fence. He looped the halter rope over the top rail, loosely, then made his way to the horse's back hip. A small, hooked, metal object was in his hand. He slapped his palm on Mac's hip as if to say, "I'm here," then ran his hand down the gelding's leg and lifted its hoof. The ease with which he did this was a miracle to William.

Steve scraped mud from inside the hoof, then lowered it

back to the ground and moved to the other side, repeating the procedure.

William climbed off the fence, then squatted down for a better look. "What are you doin'?"

"I'm cleaning Mac's feet," Steve answered.

"Why?"

"Because he can't really clean his own feet, can he?"

William thought about this question. Could a horse clean his own feet? Of course not, but that wasn't really what he wanted to know.

"But why do they need to be cleaned?" William tried again.

"Well, why wouldn't they? Come over here. I'll show you," Steve said.

William crawled closer and peered at the underside of Mac's hoof. Steve scraped dirt where it was stuck tight inside the narrow cleave of the frog. William did not yet know that the underside of a horse's hoof was called a frog, but he would giggle about it when he did.

"Does it hurt?" William asked.

"Nah. Sometimes there's a rock or two in there, and he'd just as soon get them out."

"Can I do it? With the poker thing?"

"The poker thing? You mean this?" Steve held the instrument up in the air.

William nodded.

Steve chuckled. "It's a hoof pick." He stood straight and slid it into his back pocket. "I don't think you're ready to handle the hoof pick yet. Jeezuzz . . . how much you want to learn on your first day?"

"Everything."

Dick Stinchfield's father, Leroy, had enough vision in 1930 to buy fifteen acres of wooded, rolling hills on the west side of the Shasta Valley to establish the Stinchfield Overnight Camp for what he predicted would be an eventual invasion of tourists. The American car culture, giving freedom to travel without the constraint of railroad lines, was just beginning to bring the campers and fishermen to Siskiyou, and Leroy had the forethought to jump on board.

Dick had grown up in the two-bedroom, single-story house at the campground where he still resided, but when he hadn't yet found a woman in the Kingdom Hall to marry at his age of thirty, his parents moved to the little green house in Farnsworth, removing the obstacles they imagined were keeping their son a bachelor.

In 1963, Leroy transferred ownership of the camp to Dick, then dropped dead the following Friday. Dick promptly changed the name to Pine Cone Resort, a decision his mother resented until she went to sleep for the last time.

In the early years of the camp, visitors were content to pitch tents under the pine trees, but Dick then borrowed a sum of money from Yreka Community Bank and built six rustic cabins, all with heat and private baths. The private baths were where the big money was, he had said to the bank. He advertised the improvements on the billboard south of town on the new I-5 interstate, then plastered the camp with signage and helpful tips.

"Please back vehicles into designated campsites."

"Quiet Hours Begin at 9 p.m.!"

"Glass and plastics are not to be thrown in firepits." Nor was "ammunition of any kind," added later in black felt pen.

Dick once installed a sign in the laundry room instructing guests, "Do not wash coloreds with whites." Someone later scrawled the word "duh" at the bottom.

Before the sun had risen on Monday morning, Buster Pine climbed out of the cab of his truck that he'd parked on the backside of the Weaver barn. He was an old man but would show up at the butt-crack of dawn for work, if that's what you wanted of him. He had a paper sack of needles and syringes and a portable steel forge for the B-Bar-Seven branding iron. Steve pulled in with the last of the cow-calf pairs in his stock trailer, about the same time as the sun's face was rising over the eastern hillside. Rocky Bale showed up with his horse, Snickers, and a soft poly calf rope to do the ropin'. Steve would throw the babies once Rocky had them caught. It didn't require much to do Steve's part, other than some muscle and a willingness to get banged up on the wild end of the rope. It helped to have a good man on horseback, at the other end, pulling slack, which was Rocky.

The cattle milled about in a bedlam of impatience, churning the back pens into clouds of dust as the men separated cows from calves. The pasture came alive in the chaos, driving grime and wails through the open windows of the little green house. Pansy hadn't let William leave until Dick had shown up in the Town and Country to fetch her for her first day of work. And not until William had eaten breakfast, which was toast and eggs, scrambled until dry as dust, then doused in ketchup.

Thin wafts of scorched calf hide carried the stench to Farnsworth long before William entered the pasture. On a fast run, he flew down the slope, pounding over the footbridge to join the racket. Steve had gotten himself kicked in the shin just then, cursing words that had never before come through William's ears. "Mother fuck!" he wailed, then hobbled back into the fray for another round with the calf.

"Does it hurt?" William blurted.

"Damn right, it hurts," Steve grunted. He wrestled the calf

back to the ground, and William leaned over to watch Buster cut the bull calf's balls off with a pocket knife.

Buster threw the warm testicles into a bucket. He pulled the branding iron out of the forge, its tip scorched red hot, and burned the B-Bar-Seven brand into the calf's left hip. It took a few more blinks of an eye to cut a bloody notch from its left ear.

"Does it hurt?" William again asked.

"He'll forget about it by tomorrow," Steve replied.

William retreated to the fence when Rocky roped another. Astride Snickers, Rocky pulled each calf from the chaos to the branding iron fire as Steve walked the rope, lifting each to his knees, then throwing them flat to the ground, hard enough to knock the wind out of the troublemakers. Buster stuck a needle in their necks, vaccinating against brucellosis, then shot a thick paste of de-wormer down their throats as Steve leaned heavy on their chests, bending a foreleg to keep them from rising. He gave a hard sideways glance to William, who had abandoned the security of the fence.

"Did you come over to watch or help?" Steve called out.

"Help," William said.

"Good man. Then we'll put you in charge of the gate," Steve said.

"What gate?" William asked.

"See that one behind you, in the corner? Yup, that one . . . you're now the gate man. Your job is to open it when Rocky tells you, then let the calf out to the other side." He rose to his feet, the calf bounded off to a far corner, and William ran to the far gate. "You can do that? Good boy. Just like that. Git behind 'im! Drive 'im out! Good job. Shut the gate!"

Lunch came early. Rocky speared a half-dozen hot dogs over the outside rim of the fire, and a bag of Frito-Lays got passed around. Calf testicles were sliced open, then laid flat in a hot pan of lard. Steve dusted them with a heavy handful of garlic salt, which sizzled loudly in the fat.

Steve turned a bucket upside down for a temporary stool, then rubbed his bloodied shin. "Sonofabitch, that little bastard nailed me good."

He nodded at the skillet, sitting on a rock, cooling next to a bucket of ice and orange soda pop. "What do you think about them oysters?"

"Needs ketchup," William stated. He scooped a testicle from the pan, cut lengthwise and opened like a chicken gizzard but matching the flavor and texture of its liver.

"Good to hear. Comes from the same place as hamburger. Every time you eat a hamburger, you should think about where it comes from. You can thank your local cowboy for hamburgers," Steve said.

William pondered the thought, savoring the rich fattiness on his tongue, letting some quick math rattle around his mind. "How many hamburgers do you get from a cow?"

"More'n you can eat," Rocky replied.

"Fifty?" William guessed.

"Thousands," Rocky answered.

"Thousands?" Eyes wide, William looked out to the cattle, now ranging free in the pasture. "You're gonna be rich!"

The old man, Buster, groaned in disgust.

Steve snorted. "No one gets rich." He pushed his boots out in front and laid one foot over the other. "So, big guy," he said to William. "Looks like you're plannin' to hang around."

"Yeah. I like cowboy work," William said.

"Well, just so you know . . . that dirt you're wearin' all over your backside, lookin' like you just took a bath in it? It's not just dirt." Steve looked to Rocky. "What do you think? Fifty-fifty? Half dirt, half shit?"

"Sounds about right," Rocky confirmed.

William looked as if he might barf.

"Don't go worryin' about it," said Buster. "You're wearin' them turds just fine. You'll make a good cowboy, someday."

"I'm bettin' his momma's gonna git her tit in a wringer when he gets home," Rocky said.

"Most likely, but we need to do a little fixin' before we send him home, I think." Steve made a show of rising, and his knees cracked with stiffness. He took the Frito-Lays back from Rocky. "You thinkin' what I'm thinkin'? With his name?" he asked.

"He don't look like a William to me," Rocky said.

"Nah, he don't," agreed Steve.

"He ate them oysters up pretty good. I'm thinkin' he ain't no city boy," Rocky added.

"He didn't have no problems movin' them calves out," said Buster.

Steve returned to his bucket, again sat, then slapped both hands on his knees. "Alrighty there, William. We're gonna do some fixin'."

"Fixin' what?" William asked.

"Fix the fact that you don't look like a William to me. Or to Buster, over there," tilting his head north to the old man.

"He don't look like a William to me neither," Rocky repeated, shaving a toothpick off the fence post with Buster's testicle knife.

William froze.

"Son, you need a name that don't sound like you're from the city." Steve paused to think. "You're a big damn kid." He removed his hat.

"Skeeter," Rocky suggested. "He could be Skeeter."

Steve shook his head. Nah, that wouldn't do. He grasped the side of his mustache, twisting it between his thumb and forefinger, but eventually nodded and rose from the bucket, placing his hat back on top of his head.

"We'll call you Butch."

Steve walked Butch home at the end of the day, but only to confirm what had been on their lunch menu.

"Mom won't believe me," Butch said. "We don't eat cow balls in our house."

Steve vouched for what seemed a tall tale to Pansy. Her boy had eaten them oysters up just fine, he assured her. "And we gave him a new name: Butch."

"I don't like that name," Pansy snapped. Her eyes narrowed.

"Then don't use it," Steve replied. "This is cowboy country. Nobody's gonna ask you if you like it or not."

That's a good kid, Steve said to himself when he drove home. *Would be fun to have him around.*

11

To the best of Steve's knowledge, he'd not born children by anyone. For that reason, he was poor—by his parent's choice. The youngest of three brothers, his siblings, having progeny that bore the name of Bultemeyer, were entitled by Western presumption to ownership of the B-Bar-Seven.

At one time, the Bultemeyer name carried significant weight in Siskiyou County. Grantland Bultemeyer had built the original Farnsworth icehouse in 1872, having moved out from Maine where people know a lot about icehouses. He cut ice blocks high in the winter Siskiyou's, hauled them by mule train down to the valley floor, then buried them in thick layers of sawdust inside the cold confines of a log house to sell during summer when ice was hard to come by. Siskiyou County had plenty of sawdust to go around but no ice houses, until Grantland showed up.

Two generations later, his grandson, Hazzard Bultemeyer, hobbled into attorney Pryor Haslip's estate planning office in Yreka with the sole interest of hammering out an agreement to pass the Bultemeyer ranch to his descendants. Hazzard was near to keeling over dead, and there wasn't anything to be done about it—this is how people summed up the situation in casual yet earnest conversations because a state of affairs in which nothing can be done to rectify the problem is contrary to the cowboy philosophy of self-determination.

A pervasive ambition of generations of farmers and ranchers with a Western ethic was that the most important thing one could do was to pass the land you own and what you had built on it to your children, who would then pass it to their children, and so on and so forth. It was a never-ending dream for perpetuity, the continuance of a family's legacy.

The honorable Mr. Pryor Haslip, pronounced "hays lip," was the most prominent attorney in the county. No longer a man of Siskiyou, he was a man from Siskiyou who had gone off to be educated and returned with all the trappings of refined arrogance.

Being fluent in the dialog of "life estates" and "in perpetuity," Mr. Haslip scheduled a meeting with the Bultemeyers after Hazzard's death for a discussion of the Bultemeyer Family Trust's provisions.

"Your father's goal was to pass the real property of the B-Bar-Seven Ranch to his family in perpetuity and to ensure that it functions as a working ranch for as long as the Bultemeyer bloodline exists," he said to them. "His wealth is to be enjoyed by his family, forever."

Steve groaned. Not once would his father have referred to the family's land as "wealth."

Pryor continued. "So, gentlemen, what your father desired was to place the wealth of the B-Bar-Seven landholdings, in their entirety, in trust, which was done prior to his death. I think you were aware of this when he completed the transfer. The ranch will continue to operate, much as it always has, but in trust. The trust will be responsible for upkeep and improvements from the gross income that is derived from the trust operations. The proceeds—the net income—will then be distributed in equal shares to you. This is what your father, Hazzard, desired."

There was a general murmur of understanding from the Bultemeyer sons.

"Steve, at your passing, the trust will dissolve and the property distributed outright to Hank and Maxwell, or to their issue . . . 'children,'" he clarified. "When you die, Hank, Max, or their children will become owners of the B-Bar-Seven Ranch in its entirety.

"What if they die before me?" Steve asked.

"All seven of them?" Pryor asked incredulously.

"Yeah. What if everyone gets killed, and I'm the only one left?"

"Well, Steve, your father asked the same question, but I hardly think that your brothers and all five of their progenies will die, leaving you the sole survivor. The trust does not include provisions for that circumstance. But in the meantime, assuming the rational expectation that some of you remain alive, the ranch will remain in trust. You, Steve, will work the ranch—if you choose to, of course—and are entitled to a fair income for such work. The remaining income will then be allocated equally amongst the three of you. But your brothers can't sell it while you are alive. In the event that they die first, the ranch will pass to their beneficiaries, presumably their children, on your death. Your father, as you know, wished for the ranch to stay in the family."

"I'm well aware of that," Steve said. Heartburn roiled in his belly.

"He was thinking of you when he requested these provisions," Pryor explained.

"Sure, he was," Steve grunted.

"Steve, this trust ensures that you have the right to work the ranch as long as you are alive," Pryor said.

"Exactly. I do all the work."

"Your brothers can't sell it out from under you," Pryor reiterated.

"Well, that was mighty thoughtful of him," Steve said.

"Your father indicated that your brothers are not interested in working the ranch."

"Exactly," Steve confirmed. "Neither are their kids."

Max entered the discussion. "I'm not interested. Not gonna spend my life poor."

"You *are* poor," Steve sneered. "You live in a trailer, you fuckhead."

"Well, Steve," Pryor pointed in Steve's direction, "in return for working the ranch property, the trust provides that you will live in the original ranch house, if you choose. That house was built by your grandfather if I am not mistaken."

"In 1890, the year my dad was born," Steve said.

"Yes, well your father has provided for your interests in this document." Pryor slapped it with the full force of his hand.

12

A FORTNIGHT AFTER BUTCH AND PANSY HAD SETTLED into the little green house, a lone bobwhite quail bashed itself into the kitchen window. Pansy screamed at the thump, but Butch went out to investigate and collected the carcass from where it lay in the weeds. He pulled both wings horizontally in a wide fan, fiddled with the top-notch feather at the dead bird's head, then laid it on the kitchen table, still warm and limp as a wet dishtowel. He stripped it naked, pulling skin, delicate and paper-thin, from the bird's pale breast—stretching it aloft to see the light shine through. Steve had said quail were mighty good to eat, so Pansy roasted it in a hot oven for the few minutes it took to burn the knob of each drumstick black.

By the end of August, Butch and Pansy had learned more about the ways of doing things in Farnsworth, how residents do this and visitors do that, and how everyone gets along just fine if you stay out of their business. How some people drive too fast on the only roads out to Yreka, but if you weren't in a mood to leave town, you got by with the limited selection of foods and sundries at Clark's.

The lower level of Clark's still advertised "Feed & Tack: Lawn & Garden Supplies" in blocky, red-faded-to-pink lettering, but that section of the business failed early as selling lawn and garden paraphernalia to Farnsworth residents was almost as profitable as selling air conditioning in Siberia. The larger Food-Rite Grocery had opened its doors six miles away in Yreka in 1958 with the philosophy that a proper grocery must introduce its customers to a minimum of six brands of sliced bread and four brands of instant coffee, and they guaranteed to undercut Clark's by at least five cents a pound on any cut of meat. There were still some who would instead park on Miner Street in front of the City Meat Market in Yreka and go inside for a discussion with one of the butchers. Shoppers could choose what they liked there, from a long glass case that laid out a bloody buffet of animal parts spanning the entire lengths of two walls.

On most days, the men who worked there could tell you who raised the critter from which you were contemplating purchase. That hog came from Joe Stump, they might say. It's a Yorkshire hog. You know Joe, don't you? These are some fine pork chops, you should know, and how are you plannin' on cookin' these? If there was nothing in the display case that struck your fancy, the men would disappear into the walk-in fridge, where two sides of beef and a hog were hanging by their hocks from steel hooks. There, they'd custom cut something to your desires. You couldn't follow them back to the cold locker, of course, but at one time, this was how customers preferred to purchase their dinners. Not many people from Farnsworth could afford to do it that way, not anymore.

It had only taken one visit to the campground before Dick announced that it would be better if Butch were always left at home. The campground wasn't meant for babysitting, he said, so Butch largely spent the rest of that summer in the great pasture, taking on chores that needed tending and inventing others that didn't. Bales of hay were easily separated into flakes —one alfalfa flake per horse, morning and evening. Cattle that weren't turned out to pasture were fed as much grass hay as they would eat—no need for counting flakes, as fat cows were desired. Fat horses were not.

Water troughs to fill. Gates to latch. A barn to explore. The only barrier to adventure was the responsibilities of faith. Sunday mornings were devoted to worship in the Kingdom Hall, as were Tuesday and Thursday evenings. At least one additional day per month, either a Saturday morning or a Sunday afternoon, was relegated to additional devotional hours walking the streets in what could have been considered a membership drive —searching for converts to Jehovah—a challenge in Siskiyou County. There were few churches to meet the needs of the county's pious. Most residents had the classic Western spirit of independence and didn't find their lives lacking without harsh supervision from God.

The calves had been moved out of the pasture and were now grazing east of Gregory Mountain. Steve moved a couple of breeding bulls, young and untested in their ability to sire, out to the corrals of the Weaver barn. Two rope horses were still there, and Steve had enlisted the help of Butch in cleaning manure from corrals. He slid a shovel into the wheelbarrow.

"Just pretend you're a truck driver," Steve said.

Butch bristled at the accusation. "I don't want to be a truck driver."

"You don't?"

"I'm a cowboy," Butch insisted.

"Okay. You can be a cowboy who's movin' shit." Steve pulled a handkerchief from his back pocket, then leaned over to the spigot at the water trough, drenching it. He ran it over the back of his neck. "Son of a bitch, it's hot."

"Son of a bitch, it's hot," Butch parroted.

"Jeezuzz! Don't be repeatin' me! Yer gonna get me in all kinds of trouble with your mother," Steve scolded.

"Yeah. Sorry," Butch said.

Steve walked to the truck where he had left it in the shade and lowered the tailgate for a rest. He looked back to Butch, who had abandoned the wheelbarrow and called Booger to join him on a run to the slough. A smile came over Steve. He could remember doing the same many decades earlier. A race from one point to another, for no good reason. And he thought of his father, Hazzard, a man of great patience. A man with an overwhelming desire to be a good father. Butch and Booger returned.

"Tell you what," Steve said.

"What?" Butch asked.

"Follow me."

Steve made his way back to the barn. "Let's put you up on a horse." He threw a saddle blanket and saddle on top of Speckles, a black and white Appaloosa, buckled both cinches, the breast collar, a hackamore bridle, and then mounted.

He leaned down to Butch. "Climb on up, just grab the cantle in back . . . "

"What's the cantle?" Butch was already halfway there.

"Watch where you're puttin' your feet—don't be kickin' Speckles in the belly," Steve barked.

"I wouldn't kick him in the belly!"

Together, they rode in a quick trot up to the little green house. "Hey, Mom!" Butch yelled.

Pansy emerged from the back porch. "Yes?"

"Thought I'd see if he takes to ridin' a horse," Steve explained.

"Well, a boy does need something to do," Pansy said.

"Yes, he does. School starts next week, though."

She nodded. "It does."

"You might want to put him in football," Steve suggested.

"Football? No, he doesn't need to be doing any of that," Pansy replied.

"Any of what?" Steve scowled.

"The Bible warns against organized sports and competitions. First Timothy 4:8 says, 'For bodily exercise is beneficial for a little, but Godly devotion is beneficial for all things,'" Pansy recited.

Steve grunted.

"The Bible discourages us from participating in competitive sports that may not be pleasing to Jehovah. I would be happy to share more scriptures about that if you like. If you wait here, I have some literature in my bedroom I can give you." She turned to leave.

"Woman!"

Pansy turned back.

"The day a church tells me that a kid can't play some football is the day when I'll double down on what I've always said, which you probably don't want to hear." He took a long look back at Butch. "Why don't you slide off . . . yup, just like that."

He sighed in sympathy. "All righty, then. No football for you. You know, that's really too bad. You'd make a damn good football player."

He turned Speckles in the direction of the barn but looked back to Pansy. "You know, that's a damn shame. The kid is built like me."

"Well then, perhaps *you* should play football."

Fifty-seven students showed up for grammar school in Farnsworth the Monday after Labor Day, September 9th, 1968, for instruction from Miss Lisa Becker. Seven were in the third grade with Butch, and eleven more were in that same classroom but in fourth grade. Every now and then, some local busybody stirred up trouble by advocating that all children from Farnsworth should be bussed to Yreka for their educations, as those in high school had already been doing for the previous thirty years.

Miss Lisa Becker, a young-looking thirty-something woman with soft and luminescent skin, the pale hue of marshmallows, had descended from a long line of also-pale people who had lived and taught in Siskiyou County forever. Still living with her parents at the family's original farmstead about seventeen miles south of town, she didn't often find reason to get into town during summer. When school was in session, she labored over two crucial tasks: firstly, over the specifics of her teaching responsibilities, and secondly, over her compulsion to tame her lovely but thin blonde hair that lacked the obedience to curl unless beaten into submission with a hot iron. Defiantly straight, her golden strands were the soft yellow hue of butter and belligerent about their desire to hang flat, but that's not what she wanted from hair, so each morning, she woke early to berate it with a curling iron until she had convinced three inches to stiffen into an abrupt flip, like she intended to turn it into ladles for soup. Some weeks, she parted her hair on the left, others on the right, and some days she might have gone for a straight part, right down the middle—not a single decision of which required her to re-think her flip—and she did this for the simple fact that some people don't want to be rigid in how they live, day in and day out, for all of eternity. Every now and then, people are moved to seek change, and after great thought, they make modifications to their hair and then go out to greet civilization, believing they are newly primed and coiffed to conquer the world.

On this day, Miss Becker had carved her hair into two continents of equal size, divided by a part that went right down the middle of her scalp and showed through pale, like a sharp crease cut straight through a stick of butter. She greeted Pansy warmly, thinking as she did every year on the very first day of school that she might just conquer the world.

Pansy had earlier formed a silent prayer to Jehovah in her mind but neglected to think it before reaching out to Miss Becker's proffered hand.

"So pleased to make your acquaintance. This is my son, William." She thrust him out front.

Miss Becker said, "Hello." Her hair bobbed like a coiled spring. Butch wrestled with the temptation that he could probably insert his finger into the flip tunnel.

"There is something I'd like to share with you, if you have a moment," Pansy said.

Miss Becker looked away in distraction.

"We recently moved to town," Pansy continued, "and I believe we are the only Jehovah's Witnesses in the vicinity. Are you familiar with us?"

"I am," Miss Becker replied simply. "Dick Stinchfield has shown up on my doorstep with your *Watchtower* magazines many times."

"Ah. Then you know Dick. Well, I am employed by him now, at the campground," Pansy said.

"Oh, you are? I didn't know. But you live here in Farnsworth?"

"Yes, we are staying in the little green house over on Spier Street."

"Well then, welcome to Farnsworth," Miss Becker said.

"Thank you. We are enjoying the peacefulness. It's very quiet here."

"It certainly is," Miss Becker confirmed. "We like it that way."

"Yes, well, Lisa, it's imperative for you to understand that William and I follow Bible teachings, so there are things he won't participate in, particularly around the holidays. Have you ever had a Jehovah's Witness child in your class?"

Miss Becker held her hand up, as if asking permission to speak. "Yes, well, my first name is indeed Lisa, but I prefer to go by Miss Becker here in the classroom, if you wouldn't mind."

"Oh, certainly. My mistake." Pansy again took Miss Becker's hand, then rested her other hand atop it. "Well, Miss Becker, do you know anything of our faith?"

"No, I don't believe so. I've not ever cared to take one of your magazines from Dick. William will be my first." She pulled her hand back. Her smile widened. "Perhaps we could speak of this another time? The first day of school is always so hectic."

"I can understand that, but this is an important matter. It will only take a second to clarify our position," Pansy said, firmly.

"Is there anything in particular you would like me to be aware of?" Miss Becker asked.

"Well, the obvious things," Pansy replied. "We don't celebrate holidays, of course. They aren't supported by Bible teachings, so anything you do for holidays would be something that William cannot participate in. You will need to find other activities for him during those occasions."

"All holidays?"

Were there holidays in which he could participate? Pansy couldn't think of one. "Well, let's just say that William will notify you if there is anything you do that is contrary to our beliefs. He's good that way. If he tells you he can't participate in pagan celebrations, you can trust him to be truthful. He's a very well-mannered child. Not duplicitous in any way."

Miss Becker fondled her flip.

"And the pledge of allegiance, of course. William won't participate in that, as I'm sure you can understand. And at any time, if you wish to learn more about our faith, I would be pleased to meet with you for a Bible discussion. We could even meet weekly, if you wish," Pansy offered.

Miss Becker stooped to Butch in a sweet way that children were drawn to. "Now, don't be nervous on your first day."

"Why would I be nervous?" Butch asked.

"Well, that is, indeed, the perfect question to ask. Why be nervous?" She stood, then turned back to Pansy. "I'm sure William will enjoy our school, and thank you so much for letting me know of your concerns. I'll take it from here." She made a sharp turn and guided him to her desk.

Moments later, after Pansy had left the school to walk home, Miss Becker pushed a pen and paper across her desk to William. "Let's work on a name tag so everyone will know who you are. It's not often we have a new student." The last time a new student had come to Farnsworth Elementary was in 1963.

Butch did not lift the pen from her desk.

Miss Becker leaned over to him. "How do you spell William?" Perhaps Jehovah's Witnesses didn't teach their children to write?

"I know how to spell William," Butch replied. "I'm eight. But people call me 'Butch.' I know how to spell Butch, too."

"Your mother said your name is William," Miss Becker said.

"My mom likes William. I like Butch." He looked up to her, transparent in his honesty. "You can ask Cowboy Steve. Mr. Bultemeyer. He gave me that name."

"Steve Bultemeyer? Oh, he did, did he?" Her lips spread into a wide smile. "Well, that sounds like something Steve would do, so I guess we'll call you Butch. That's a fine name, and I like it, too."

Mother won't like this, Butch thought. He'd tell her later, but not today. He looked over the room where indoor chaos had reached a crescendo as students reconnected after the long isolation of summer. Few resided in town. Most lived outside of Farnsworth, within a thirty-mile eastern radius. Families on the west side sent their kids to school in Yreka.

Miss Becker turned Butch to face the class, introducing him, then whispered in his ear, "How about walking these papers to the front office for me?" She tucked a folder into his hands, then clapped loudly. "Howard! Would you like to lead us in the pledge?"

A half-hour later, a blond boy, Calvin Broadus, showed up for class. Living twenty-seven miles east of town on the edge of the Cistern Plateau, he had to take a long ride into town with his dad every weekday if he had any hopes of making it to school. Sometimes his dad would forget it happens that way, and Calvin would then be stranded at home to clean horse stalls and make peanut butter sandwiches for his momma, who was rumored bedridden with migraines. Or malaria. No one was exactly sure what ailed her. Some thought it was hereditary.

Wally Barker again passed out flyers for the local Cub Scout troop. The previous year, he'd forged signatures from kids who hadn't any interest in the foolery of Scouts. Designed for bored city boys who had abundant hours of free time, the Scouting life rarely drew interest from the youngsters in Siskiyou County who were busy learning to cope with real-life situations, like pulling bull calves out of the mud each spring to cut their testicles off. Or getting through the last round of an alfalfa harvest before the rains came in the fall. Or conscious decisions to kill during hunting seasons. The opening day of dove season was considered an admirable excuse for skipping school in Siskiyou County.

The weather turned foul just before the Thanksgiving break, and the sky collapsed in vast sheets of rain as if it could do nothing more than rain forever. Brother Stinchfield added his own embellishment to the Sunday public talk, harping about Jehovah having once sent the great flood of Noah to destroy the wicked —this current rain could be a reminder of God's wrath. "Some food for thought," he added.

Calvin Broadus missed four days of class because his dad's truck got stuck in the mud. Miss Becker stayed late after school for three whole days, holed up inside until well past dinner, cutting brown grocery paper into one-dimensional decorative turkeys and inscribing each with a student's name in her cursive teacher-letters. Butch did not get a paper turkey, nor would Miss Becker have tempted him so. She asked him to distribute the stack for personalization with each child's choice of decorations, which was her way of letting him participate in the holiday without the guilt of offending God. Butch gathered the stack in his arms and read the name on the first bird before it slid off to the floor.

"Calvin . . . here's your turkey," he said. "On the floor. I dropped it."

"Lisa . . . your turkey."

He stalled at the next one. "Beverly?" He got close to Beverly, or Belinda, unsure of specifics. "Which one is Beverly?"

"Who cares?" Calvin blurted out, which sent the entire class into hysterics. Beverly Buffet was Belinda Buffet's twin, but not identical, so they only looked like they were possibly related, perhaps cousins, but twins wouldn't have been anyone's first guess. They couldn't talk, so they were ignored during social activities and abandoned to pursue their own devices, which meant they mostly just tucked their heads into a tight little pow-wow to whisper about whatever occupied their private little world. Everyone then recognized that the Buffet sisters could genuinely communicate. They didn't choose to do it with anyone else. Everyone who had ever met them eventually gave up on being friends and let them go, on their own, to do their whispering.

Miss Becker said the girls had challenges, but no one put serious stock in her diagnosis. Calvin Broadus had challenges. He could end up with migraines. Or malaria.

Howard, being helpful and all, offered an overheard analysis of the situation. "My dad says they're socially retarded," which he didn't repeat with any intention of being mean. He was not that sort. He was just helpful, but Miss Becker turned purple as an eggplant and waved her arms about the room and forgot that Howard just liked to be that way. Helpful. She threatened to rescind his eraser cleaning privileges and then went off on another tangent about the girls having challenges, but everyone knew that Howard lived about fifty acres away from the Buffets' house on the other side of the alfalfa pasture that backed up to their property at the 6.73 mile marker off of Chutes Road, so he ought to know something about what the girls were all about. They practically live next door.

Later that day, being helpful and all, Howard Haffner sidled up to Butch with some words of friendship.

"I don't really give a turkey shit if they can talk or not," Howard whispered.

Butch then relayed the conversation in exacting detail at home.

Pansy gasped. "How is it that your language has become so crude?"

"It hasn't. Howard said 'shit,' but that's a cuss word, so I'll say turd. I don't give a turkey turd," Butch said.

"That's crude," Pansy insisted.

"But turd isn't a cuss word," Butch argued.

"No, it isn't," Pansy conceded.

"Then it's okay to say it."

When December arrived, the long hours of evening darkness meant livestock got fed first thing after school, by 4 p.m., about the time the sun started slipping behind the Siskiyous. Steve then sent his steers to auction. The bulls and breeding cows were trucked out to winter pasture on the far side of Ball Mountain, the rope horses went back to the B-Bar-Seven homesite, and Butch found himself with nothing to do.

Dick Stinchfield leaned against the kitchen sink in his parents' home, now Pansy's. He was over for an afternoon meal one week after Christmas—his first social visit since she had moved in, and on a Sunday, as he had requested. There's nothing on TV, he had said, not on Sunday. It would be good to get together for some socializing, and dinner could be early, maybe shortly after the *Watchtower* study at the Kingdom Hall.

Pansy nearly exploded at the prospect. "Like brunch! I'll cook breakfast, and we'll call it brunch. Two o'clock is a perfect time for brunch!"

Readers Digest had written that one could serve just about anything for brunch—some items should be hot and others cold —but warm, soft-cooked eggs were always a hit, so Pansy walked to the southern end of Spier Street and bought a dozen eggs from Trixie Bleaker for fifty cents, pleased that she had saved three cents over the price at Clark's Grocery. Returned home to her kitchen and having little faith in her ability to cook things in a manner she'd never before seen, she practiced poaching four, one by one, in the way recommended by *Reader's Digest*, which was to gently slide them into a pan of hot water until somewhat congealed but still runny.

Poaching didn't reveal itself to be difficult; each egg turned out just fine, and having plenty of faith in her magazine, she ate all four experiments with a spoon, telling herself that eggs really did not need cooking to the point of death, as she had previously been led to believe. Undercooked eggs could make people sick; she'd heard of this but had never known someone who had gotten ill in that way, so she pushed the fear aside. If *Reader's Digest* said you could eat eggs nearly raw, that was good enough for her. The magazine should know something about the facts. Millions of people paid thirty-five cents to read what *Reader's Digest* had to say.

Brother Stinchfield showed up for brunch at precisely 2 p.m. He was a punctual man, and while she pushed flat potato slices around a skillet of hot bacon grease for brunch, he ran cold water in the sink, then hot, watching it spiral down the drain, and declared everything to be in good working condition. He asked if everything else in the little green house was working well, and Pansy stated that she thought things were functioning as they should. She said she was thinking of getting a television set, but it didn't have to be a new one with color. She would be content with an old black-and-white unit if Dick knew anyone who might have one for sale. Cheap. Dick thought Pansy couldn't have any use for a television. It was a waste of time, he insisted. Pansy had never owned a television, and Butch wanted to watch the Cowboy Dan show, she said, at which point Butch thought the best way to enter the discussion was to sing the theme song at the top of his lungs.

"Cowboy Dan was a maaan. Was a BIIIIIG man. But the bear was bigger, so he ran like a hm-hm up a tree!"

He collapsed in giggles.

"Like a 'hm-hm'?" Pansy asked.

Butch pulled himself off the floor and described the lyrics in detail, as he had heard them sung at school. "But I can't sing that word. It's a bad word. But we sing it at school."

"How bad?" Dick pressed.

"It's the word for Black people. The bad word for Black people," Butch explained.

"The N-word!?" Pansy shrieked.

Butch nodded.

"It makes no sense to use that word!" Pansy shouted, so upset that she forgot about pushing her potatoes. "Why put that word in the song? Why wouldn't they just sing the song about a Chinaman climbing a tree?"

"Chinaman doesn't rhyme with bigger. The bad word rhymes with bigger," Butch said.

"That's beside the point!" Pansy snapped. "How would you feel if they sang that song in front of one of the Black sisters from Fresno? Sister White, for example?"

"Mom, Sister White is too old to climb trees." This assertion set Butch to again convulsing with laughter, which was the wrong thing to do as Pansy said it clearly demonstrated an unwillingness to comprehend the seriousness of the situation.

Butch had not seen any Black people in Farnsworth, which he then said out loud as if to clarify that no one could be offended by something they weren't around to hear, but that was beside the point, Pansy again replied. It was an offensive word and shouldn't ever be part of one's vocabulary. Dick then added that if any of the Coloreds were to travel to Farnsworth, for what, he couldn't imagine, it wouldn't take them long to turn around and hightail it back to where they had come from.

Pansy turned to Dick in sharp rebuke. "And just why would a Black person run out of Farnsworth?"

"Well," Dick replied, "it's not that I got anything against the Coloreds, but if you were a Colored and there wasn't another person within a hundred miles who looked like you . . . would you stick around?"

Pansy paced hard to the silverware drawer and removed three forks for brunch. "I've known many wonderful Black people in my life," she snapped.

"They say Jehovah will turn the Coloreds white in the new system," Dick mused.

"We don't believe *that*, anymore," Pansy muttered. Dick stood nearby, still leaning heavy on the sink, and she wondered if he might take issue with the way in which she used things that had once belonged to his mother. Cora had done things this-a-way and that-a-way, he had sometimes reminded her. Pansy's utensil drawer had not been used by Cora for that purpose—she was certain of this because she had moved Cora's old silverware out of one drawer and to another—and she waited for Dick to comment on what she had done.

"There's not a soul in this county who isn't White," Dick continued. "Except for that Oriental man over there in Mt. Shasta. Couldn't tell you his name. But he's an Oriental. The only one I know of in Siskiyou. And there's still some Indians, of course, but they don't count. Otherwise, there's no Coloreds anywhere near here."

Pansy slid three plates of soft-cooked eggs stacked atop fried potatoes across the table—still hot, which everyone could see by the steam lifting high, proving she had done proper justice to the *Reader's Digest* instructions.

Unprompted, Dick took the chair his father had occupied a

decade earlier. He leaned back to view the meal, stretching his arms out wide as if intending to gather hordes of onlookers, and blared, "Well! It just don't get any better than this, does it?" This proclamation meant different things to everyone, Dick not taking the statement literally, of course, but believing it to be a passive way of thanking Pansy for feeding him eggs.

Pansy imagined the declaration as an attempt to establish familial ties—as if he might come back, like a relative who lives just a little ways down the road and believes it acceptable to swing by on a whim, expecting eggs and potatoes whenever one likes, which was not what she had perceived this social gathering to have committed her to.

Butch thought Dick was completely full of himself because just about anyone could see that brunch with Brother Stinchfield couldn't possibly be as good as things could get. A cheeseburger at the Mammoth Orange Hamburger stand in Fresno was probably about as good as things could get. Was this as good as that? Nope. Definitely not. This wasn't even as good as a lunchtime plate of stewed chicken over rice in the Farnsworth school cafeteria.

But the meal had been put out for all to enjoy, so Dick stated, "Shall we bow our heads?" which was the only sentence in which he found use for the word "shall." But that's how he had learned to begin prayer—with the common refrain that is often stated in the tone of a question by people who think it important to send words to God before putting food into their mouths. "Shall we bow our heads?" Dick asked, but people who are familiar with this procedure know good and well that it isn't a question at all. It is, in fact, a simple command to lower your head to an angle where, even if you dare to disobey the other half of the rule and open your eyes during this prerequisite for eating, you won't know if anyone else has dared to do likewise. Jehovah apparently prefers people to not have a clue what anyone else is doing during prayers. No one knows why this is so, but after all three had tucked their heads into the appropriate position, Brother Stinchfield gave the standard invocation in which he thanked Jehovah for the food and asked for protection of the brothers and sisters in Malawi who were being persecuted.

Prayers for Malawi were encouraged at the Kingdom Hall—going on more than a decade now. Only a week earlier, Butch had prayed in this way over toast and jelly at breakfast and then later asked Miss Sanders where Malawi was. She didn't know, which made it seem clear that Malawi couldn't really be all that important if a third-grade teacher didn't know about it. Miss Sanders climbed to the top of a footstool and pulled the entire collection of encyclopedias off the upper shelf to investigate the matter because they claimed to have truthful answers to every question people could ask, which turned out to be a lie. They didn't know about Malawi, either, so Miss Sanders then inquired of another teacher who only knew that Malawi was in Africa. When asked where in Africa, she said she had no idea.

But Butch put those concerns aside and murmured amen, then pondered the oddity of the brunch food his mother had prepared, realizing that Jehovah hadn't provided any of it. He thought of pointing this out but felt that the previous discussion of the N-word had put him in a tenuous place where his mother might label him obstinate for doing so. But Butch had been thinking of this recently: the contents of prayers and giving gratitude to God for providing something that couldn't possibly be verified, and it all seemed silly. He thought of Trixie Bleaker, who had given him a half-dozen brown eggs a few weeks prior—as a sample, she had said.

"Hiya, handsome! Give these to your momma," she had instructed, "and tell her that she can buy a whole dozen for a half-dollar, anytime she would like." Trixie, a stranger, was the only woman in Siskiyou County known to wear flip-flops. Pink ones. People had seen her wandering the neighborhood thusly in search of wayward chickens, pink toenails stickin' out the front of her pink flip-flops. She was rumored to be weird that way—an oddness that was confirmed when she announced that she would soon travel to Medford to buy a new pair. She posted details of her trip on a three-by-five index card and tacked it to the bulletin board outside of Clark's Grocery, next to all the other cards announcing local services. Got a problem with your septic? There was a card for that at Clark's. Need to get your hay cut, or looking for a 1942 John Deere with a bad clutch? Flip-flops from Medford? All were offered on Clark's bulletin board.

Butch speculated that maybe they could pray to Jehovah and thank him for Trixie's eggs, but only for that one time when she had given them for free because she was now demanding fifty cents, and you can't really thank Jehovah for giving you eggs if you traded two quarters for them. But really, free eggs shouldn't be mentioned in your prayers, Butch thought, because it simply wasn't believable. As if Jehovah had nothing better to do than send women around the country with eggs. And if Jehovah *had* prompted Trixie to bring them over that first time for free, he'd probably have sent her over with a full dozen, instead of half, given that she claimed to have eggs coming out her ears. And somehow Jehovah can't find time to help the Witnesses in Malawi who are dying from persecution, but he's got time to send crazy women in flip-flops over to your house with eggs.

Pansy, being committed to the *Reader's Digest* philosophy that one can't discuss work and cleaning responsibilities over what is meant to be a social occasion, made a point to not mention them during brunch. Dick was committed to thinking that one can't discuss Kingdom Hall business at all times of the day, so he made a point to not bring that up. Their brunch chatter was stilted and awkward until Pansy explained that *Reader's Digest* had recommended preparing eggs in this way—soft-cooked so the yolks would run over the plate and bathe the potatoes in yellow fattiness, a spoonful of chopped pickle relish placed on top, right in the center. Dick said he preferred scrambled eggs. Perhaps they could do this again, he wondered, and maybe she'd cook eggs to his liking the next time, just to switch things up a bit.

All mumbled some quiet words of joy at Pansy's brunch presentation, then labored through an extended silence. Dick chewed loudly, his mouth wide open. How had she not noticed this earlier, she wondered.

Reader's Digest had recommended that brunch conversations be lively, so Pansy announced that she wanted to learn the ukulele in the new system, after Armageddon arrived. She'd always loved the ukulele, she said, though Butch didn't remember her ever saying this before. It was news to him, and about as preposterous as the day she announced an intention to can peaches in Farnsworth.

"Don't you just love the ukulele?" she asked Dick.

Dick paused to think of this, his fork suspended in midair. "Your fingers are too fat," he stated in a way that made him sound like he knew everything about ukuleles. Pansy bristled at the word "fat."

"Jehovah will make me perfect in the new system," she retorted. She wouldn't have fat fingers, and she intended to play the ukulele all she liked when she got there. In fact, she thought Jehovah would probably make Dick taller and thinner in the new system, which she said out loud as if the thought may have never occurred to him.

Dick pushed his plate across the table, then stood to leave. At the door, he reminded Pansy that he would again pick her up for work at 7 a.m. "Don't be late," he added.

"I have never once been late," Pansy replied.

A wet spring arrived in the Shasta Valley in 1969. The days turned warm, and the slope behind the little green house seeped in runoff to the pasture below. At the B-Bar-Seven Ranch house stood three neglected peach trees, twisted with age but glistening each morning with a fleeting blanket of dew, their blossoms at popcorn stage and on the edge of bursting. Blackberry thickets had swallowed portions of the creek on the east side. One last Pippin apple tree, gnarled and unpruned since his mother had passed, not yet into its bloom and not yet dead in spite of Steve wishing it to be, leaned south to the morning sun. "It's just an old sour apple," he described to anyone who asked. "My mother used to bake pies out of them apples, but no one around here does that sort of thing anymore. If I want pie, I can get one at the Food-Rite for a buck-fifty."

The Bultemeyer family, save for Steve, did not welcome Butch into the folds of ranch life with graciousness, but he hadn't yet noticed. Max had complained, "God damn. You should just adopt that kid." Max, divorced and single, lived in a single-wide trailer three miles north of Yreka and ten miles from the main Bultemeyer ranch property. His hair grew long, well below his shoulders, and was always bound into a long gray ponytail. This led many to look at him with suspicion, as that style was anything but normal in Siskiyou, unless on a woman, which Max was not.

Hank Bultemeyer lived a mile from the Bultemeyer property, further down Little Shasta Road. This only came to be after a short battle with Siskiyou County over the specifics of how the West Corner Bridge that had been washed out by winter runoff in the big storm of 1958 was to be rebuilt. The county demanded money and engineering calculations, so the Bulte-meyers and two other farming families who relied upon that access point dragged an eight-by-eight Douglas fir beam across the span, twenty-three feet long and ten feet above the creek bottom, and navigated it by foot each day to ferry groceries to other vehicles.

Hank designed a new bridge on his own, and under the cover of winter skies and the fact that the county had little reason to find themselves on private land, he and Lee Amos from the Amos Ranch rebuilt it themselves. It took the county two years to discover the structure, after which they sent a three-man team out to interrogate residents, none of whom pointed fingers.

The county stiffs climbed up and down the new bridge. After rigorous examination that failed to identify any structural defects or code violations—other than the obvious one that the bridge had been built without paying the county for the privilege of doing so—the inspectors drove back to the office in Yreka where travesties of this sort were discussed. They weighed the pros and cons of waging what would have been a public battle with the Bultemeyer family. With no residents willing to take ownership or responsibility for the bridge, the county added photos and investigatory details of the illegal structure to a thick binder of all known bridges in Siskiyou, labeled with a big red sticker as "non-permitted."

Five years later, the county building department trotted out this binder when Hank applied for a building permit to enlarge the kitchen on his B-Bar-Seven Ranch home. His kitchen remodel project was approved, contingent upon his first pulling a permit to rebuild the illegal bridge. Being the sort of man who got loud fast, he told everyone to go fuck themselves, then moved off the ranch to a new home just a mile down the road on a one-acre lot strewn with lava rock. That was how the B-

Bar-Seven found itself with no residents who would continue the dreams of Hazzard Bultemeyer.

Steve remained in the original one-bedroom house in which he had been born. The larger Bultemeyer home that had been vacated by Hank was rented out to Dave Lunardi—a married man who drove a water truck for Lunardi Well and Pump. The $215 collected from Dave each month was added to the ranch coffers to be shared equally amongst the Bultemeyer boys, and the ranch began its slow decline with no Bultemeyer offspring, save for Steve, interested in operating it.

Steve had driven Butch out to the property one spring morning, with Pansy's permission, then parked in the weed patch on the north side of the apple tree where corn and tomatoes were at one time grown. Butch opened the passenger door and slid to the ground, then hollered for Booger to jump out of the truck bed. "Come on, Booger! Let's go feed the cows!" He scurried to the far corrals, where he caught his shirt on a stretch of barbed wire.

He returned to Steve to lament over the situation.

"Might want to work on staying farther from the barbed wire next time," Steve said.

Butch thrust his finger through the hole. "Mom's gonna be mad."

"Nah . . . she can fix that right up, I'm sure," Steve said.

"How are you sure?" Butch asked.

"Because it's not a big deal." Steve poked his own finger at the tear. "It won't take more'n a couple of minutes to stitch that up . . . my mother coulda done it."

Butch rubbed the torn edges between his fingers. "But how do you know my mom can do it? Can *you* do it?"

"Well, no, I don't sew. But I'll bet I could figure it out if I had to. Sometimes, things aren't as difficult as people make them out to be."

"Well, maybe you can figure it out. Before I go home," Butch suggested.

"All right, let's see if we can do something about that." Steve turned for the back door. "Let's go find my mother's sewing kit." He led Butch into his kitchen.

Butch rolled his eyes around the devastation. Boxes of pink eye medicine for doctoring cows were piled atop the kitchen table. The sink overflowed with dirty dishes. Steve appeared to own entirely too much stuff and hadn't learned to put any of it away.

"Your house is a mess!" Butch exclaimed.

"Yup. That's my number one goal in life. My brothers can clean it up after I die."

"My mom would have a heart attack." Butch gazed at the mountains of rubble. "I don't think she would let me come over if she knew you were so messy. She doesn't like messy."

"Well then, I'd say you'll want to keep that information to yourself."

13

PANSY WOULD NOT ENTERTAIN HERSELF OUT OF doors. Not near the cherry plum thicket on the east side, nor in back where she hung laundry every Saturday afternoon. The little green house had no lawn in front. Unintended vegetation grew in unorganized abandonment, as it wished and in the seasons when prompted. There were bushes out front, of varieties Pansy did not care to know. Spring had brought brief colonies of paperwhite blossoms near the back steps. Their fragrance drifted through the kitchen window and spilled all the way to Spier Street.

On the 6th of June, school let out for the summer. The days were warm, but the Shasta River still ran cold, and the delay of sunset pushed the summer feeding chores to 6 p.m., with four more hours to spare before nightfall. Two dozen cow and calf pairs had again been turned out to the great pasture for summer grazing. Three rope horses were penned up at the barn, needing to be fed each day.

The first time Pansy stood at her kitchen sink and looked out to see Butch astride a horse, she thought to rush down and plead for him to dismount. Butch looked secure, content, and unmarred by fear. Now wearing cowboy boots, a cast-off gift from Steve's nephew Rumford, Butch did chores, invented others, climbed to the barn loft, and rode Speckles from one corner to the next.

The second cutting of alfalfa had been baled two weeks prior. Steve rolled a long steel conveyor contraption up to the barn to send bales up to the second floor, where Butch helped stack them in a crisscross pattern so they wouldn't fall over. Butch climbed atop the stack to gaze over the pasture and beyond from the open door—standing tall, announcing that potential invaders would be shot.

Butch and Pansy were enjoying their second summer in the little green house. Their routines were set; they knew people, but not well. They had spoken to the neighbors on both far sides of their property without any intent to socialize. Pansy had found a used black-and-white television, but Butch rarely lounged in front of it. Pansy had yet to find a Bible study with anyone. Her search for the desperate had yet to churn up anyone willing to devote life to The Truth.

Pansy was the first to leave the Kingdom Hall after each meeting. She wouldn't bring social activities into the privacy of her home. She walked to Dick's Town and Country after the last song had been sung, waiting for him to lock up, and he then drove her and Butch home.

Dick Stinchfield announced plans for Butch to accompany Pansy to the campground. "He could help with chores," Dick suggested. "You'll have to pack a lunch for him, of course. It will teach him responsibility. And besides, you can't just have him sit at home all by himself for the whole summer, can you?"

"Why wouldn't I?" Pansy replied. "When we moved here, you told us nothing bad can happen to a child in Farnsworth."

She looked at him with some irritation, waiting for an explanation. "Do you remember telling us that?"

Dick waved a stubby finger in her direction. "Responsibility is what every kid needs to learn these days."

The telephone rang in the little green house at eight o'clock that evening, but Pansy waited until the fourth ring to answer it. After a short conversation with the caller, she strode out front to locate Butch, who was stacking three rocks and a collection of sticks in what he described as a quail trap. "I'm catching quail for dinner," he asserted.

"Brother Stinchfield says he would like you to come to camp with me this summer," Pansy said.

"What for?"

"He thinks you might enjoy having some work at camp."

Butch shook his head in refusal. "I can't. Steve's gonna teach me fishing."

"What have I told you about that?" Pansy scolded.

"Not to say that word."

"It's *not* a word. There's no listing in a dictionary for 'gonna.'"

"Steve said he's going to take me fishing," Butch said.

"Better." Pansy turned for the house. Halfway there, she looked back to Butch. "Okay. It's decided. I'll tell Dick you're busy fishing." Nearing the front door, she yelled down the lilac tunnel. "Maybe you should give a fish to Dick! You can tell him to cook it for dinner!"

"Brother Stinchfield doesn't like fish!" Butch yelled back.

"Exactly," Pansy muttered.

The next day, Saturday, Pansy sent Butch over to Trixie Bleaker's house with four quarters for two dozen eggs. The early morning light was still dim. Most people hadn't yet stirred for coffee. Steve's truck was parked in the empty field out front.

On her front porch, Trixie mumbled about Butch getting an early start to the day, collected his change, then handed two paper sacks to him, a dozen loose eggs in each.

"Thank you," he said. Trixie reached across the threshold to caress his cheek.

"You're sure a handsome boy," she said. "You're gonna have to come back to see me when you grow up."

"Okay," Butch said. "I'll be back when Mom needs more eggs."

Trixie smiled. "Yes, you do that."

Steve emerged from the depths of her kitchen, his hat in hand. "Thanks," he mumbled to Trixie, nodded "good morning" to Butch, then strode off to his truck across the road. Butch followed.

"What are you doin' over here?" Butch asked.

"Ahh . . . just came over to get me some eggs," he said.

Steve settled into the front seat of his truck, then rolled down his window.

"Where's your eggs?" Butch asked.

"Uhh . . . Trixie ran out." Steve turned the ignition. "You want a ride home?"

Butch hustled around to the passenger side and climbed in, laying his eggs on the seat between them. He went silent for the drive, all three blocks. When Steve pulled up to the lilac tunnel, Butch lifted one of the sacks. "You want some of our eggs?"

"Nah, I don't really need any eggs right now," Steve answered.

Butch opened the truck door to leave.

"Tell you what. Let's head over to Yreka. You wanna go?" Steve asked.

"What for?" Butch asked.

"Need to stop at the feed store for grain."

Steve roared with laughter on their drive.

Butch had complained that Trixie's rooster was scary.

"Did he chase you out of the pasture?" Steve asked.

Butch nodded, yes.

"You got whooped by a rooster!" Steve teased.

Butch again nodded. "He's mean!"

"Well then, you need to cowboy up. No reason to get whooped by a chicken. Just grab a stick and smack him once. Then he'll know you're the boss." He again broke into serious laughter, making Butch wonder if Steve had ever driven off the road. Butch asked that question, had Steve ever driven off the road, but Steve replied, "Of course not." Butch didn't ask for more as he was of the nature that he should believe answers that had been given. Steve said he was a very good driver, which Butch could accept as fact, as Steve said he had never once driven off the road.

"Brother Stinchfield wants me to work at the camp this summer. Mom said he's tryin' to get something for free—or two for the price of one," Butch said.

"What do you think he wants?" Steve asked.

"Two for the price of one."

"Well then, let's see what we can do about that when I get you home."

"What are you gonna do?" Butch asked.

"Don't know yet."

They returned to the pasture thirty minutes later, unloaded five fifty-pound sacks of grain, then Steve put a saddle on Speckles. "Alrighty, time to go talk to your momma," he announced. "Climb up."

They rode Speckles up the slope at a hard gallop. At the fence, Steve hollered for Pansy to come out from the little green house.

She emerged from the back porch and walked to the barbed wire.

"Good mornin'," Steve said.

"Good morning," Pansy repeated.

"It's a beautiful morning, isn't it? Almost time for lunch, maybe?"

"Is there anything you want?"

"Maybe I just came by to say hello," Steve said.

"Okay. Hello," Pansy mimicked.

"Maybe I came by to see if you have some ice."

"Ice?" Pansy asked.

Butch interrupted. "Mom! Steve wants to ask you something."

"Yes, I do." Steve turned back to Butch. "Slide off."

He waved a finger in Pansy's direction. "So, been thinking about something. You've got a great kid here," pointing at Butch. "I'm thinkin' he doesn't have much to keep himself busy during the summer. Sometimes I don't wanna drive out every morning, so was thinkin' that I'd be willin' to pay him to help me out . . . maybe a buck every week. It might help him out, too, for a young guy to have a bit of spending money. Whadya think about that?"

Pansy blinked.

"Whadya think?" Steve repeated.

"Well, I don't know. What would you have him do?" Pansy asked.

"There's plenty to do. Just ask him," Steve nodded to Butch and winked.

"I'm a cowboy. There's always work to do," Butch said.

"Oh, you are, are you?" Pansy was skeptical. "What exactly would cowboys do out there?"

"The animals come first. And I can walk fence, too."

"Well then, let's write everything down." Pansy disappeared into the house but quickly returned with a pen and paper in hand. "It's always best to make a list. Just tell me what needs to be done first, at eight, and I'll write it down for you. Then maybe something new at eight-fifteen, and eight-thirty." She might have suggested that Steve open an ice cream shop at the edge of the great pasture from which to sell pancakes.

"Mom," Butch said. "Cowboys don't need lists."

"Why wouldn't they? It's always best to have a list," Pansy stated.

"Because cowboys think for themselves." Butch looked at Steve when he answered.

"And how do you know this?" Pansy asked.

Butch giggled. "Because I have a brain."

Pansy looked to Steve. "I suppose you taught him that."

That evening, over bowls of chocolate ice cream, Pansy brought a pad of paper to the kitchen table. "It's always best to have a list," she said to Butch. "So, what's the first thing on the list?"

"Feed the horses," he replied, conceding to the will of his mother. "That's the first thing."

"Got it." Pansy looked up from her note-taking. "What else?"

"Smack Trixie's rooster with a stick," Butch said.

"And why would you beat Trixie's chicken?"

"Steve said I need to show the rooster who's boss."

"Well, I'm not adding that to your list, Pansy replied. "We should keep it to reasonable expectations for job responsibilities."

Butch jabbed a spoon at his ice cream. "Steve was over at Trixie's house this morning."

"He was? That early?" Pansy laid her pencil on the table. "What for?"

"He said for eggs, but she ran out," Butch said.

"Trixie ran out of eggs?"

"That's what Steve said."

Pansy sniffed. "Well, God bless him. Good to hear he's only over there for eggs. Wouldn't want to think she's offering other items from the menu."

Attempting to time the unpredictable peaks and valleys of the cattle market, Steve was convinced that splitting his herd, half going to steer production and the other going to a cow-calf operation where the calves would be sold at auction and finished elsewhere, would even out the cash flow of the B-Bar-Seven. Most calves would be born during a two-week period on the ranch, which was happening now, on a Friday morning in June while Pansy was cleaning cabins at the campground, and Butch was knee-deep in watching calves spill from their mothers at the B-Bar-Seven.

It seemed a miracle when calves pushed from their wombs in slimy shrouds of afterbirth. Those lives that were encouraged, developed, and then nurtured by cowboys held Butch's thoughts for most of the day.

They drove back to town early in the afternoon, Steve asking Butch if he wanted to be dropped off at home. "Nope. The pasture." Steve parked near the barn, lowered his tailgate, and then sat, gazing in the direction of the Siskiyou Range. Butch sat next to him.

Steve reached into his back pocket and removed a dollar bill from his wallet. "Thank you, young man, for your help. You're a good cowboy."

Butch ironed it flat on his thigh. "It's my first cowboy dollar."

"You can have weekends off, if you want," Steve offered.

Butch shook his head in rejection of the offer. He folded the bill, then slid it into his pocket.

"What are you gonna do with it?" Steve asked.

"Can I buy the pasture when I grow up?"

"Should be able to trust a man's promises," Steve often said. True to his word, he pulled an old fishing pole and spinning reel from Dave Lunardi's garage, then walked Butch to the Shasta River with a five-gallon bucket. They caught grasshoppers in the tall grass, and Butch brought two ten-inch trout home. He worked little that summer but would say differently, if asked. The list was short: Feed in the morning. Then, do anything that makes you happy. Walk the fence for no reason. Climb onto Speckle's back. Ride around. Fish the Shasta.

Butch stashed his savings on the second floor of the barn, sealed tight in a mason jar. Pansy inquired for details. "Where are you hiding it? It would be a tragedy to lose your money," she said.

"It's a secret. I'm saving it."

"Why are you saving it?" she asked.

"To buy the pasture."

"When are you planning to do that?"

"When I grow up," Butch replied.

"Armageddon will be here long before you save enough money to buy the pasture. And Steve is not going to make it into the new system, so you can probably have the whole place if you want it. No one else is going to get excited about an old barn, that's for sure."

Trixie Bleaker volunteered to head the Siskiyou County Cattlewomen's Club that summer after she intentionally walked in on their emergency meeting at the abandoned shoe store on Eleventh Street. Being occupied for the first time in over a decade, and only for this impromptu meeting where the cattle-women had hastily rounded up their membership to replace the president who had just up and died, Trixie barged inside to see what was going on and learned that the previous leader, Elsa Sullivan of Farnsworth, had somehow ridden her horse into a fence. The cattle ladies got all riled up and pulled emergency copies of the association phone tree from hiding. Calls then crisscrossed the county and before anyone knew it, most had gathered at the old shoe store to sympathize over her passing.

Being the youngest person in the room, age thirty-seven, Trixie stuck herself in the middle of the discussion. Youth has advantages, she asserted. "None of you are spring chickens," she said, the exception being herself. "You're all about to keel over from old age. You need some young blood to get things fired up." She then volunteered to assume the official duties of head cattlewoman, until someone pointed out that Trixie had no cattle, to which she replied that she had seventy-six chickens and three roosters in her backyard, and let's face it, there's not a lot of difference between a chicken and a cow.

"Both are domesticated farm animals, so if you're looking for a new president, I'd be happy to take the job. I'm very effective at getting things done," she assured them. "Just look at my chicken business. I sell a lot of eggs in this town."

Lucille Pittsenbarger stated that keeping chickens isn't

anything like herding cows into pasture, to which Trixie insisted that a fence is a fence. You build a fence to keep chickens, or you build a fence to keep cows. Doesn't seem to make much difference. A fence is a fence. Birdie Johnson declared that there's a world of difference, bein' that cows don't fly. Takes a different sort of fence to keep them in, but Trixie just plain couldn't see her point. Birdie snapped back in frustration—the explanation was right there, plain as day: cows, don't, fly. But Trixie still couldn't see it until someone grew weary of both unwavering sides of the debate and asked if she owned any cowboy boots. Cattlewomen don't wear flip-flops. Trixie looked down to her pink toenails and surrendered.

In the end, the job was given to Susan Leadbetter who had never owned a cow, but she did have a pair of boots in the back of her closet. Her husband, Earl, cut the hair of most ranchers in the vicinity at his barbershop in Yreka. Earl knew just about everything that went on in the ranching world, given that the cowboys who had been sitting in his chair for the last forty years usually brought their afflictions with diarrhea of the mouth, and that satisfied everyone, including Trixie, who said she could see the logic of that. Susan would make a fine president, she conceded. Susan then thanked everyone for their support, and someone banged a gavel on the foldout table three times, and just like that, Susan Leadbetter was president of the Siskiyou County Cattlewomen's Club.

Every Saturday afternoon at 2 p.m., when the house squeaked of cleanliness, Pansy walked to Clark's Grocery with a list of what should be purchased for the upcoming week. Grateful for all that Farnsworth had given her, the limited selection at the town's only grocery had begun to put a heavy layer of constraint on her shopping experience. One could find canned peas or creamed corn and one-pound packages of ground beef whenever desired, but she wished for Clark's to do what one expected from a grocery. Signs could be hung in windows, letting you know what was on sale or what they most hoped to be rid of. Like canned green beans for eighteen cents, available this week only. But Clark's didn't do this. Nothing hung in their windows. It would eventually abandon the grocery business and nail sheets of plywood over every orifice, but until then, which Pansy could see, the store lacked hope for existence. Nothing could rile her more than having no hope for the future.

Two weeks earlier, she had asked Dick to stop at the Food-Rite in Yreka. The moment she uttered that request, she felt controlled by his car keys and willingness to indulge her needs, but more than anything, the arrangement had begun to offend her honor.

The following Friday, after work, neither attempted conversation on their drive to Farnsworth. Not an unusual thing, but when Dick pulled up to the lilac tunnel, Pansy invited him inside, saying she had some business to discuss.

A bowl of yellow cherry plums that she had harvested from the east side of the house sat in a bowl near the sink. Dick plopped one into his mouth. "Used to eat these when my folks were alive." He spat the pit into his hand. "Mother used to make jam out of them."

"Maybe I'll make jam, someday," Pansy said. She took a seat at her kitchen table and unfolded the *Yreka Herald*. "Brother Stinchfield, the reason I have asked you into my home is because I have been giving some thought to our arrangement here, with us living in Farnsworth. I have done some simple math, wanting to better understand our options."

Dick paled. He slid the moist plum pit into the front pocket of his pants.

"As much as I appreciate living in your house, William and I don't need to live in Farnsworth, where we are dependent on you for transportation. Homes can be rented in Yreka for $75 a month." She stood from the table. "And I intend to purchase a car."

Dick licked his lips. "A car? You know how to drive?"

"I do not. But I can learn. And my point is this. The Siskiyou Manor Motel has posted a job offering in the paper for a maid and is offering $2.50 an hour for the position. I don't know if you saw that," Pansy said.

"I don't take the paper. Not much of a need to, in my opinion," he replied.

"There is plenty of useful information in the paper," Pansy stated. "I am proposing that I pay rent to you in an amount that is reasonable in comparison to what I could rent elsewhere. And I am asking you to treat us fairly."

Pansy fingered the corner of the Classifieds. She rotated the paper sideways, turning it in his direction. "You have been paying me $1.50 an hour. Apparently, the standard compensation for a qualified cleaning woman is $2.50 an hour, if you can find one." She slid it to the center of her table. "The Siskiyou Manor appears to be having a difficult time finding one."

Dick stared at her.

"So, what I propose is an hourly wage of $2.50 an hour. The minimum wage just went up this past January to two dollars, so it's not unreasonable to ask for fifty cents more. In return for being paid fairly, I will, in return, pay you seventy-five dollars a month for rent. That's how much houses rent for in the vicinity."

Dick slapped both hands on the table. "If I accept rent money from you, I'll have to report it for tax purposes! You'll cost me money by having to do that!"

"The honesty of your tax return is a private concern between you and Jehovah," Pansy retorted sharply.

Dick turned away, facing the great pasture. "Let me think on it. I'll have an answer for you in the morning." He left the house and drove away.

A quick summer cloudburst blew through the next morning, a typical mountain storm when clouds roil and bellow in short squalls, the precipitation brief but heavy. It then rolled over the ridgeline, leaving a freshness in its wake. The rain had stopped now, and the quail were skittering across the gravel of Spier Street, paired for mating season. Trails of puffy hatchlings would soon follow. Pansy walked to the end of the drive, the green house behind her, and watched two pairs. Off their nests, the parents gorged with abandon in the clearing, then blasted over the road in a reckless run as if Satan's fire had lit their tails ablaze. After their babies were raised, all would abandon their pairings and congregate into vast social coveys as quail can't survive without the social intimacy and protection of a crowd.

Five blocks over at the corner of South Twelfth Street and Farnsworth Road, Celeste Stuttengraph had left her blue Toyota Corona where she hoped it to be most visible. Pansy walked around it twice, circling to inspect what, she didn't know. She asked Celeste how much she wanted for the vehicle.

Celeste asked if Pansy had seen the price posted in the *Herald*. "Page seventeen," she stated. Three hundred and fifty dollars. That's what she had posted.

Celeste had been running her ad for an entire month, Pansy pointed out. "If it was worth $350, someone would have already bought it."

"She has a name," Celeste said.

"She? A name?" Pansy asked.

"Well, sure! She should have a name, don't you think?" Celeste burst into an oversized smile at the thought that Pansy could be persuaded into the deal, befriended even, if she were introduced, on a personal level, to the Toyota. "Didn't you name your last car?"

Pansy opened the driver's door. "I've never owned a car." She lowered herself into the seat and contemplated its narrowness, a bit snug for a woman her size . . . then decided this was how it should be when in the driver's seat. Snug and secure, the way she thought would be most appropriate when driving. "The radio works?" she asked, without testing it for herself.

"Everything works," Celeste answered. "That's why I'm asking $350."

The car eventually changed hands for $335. Both felt they had been taken advantage of. Shortly after Pansy returned home, she realized that she had failed to ask Celeste for the name.

Roger Dodger was the insurance man in Yreka, but people knew him as Cliff. "Roger Dodger Insurance Agency! Keeping back-sides covered for thirty-two years!" By phone, Pansy asked Cliff if he made house calls. On Saturdays. She couldn't drive to Yreka to see him, of course, not having insurance and all.

"Can get you signed up in less than five minutes," Cliff assured her. "You are employed? By Dick Stinchfield? Well, we could get him some insurance, too."

"I'm sure Dick has insurance elsewhere," Pansy said.

"He doesn't," Cliff replied. "I've already asked. Repeatedly. I can get you a discount if you can get him to sign up," he offered.

"Well, on second thought, I'll give you his home number," Pansy responded.

Pansy then made another phone call. "I truly appreciate everything you do for us," she said to Steve.

"You're mighty welcome," he replied. "Your boy's a good kid, so it's my pleasure."

Pansy asked if she might impose upon him for driving lessons. She was a quick learner, she guaranteed, and Steve spent an hour on Sunday evening driving up and down Ball Mountain Road with Pansy Blackwell.

"Keep the tires on the road, somewhere between the fence-posts. That's all you gotta remember," Steve instructed, which Pansy agreed to abide by.

That evening, she parked the Toyota outside the little green house, ensconced inside the lilac tunnel. Over a dinner of ground beef soaked in gravy and spooned atop slices of white bread, Pansy asked Butch to again thank Steve for his kindness. She deliberated over short contemplations of the man, then finally settled on a solid statement of truth. "Steve's a good man, don't you think?"

Butch nodded.

Pansy sopped gravy with a crust of white bread, then seemed to go vacant in thought at the realization that Steve would soon die at Armageddon. She sighed. "It's really too bad that things are as they are ... "

The next day, inside the Weaver barn, Butch asked Steve, "Do you think my mom is pretty?"

Like a plain piece of paper, Steve thought.

"You should think of it this way," he said. "Like when you get presents, and one is wrapped in somethin' special. Another is wrapped in a grocery bag. It don't look special, but then you open it and see that it's just as special as the one in the fancy paper. You understand me?"

Butch did not.

"You should think of your mother that way . . . she's just as special as everyone else's mom. Got it?"

"We don't get presents," Butch said.

"Never?"

The price for beef cattle rose by five cents a pound, which was unusual for August, so Steve was sending some steers to auction early. He hitched his truck to his largest stock trailer on Friday and loaded a dozen for transport to Medford. He'd asked Pansy if Butch could go, but she had drawn an imaginary boundary for their travels together: the borders of Siskiyou County.

When Steve returned, he drove to Pansy's house. His empty trailer stretched a good length of Spier's Street in the dark of evening. When Pansy answered her door, he marched inside.

"Got something for you," he said to Butch. He walked to the kitchen and laid a package, wrapped in brown paper sacks, on the table. "It's a present."

"It's my first present!" Butch declared.

"Yes, I know," Steve said, as Pansy thought back to her own, delivered in brown Kraft paper, unwrapped by her mother in the dim light of a Denver bedroom. Butch had already stripped the paper from the box and pulled out a straw cowboy hat.

"It's a little big, but let me show you how we can fix that." Steve looked to Pansy. "Do you have a newspaper or something? Even a napkin will work."

She pushed the *Herald* across the table to him.

Steve stripped a half-sheet, folded it lengthwise, then again, and one more time until an inch wide. "Now look here," he motioned to Butch. "We fold a piece of paper like so, and then we tuck it inside the sweatband. Just like that." He handed it over. "And as you get bigger, we put a new piece of paper inside to get your hat to stay where you want it."

Butch shoved the hat onto his head. "It won't come off."

Steve reached across the table and turned the hat in the opposite direction. "We'll need to conversate about which end is the front. You don't want your hat backwards."

"Okay," Butch said.

"And another thing. Don't let people mess with your hat," Steve instructed.

"Why?" Butch asked.

"Why *not*," Pansy corrected.

"Why not?" Butch repeated.

"Because cowboys don't let other people mess with our hats. It's a rule," Steve explained.

"Okay," Butch agreed.

"And one more rule. This is really important. A good cowboy never lays his hat on the bed. *Ever.* You put your hat on the bed, and that's where you're gonna end up. In bed. Hurtin' or dead. It's a bad omen," Steve said.

"That sounds like superstition," Pansy stated. Her voice rose.

"You can call it what you like," Steve retorted.

"We don't believe in superstition. Satan uses it to draw people away from Jehovah."

"Cowboy hats will draw you away from Jehovah? Good God. You want me to take it back?" Steve asked.

"No, no." She glanced at Butch. "There's nothing wrong with the hat. I am just saying that we don't participate in superstitions."

"So, the hat's okay . . . " Steve paused in thought. "I'm just trying to wrap my head around what your problem is."

"I don't have a problem," Pansy snapped. "I am explaining to you that I intend to raise my child in a manner that is pleasing to Jehovah. There is no room for superstitions or demonic worship in our faith."

"Fine." Steve turned back to Butch. "So, your mom says you can keep it. We just won't talk about Satan. And don't put your hat on the bed."

"I won't," Butch promised.

The right side of Steve's mustache curled upwards. "Good man." He patted Butch on the shoulder, then leaned to Pansy. "That's a good boy you got there." On his way out, he looked back to her, one eyebrow rising north. "Just so you know."

The next morning, Butch slapped his hat on his head and ran to the barn. In her kitchen, Pansy turned from her view of the pasture and thought that she may have been rude the previous evening. She looked around her home. A feeling of comfort took her thoughts. Maybe she should invite Steve over for supper. She went out front, then backed her Toyota out of the lilac tunnel and drove to the north side of town. Creeping along Farnsworth Road, a mile away, she turned around at Gravel Pit Road, then headed south to Ball Mountain Road. Four miles east, she pulled over where the road signs warned of a sharp curve ahead. On her left, a mature growth of alfalfa rippled. An ocean of blue-flowered stalks waved in the breeze, waiting for a second cutting of the season. On her right, the north flank of Gregory Mountain. The B-Bar-Seven was just a little further down the road, she knew. She turned her car around and drove home.

Farnsworth Elementary flung its doors wide open for school on September 8th, and Butch started fourth grade. Steve killed a stray dog in his pasture. Butch found blowflies feasting on its carcass two days after, hung by its head from the barbed-wire fence.

Steve's .22 Remington still rested in the gun rack mounted to the back window of his truck. It seemed to Butch that most people around Farnsworth had guns. Trixie Bleaker had a gun, so she said.

"Whose dog was it?" he asked.

Steve shrugged. "Don't know. But a dog that chases livestock isn't welcome in cattle country."

Butch looked to Booger. "I hope no one shoots Booger."

"No one's gonna shoot Booger unless he's chasin' their animals, and then they're within their rights to put him down." Steve laid out the truth of dog killing: your dog chases horses, you should know to keep him chained up in your own yard.

He pulled his unloaded .22 from the truck, slid the bolt open, then handed it to Butch. "First thing to understand, most important thing to know, is that a gun is not a toy. A gun is a tool. The purpose of a gun is to kill."

They discussed the tools for killing. A deer rifle, for the obvious. Shotguns, for quail hunting. Rabbit hunting, but not until winter, when the weather turns cold. Maybe just before Christmas. "We'll go chase some rabbits around Christmas," Steve said. "Tastes just like chicken."

"Okay," Butch agreed. "Can I shoot your gun now?"

"Tomorrow. But only the .22. You're not ready for the big guns, not yet," Steve said.

"Why not?" Butch asked.

"They'll knock you on your ass. You need to know gun safety before you fire somethin' that could blow your head off."

"That wouldn't be good," Butch mused.

"Nope. Your mom would be really pissed if I sent you home without a head."

Butch aimed a blank stare at Steve.

"It's a joke. You're supposed to laugh," Steve said.

"Your jokes aren't very funny."

"You don't think? I'll work on that," Steve promised. "And we'll take a few shots out in the pasture tomorrow morning. Only if your mom gives permission. You can ask her to come watch."

"She can't come watch. Tomorrow is Saturday. Mom cleans house," Butch answered.

"She could clean house after you get back. Or clean the dang house on Sunday. It can't take that long to clean house."

"Mom doesn't clean house on Sunday. She cleans on Saturday. That's the way she does things, and she doesn't like it when people up and change things on her."

"Okay, fine, then why don't you head over here on Sunday morning? Bring her with you," Steve suggested.

"We go to the Kingdom Hall on Sunday," Butch said.

"Well, I know that. I've been watching you go to church every Sunday since you got here. Can't you skip church this weekend?"

"It's not a church. We go to a Kingdom Hall. It's different than a church," Butch explained.

"How is it different?" Steve asked.

"Churches are where worldly people go."

"Worldly people? Who is worldly?"

"People who aren't in The Truth," Butch replied.

"The Truth?" Steve asked.

"Jehovah's Witnesses. We have The Truth," Butch answered.

"I see." Steve removed his hat, then rubbed his head vigorously. "So, am I worldly?"

"Yeah, but you don't go to church."

"No, I don't. But I'm still worldly?" Steve asked.

"Yeah," Butch said.

"Good to know."

"You're officially a publisher, now," Brother Stinchfield said to Butch. "You'll witness to Steve again, right?"

Butch nodded.

"So, this will be your first field service report. We'll count your witnessing to Steve as a half hour." Dick turned the paper to face Butch. He pointed to a box in the third column. "Right there." He moved his finger to a footnote at the bottom of the document. "See what it says there? Sixty hours of preaching is the requirement, every month. Think you can do that?"

"Sixty?"

14

THE WINTER COLD HAD PUSHED THE GREAT PASTURE into its time of rest. The last storm came through wet but icy. Each morning, the mud was hardened with frost. Steve sent the last of his steers to the auction in Medford. Breeding cows were fed from hay in storage.

When Christmas arrived in Siskiyou, the county shut down as if the entire world was about to end. Rural people took the holiday seriously. Jesus played little part in the celebration, but commercial establishments locked up tight for the three-day period, which Pansy had learned. This year, prepared for the shutdown, she had stocked her kitchen for the week.

Her first frozen turkey, purchased from the Food-Rite Grocery and hard as a cannonball, laid on the washing machine to thaw in the winter chill of her back porch. She had given it plenty of thought, analyzing the difference between doing something *for* Christmas or *on* Christmas. On the morning of the twenty-fifth, the bird yawed open in preparation for stuffing, slathered in a half pound of butter. *Reader's Digest* had recommended one not to skimp. A good turkey could be ruined without butter, it said. She slathered it again after pulling it from the oven.

An early dinner, Butch pulled a leg and a thigh to his plate. "We should do this every year!"

Pansy smiled at his request. "Okay," she said.

"Okay, what?" Butch asked.

"We'll do this every year. Turkey dinner, on Christmas day, but only because turkey is on sale, and only until Armageddon comes. We won't be eating turkey in the new system."

The Yreka Feed and Tack was selling off their entire supply of men's clothing two days after Christmas as if they wouldn't survive to see another holiday unless the entire store were immediately liquidated. Jeans were on a drastic discount.

Steve drove Butch there. His tires rumbled on the asphalt. The chill of a winter day flooded the interior of his truck.

"Hey, buddy, put some glass in that hole," Steve barked.

"What?!" Butch asked.

"Roll the dang window up. It's cold out there."

In the back corner of Yreka Feed, Steve asked Butch for a gift suggestion. "For your mother."

"We don't celebrate Christmas," Butch said.

"Yes, I know. Christmas was three days ago."

"She'll think you're weird. Make sure it doesn't look like Christmas." Butch laid a pair of Wranglers back on the shelf. "You probably shouldn't buy these. It will look like a Christmas present."

Steve handed them back to Butch. "You need pants. Take them over to the register."

"Fuckin' retarded thing," he muttered under his breath after Butch had walked away.

On their way out the door, Butch asked, "Are you gonna buy something for my mom?"

"I intend to," Steve said.

"She'll think you're weird. She doesn't get presents."

"She can think whatever she dang well pleases. It would be nice to get her something to repay her for the help you give to me. That's not such a bad thing, is it? Just tell me what she would like," Steve demanded.

"She's in love with Tom Jones."

Steve found a Tom Jones album, *Delilah*, and the day after he drove it over to Pansy, she went to the Sears and Roebuck catalog office in Yreka and ordered a hi-fi stereo to be delivered.

She taped two photos of Tom to her living room wall, torn from *Celeb Scoop* magazine that she sometimes purchased at the Food-Rite. Her two God dolls, constant companions since leaving Denver a decade earlier, were now in the middle of her kitchen table, back-to-back in vertical precision, centered on a white doily from Mrs. Stinchfield's collection.

"Don't you just love Tom Jones?" Pansy asked Dick. He was standing in her kitchen. She pointed to the God dolls. "Aren't they pretty? Those are my momma's God dolls."

"God dolls? From the Catholics?" Dick shook his head. "Satan is clever that way."

On Monday, at camp, Dick drew an *Awake!* magazine from his desk. He pushed it across the counter to Pansy, opened to an article that expounded on biblical logic for why a woman should not exercise authority over a man. The female skull was ten percent smaller than that of the male, it said. A larger brain had an advantage. Women must learn the art of "eternal acquiescence" in dealing with their husbands if they wished for true happiness.

A smugness came to Dick, and he thought of the Great Jehovah, whom he wished to serve. "Satan is very clever," he said to Pansy. "He may have found his way into your home with those God dolls there, in your kitchen. This is why Jehovah has established the man as the head of his organization."

When Pansy returned home, she pulled the wooden cutting board from its cabinet and placed it on the counter. She laid the two God dolls on top, then slammed a heavy cast-iron skillet on both. She swept the rubble into a dustpan and calmly carried it out to the street.

15

MANY SEASONS HAD COME AND GONE; THE YEAR 1975 was just a half-year past, which had caused great crisis amongst Jehovah's Witness congregations around the globe when Armageddon did not materialize. Pansy accepted the explanation from the Witness headquarters that the world's failure to meet its predicted destruction was a simple test of faith. "Trust in Jehovah," the brothers said.

Brother Les Kinsey and his wife, Regina, had sold their home two years earlier, as had many others, and spent the proceeds being unemployed full-time servants of God. When their bank account was empty and The End was nowhere to be seen, Brother Les took a half-time job at the Yreka Feed and Tack and Sister Kinsey concluded that the Witnesses were false prophets and did the nasty with Tim at Tim's Tire and Transmission. She then went home and confessed to her husband, which drove him to seek permission from Brother Stinchfield to divorce.

In a great religious restructuring, the Witnesses had just armed Dick with the newly adopted title of elder. The Sacramento circuit overseer had driven up to Farnsworth to deliver a sixty-three-page document of procedures and punishments related to fornication, rebellious wives, and bigamist husbands.

Ever so happy to uphold the duties and philosophies of The Truth, Dick met with Les Kinsey twice to resolve the complications of what could have been a very consensual divorce. In order to grant the separation, as requested by Les and presumably agreed to by Regina, he was required to verify that Regina had, in fact, committed adultery—the only permissible Scriptural grounds for divorce. In the absence of a required two-witness minimum to the adulterous act, Dick was instructed to convene an investigatory meeting with a minimum of three elders in order for Regina to admit to the specifics of her sin. Regina must consent to such a meeting, but she had stubbornly refused to do so.

Dick lay in bed each night for a solid week, unable to sleep without Regina's confession to out-of-wedlock vaginal intercourse. A simple blow job or any other form of sexual enjoyment would not have met the classification of adultery. Such activities, having been banned as "sexual perversions," would have labeled Regina as "unclean," the consequences of which would have been disfellowshipping from the congregation if she didn't show a willingness to repent, but this is not what Les was asking for.

What Les wanted was a simple divorce from an unfaithful wife, but his simple request could not be granted without lengthy debate because the rules for dealing with such matters in a congregation of Jehovah's Witnesses aren't simple. They are rigid and complex. In order to consent to the divorce, Dick must know if Regina had vaginally fucked Tim the Tire Man at any time during her marriage to Les. He must also know if Les had vaginally fucked Regina after learning of her purported fucking of Tim, which would imply that Les had forgiven her indiscretion. A post-fuck fucking, on the part of Les, would prohibit the granting of divorce. As one can see, there are numerous details of the fucking that Dick must ascertain in order to keep the Jehovah's Witness organization clean from an adulterous woman.

At his wit's end, Les drove over to the auto shop and pleaded with Tim to have some words with Regina. "You understand what I mean," Les had asked, "man to man," but Tim did not understand as he had never been a Witness, forcing Les to explain that he would never again have sex if Regina would not assist him with getting permission for divorce. "If I can't get permission for divorce, I can't ever marry again. If I can't remarry, I will never again get laid."

Two weeks later, Regina returned Dick's calls and admitted to the back-room fucking. No, she would not submit to a judicial committee. She was no longer playing by JW rules, but yes, she admitted, she had indeed fucked Tim, and no, she had never once been intimate with Les afterwards.

The following Sunday, Dick stood at the podium and announced that Regina Kinsey was no longer a Jehovah's Witness for "conduct unbecoming to Jehovah."

Les, who came to realize that the only single female Jehovah's Witness in Siskiyou County was Pansy Blackwell, moved south to a Sacramento congregation, bringing many available women to sit near him in the Kingdom Hall. Three months later, Les remarried, and his short dry period of not having someone to fuck came to an end.

16

"BREAKFAST?" ASKED PANSY.

Butch sat at the head of the table, pulling boots on both feet. Now sixteen, he spent much of his free time driving one of Steve's trucks from the pasture to the ranch or to the grazing land northeast of Gregory Mountain. Butch could saddle any horse in the pen without fear on the part of others that he might ruin their best mount. He had developed a light hand on the reins, never rough on a horse's mouth.

In another month, he would enter Yreka High for eleventh grade. Now shaving, his voice deepened, Butch was six foot four and hadn't finished with that, yet. "Have you ever known me to skip breakfast?" he replied.

"No, I certainly haven't," Pansy said. She rose to scramble eggs. Three of them. She then asked if he wanted ketchup. Butch questioned if she'd ever seen him opt for eggs without ketchup.

Afterwards, Pansy squeezed her hips between the armrests of Cora's wing-backed chair to prepare for the next day's *Watchtower* study, highlighting text with blue and red pens. A month earlier, she had hung orange polyester curtains across the front window, blocking most of the sunlight that now found its way inside after Dick thinned much of the lilac tunnel out front.

Pansy leaned forward and moved her curtain aside, watching a quick burst of rain fall in thick, heavy drops. "You could join me. We could complete our meeting preparation together."

"I'm not going to the Kingdom Hall tomorrow. I'm goin' huntin' with Steve," Butch replied.

Pansy laid the *Watchtower* in her lap. "Why would you schedule a hunting trip on a meeting day?"

"Sunday's the day when Steve wants to go," Butch said.

"You missed Thursday's meeting," Pansy snapped. "You will appear weak in your faith if you miss another."

"I've been going to meetings every Sunday of my entire life. I don't think Jehovah's gonna get all irritated if I miss a few."

"Brother Stinchfield will not be happy," Pansy stated.

"Name any Sunday since we came to Farnsworth that we didn't go to the Kingdom Hall," Butch demanded from her.

"You need to call Dick," Pansy said.

Half the size it once was, the Kingdom Hall no longer held a membership of a functional size. Dick was under heavy pressure from the Sacramento circuit overseer to grow the faithful in Siskiyou. Pansy had found a new fervor in her faith. Her comments during the *Watchtower* study turned to her own thoughts and vocabulary, until Dick reproved her, privately. No need to be going off track, he said. Stick to the words printed. Just read what's there. No need to add more.

Steve set out for an overnight trip to the eastern Siskiyous with Butch on the afternoon of July 26th. Two cardboard boxes of camping gear went into the bed of the truck, and Steve's

Winchester .243 rested upside down in the gun rack on the back window.

"It's ninety frickin' degrees today," Steve complained. "It's a damn stupid time to be huntin' deer. They do it right, up in Oregon. Deer season doesn't open for another two months up there. Jesus Christ, California does everything wrong these days. Things were a lot different when I was a kid. Can't shoot bears anymore. There's too damn many people moving to the state, and too damn many bears."

"There's a couple bucks hanging out near Hat Creek, behind Gregory. We could kill one there and still get home for breakfast," Butch suggested.

"Are you starving?" Steve asked.

"Not hardly," Butch replied. "I'm two hundred and forty-something pounds. I think that means I'm not starving. I qualified for the free lunch at school this year." He laughed. "They wouldn't have done that if they knew how much I eat."

Steve grinned.

"They asked how much my mom makes, working for Dick. I didn't tell 'em about the money you pay me. I probably wouldn't have gotten a free lunch if I had."

"The day the Feds expect a kid to pony up his own pocket money for lunch, is the day I'd tell them to fuck off. Just another example of damn government overreach, if you ask me. And another thing: deer hunting isn't always about shooting whatever you see—unless you're starving. The bucks out on Gregory can go to them guys from the city. Most of them don't want to put any work into a hunt anyway," Steve said.

"I'll bet they taste the same. A deer's a deer."

Steve turned his head to look Butch in the eye. "There's something special up there in the mountains, where we're headed. Just enjoy the ride."

"Okay," Butch promised.

"The way people are moving into the area now, it won't be long before someone gets the idea to put another city up here," Steve said. "The government will let that happen. You can't trust government. They're still trying to grab every drop of water from Siskiyou and send it down to Los Angeles."

Butch nodded.

"Everything is going to change soon. It's the way people are. They see something beautiful and decide they need to own it, control it. And then they ruin it. As much as you like to fish, you might want to get up here and chase some salmon before things change. There's nowhere near as many salmon as when I was a kid. The salmon are all gonna be gone someday," Steve predicted.

The two men gave in to their quiet thoughts on a quiet mountain drive. Just past the Scott River confluence, Steve turned his gaze to a squat cabin across the river. Three men were unloading gear from the back of a truck. Steve pointed in their direction. "My grandfather built that cabin."

"Really? You own a cabin?" Butch asked.

"Nah. Gramps sold it to Earl Hudson back in 1957, but even after that, we used it when we were hunting. It was always open to anyone, no matter who you were. If you found it empty, you were welcome to spend the night when you were hunting. It would never happen that way now. You let strangers in your cabin these days, and they're likely to burn it down. People are stupid, today." He snorted. "Speaking of stupid . . . did you ask Dick for permission to hunt?"

Butch grunted. "I don't need his permission. I just told him I was going huntin'. He was fairly pissy about it."

"Of course, he was. What's he got against huntin'?"

"Hunting isn't the problem. The problem is that I missed the meeting last Thursday, which is your fault, by the way. Hauling horses down to Mt. Shasta isn't an acceptable excuse for missing a meeting. There's not enough guys in the hall to give the Bible readings on Thursdays, so if he doesn't give one to me, he has to do it himself, and that's enough to piss him off. He's tired of having to do all the talks himself, and I'm tired of having to do it just about every damn Thursday," Butch groused.

"No shit? You give talks? At sixteen?"

"Not the real talks. Just the small ones on Thursdays. Been doin' it since I was ten," Butch explained. "All Witness boys do it, except there aren't any, other than me. It's only four minutes long, but I'm the only boy in the hall, so if I don't do it, Dick has to. Or Brother Stevenson from Seiad Valley, who can't ever show up on time. Sometimes the Medford congregation sends people down to fill chairs."

"Does your Bible tell you that you can't miss church twice in a row, or is Dick makin' up shit to annoy you?" Steve wondered.

"Dick, making up shit. He's become an ass."

"Right. Like he was something different before."

"True," Butch agreed.

Steve laughed aloud. "Something my dad always said is, 'Sometimes people change. But not much.'"

Butch threw his fingers up in mock quotation marks. "'Sometimes people change. But not much.' Words of wisdom from Steve Bultemeyer. I've heard you say that at least fifty-seven times since I've known you."

Steve's mustache tilted. "Fifty-seven?"

"It's a joke. You're supposed to laugh." Butch grinned.

Steve pulled up to a thick stand of Douglas fir. "Alrighty, this is our camp spot for the night. In the mornin' we'll hike halfway up that ridge." He opened his door, walked to the tailgate, then reached over to rustle in a box. "I brought a box of these space bars. Food Sticks. Saw 'em on TV. They say the astronauts took these to the moon. If they're good enough for astronauts, they're good enough for me."

"You brought astronaut food?" Butch asked.

"You still worried about starvin' to death?"

"Hell, you mighta thought to tell me to pack a sandwich. We could be here for a while," Butch complained.

"We'll be home tomorrow. You'll shoot something up on the ridge in the morning. Until then, we have a box of astronaut food and a sack of peanuts. Grab those sleeping bags in back. Roll 'em out right over there under the trees." He thought to mention the pine needles being dry but stopped himself. Butch had camped with Steve many times. There was a point where a man should be treated as a man.

They collected fire material nearby, cleared a bare-dirt circle for a low blaze, then lounged near it, reclining on flannel sleeping bags. At its lowest point, the Klamath River crawled alongside in patient progression to the coast. The sun settled below the western ridgeline.

"What do we do now?" Butch asked.

"Sit around the fire and conversate," Steve replied.

"Conversate isn't a word. Just ask my mother."

"It certainly is a word. Don't care what your mother says," Steve countered.

"I'll be sure to use it when I get home. I'll let you know how long it takes her to get all fired up." Fully clothed, Butch kicked off his boots, then thrust his legs deep into his sleeping bag. He pulled the end over his head. "You can conversate all you want, but I'm going to sleep."

Steve loaded his .357 Magnum, an intentional shell in the chamber, and laid it near his head.

Steve woke early, rousing Butch with a shove of his foot. "Get up!" he said.

He threw breakfast to Butch. Two food sticks.

The trail was an easy hike, free of brush, in the morning light. After twenty minutes, they came to the top of a wide clearing. A flat saddle of grass stretched below, a good hundred yards over the river bottom. Steve made his way to a sheer outcropping of granite. Two Douglas fir trees acted as sentries on the north side. Steve settled against a ledge of stone.

The fog rolled back to the ocean. The mist carried the odor of conifers, the land, and the deep musk of deer.

"Keep an eye out for somethin' comin' out on that mesa," Steve said. "The grass is good, there. Brings the does in. The bucks follow."

The fog was rushing in a wet haste to peel itself over the ridgeline, revealing depths of dark shadow under the forest. The sunlight grew and expanded until the first darts of light hit the canyon floor below.

Butch let tranquility enter his being as the sounds of the Klamath came to his ears.

Steve sighed with contentment. "Sat here many times, long before you were born. Shot a lot of bucks from up on this ridge."

"Hope we see something soon," Butch said.

"You will. It was my grandfather's favorite spot. Never disappointed him, or me, for more reasons than you might know." He pointed downslope. "See that big Doug fir, down there? The biggest one?"

Butch nodded, yes.

"Scattered my grandfather's ashes there. When I visit this place, I'm visiting him. When I kick off and die, my ashes are joining his. Told my brothers, that's where I want to go." He grunted. "Don't know if the shitheads will remember, when that day comes."

Butch drew his knees up to his chest, resting his rifle

upwards. "So, if we're shootin' a buck down there, maybe we should have stayed down there."

"There's no other place in the entire world like this spot. Just be happy that you're here," Steve instructed.

Butch looked around. "It's like a tree fort."

"That's right. My grandfather brought me up here when I was a kid, and now I'm passing it on to you. Just appreciate it. That's all you gotta do."

"Does everything look the same?" Butch asked.

"It does. But that's gonna change. Too damn many people moving to this state, and too many of 'em tellin' everyone else what to do." He looked to Butch. "Someday, you're gonna get tired of another man tellin' you what to do."

Butch didn't respond.

"Especially when the guy uses his Bible to invent what he wants, and if he can't find it there, he just pulls demands out of his ass to show he has the power to do it," Steve said. "There's a word for that kind of crap. Don't know what it is, though. You can ask your mom. She'll know." He laughed.

"I don't need to ask my mom. The word is 'arbitrary.'"

"Sure. Arbitrary, that's it. Makin' up shit as you go. People are known to do that. Especially if they go to church. That's where they learn it. My grandfather didn't believe in God. Neither do I, as you know, but he was convinced that if there is a God, this is where you'll find him." He again snorted lightly. "'God won't ever be found in a church,' my grandfather said."

Butch turned his thoughts to drama and authority. He thought of the little green house and the people in town who impressed him with their resolve to be stout in the face of difficulty. The repetitive push from Dick to be baptized—making a lifetime commitment to Jehovah.

Steve whispered, "Right down there . . . on the edge of the timber. He's about to make his way out."

"I see him," Butch said.

A young buck emerged from the underbrush, facing away from the Klamath.

"Looks like a three-point," Steve whispered.

"Two points on the left," Butch answered.

"Is he big enough for you? For your first?"

"He is. I won't be eating the horns." Butch lowered the rifle bolt from its half-cocked position, then pushed the safety forward with his thumb. With agonizing slowness, he raised the .243 to his shoulder, resting his left elbow and the rifle on his thigh. His breathing was calm, measured. Steve watched the young man wait for the buck to turn and offer a clear vital zone. Proud of what he had passed on to Butch, thinking of the day when his grandfather had done the same for him.

They gathered over the carcass. A bloodied tongue rolled from the buck's mouth in a final gasp for life. Blood seeped from a single bullet hole behind its left shoulder.

"Need to get him dressed out and cooled off," Steve said.

"Yeah," Butch agreed.

Butch flicked his Buck knife open and cut the deer's belly to expose its innards. He slit the brisket, pulled his shirt off, and plunged his arms into the warm cavity. A damp heat rose, bloody wafts of iron and minerals, and he pulled the heart from inside, shredded by his slug of lead. He found the liver, intact, and pulled it free. Undamaged. Warm. Beautiful. He held it aloft. "How hungry are you?"

"Not *that* hungry," Steve said.

"You don't like liver?"

"Nope. But we'll take it home anyway. There's always someone else who will eat it," Steve reasoned.

"Like me! I'm not givin' it away!"

"Suit yourself," Steve said. "How you cookin' it?"

"Haven't a clue."

They delivered the buck for processing to the Meat Market in Yreka, then returned to Farnsworth before the sun set. The horns, cut from the carcass with a hacksaw by one of the meat men, lay in back of Steve's truck. Brother Stinchfield was visiting Pansy. When Butch lifted the rack from the truck bed, Dick sniffed.

"Only a three-point?" Dick whined. "It took you two days to shoot a three-point?"

Butch glared but retrieved a sack from the cab. He held it up as a visual. "I kept the liver."

"Not interested in the liver, but I wouldn't mind a couple packages of backstrap," Dick said.

Steve spluttered loudly. "Yeah, well, people in hell want ice water too, but that ain't gonna happen."

Dick jerked his head in Steve's direction.

"Oh, that's right. You don't believe in hell. But I'm tellin' you, it takes balls to be an ass about the kid's first deer and then ask for the best cut of meat," Steve said.

Dick stomped to his car. Steve looked to Pansy. "There's somethin' wrong with that man's head."

The next day, Saturday, Steve drove the stock trailer over to the pasture. He backed it up to the loading chute, Butch unhitched the trailer, and then Steve moved his pickup to the far alfalfa stack. His rear hitch rocked the backside of the bales.

"Maybe you should try to get a little closer," Butch joked.

Steve scowled, then climbed the stack and heaved a bale into the truck bed. "You here for the day?" he asked.

"Yup. All day. Mom's gone treasure huntin' with Dick," Butch said.

"They're what?"

"They're hittin' up the garage sales in Yreka. There's two listed in the *Herald*," Butch explained.

Steve lifted another bale to his knees. "What, Dick needs another toaster?"

"I don't think he's lookin' for toasters. He's huntin' for treasures. He says you can buy things for pennies on the dollar. That means cheap."

Steve threw a third bale. "I know what it means. Sounds like something Dick would do, tryin' to get somethin' for nothin'."

"Dick says he once bought an Indian rug, Navajo, he said, for just about nothing at a garage sale."

"Sounds like he stole it," Steve retorted.

"You're sure in a snotty mood," Butch answered.

"Yeah, I'm a little irritated right now, so why don't we just concentrate on puttin' this hay in the back of my truck? I'll throw, you stack, and then I'll tell you about it after we're done."

"Okay, sure." Six bales on the bottom, lengthwise. Butch set them in square, just between the wheel wells. Eight on top, just to the edge of the truck walls. Truck beds might have been designed with hay bales in mind. Fourteen bales fit perfectly in two layers—more if you wanted to go higher.

Butch leaned on the tailgate. "Okay, done. Now, what the heck are you so irritated about?"

"I'm a little pissed off at my brother right now, but that's neither here nor there. You don't need to know about that. Max can be a fuckin' dickhead sometimes," Steve said.

"Yeah, I know," Butch agreed.

"And then we got Dickhead Stinchfield, who just irritates the snot out of me. So, here's what I think about his treasure huntin'. You remember that gelding I bought from Tom Stout last year?" Steve asked.

Butch nodded.

"I didn't really need another horse, right? But Tom was in a world of hurt, lost his job and I don't know what else, but he was down to sellin' off his horse to get out of a rough spot. He probably would have sold him for just about nothin', 'pennies on the dollar' as Dick might say, but it's not right to take advantage of a man when he's down. I coulda got that horse for about five hundred bucks, if I was that kind of guy, but I paid Tom what the horse was worth, which was probably three times what he would have taken," Steve said. "Fifteen hundred bucks is what I gave for that horse, just because it was the right thing to do."

"You didn't buy him at a garage sale," Butch said.

"What difference does *that* make?" His irritation grew, and Steve stretched his arms wide, in the shape of a cross, palms upward. "The right thing is the right thing! Here's what a man like Dick would do. Let's suppose Dick goes to some garage sale today where a little old lady is selling off everything she owns. She's about to move to that board and care home just down Interstate 5 and needs all the money she can get. She's got some old toaster she's sellin' for a buck, and Dick buys it for a buck because he wants a toaster. A used toaster is worth a buck. No problem there. But she's also got some treasure for sale, only she doesn't know it's treasure. Maybe it's one of those Navajo rugs, and she's askin' ten bucks for it, but Dick knows it's worth a hundred. It's a real treasure. You think he'd tell her what it's worth, just to help her out? He knows she's in a tight spot. That's why she's sellin' her stuff."

"No, of course not. Dick would be happy to get it for ten bucks," Butch replied.

"No, he wouldn't! That's where you're wrong. Dick would offer her five," Steve said.

Butch whistled softly. "Damn. You're right."

"I know I'm right. The man's an ass. There's right things, and there's wrong things. Doin' the right thing is usually the better choice." Steve pointed his finger at Butch. "And the other thing you should learn from this is that when a man shows you what kind of man he is, don't expect him to ever do things different."

Butch and Steve set out for Medford the next afternoon, pulling a loaded trailer of weaned calves. The auction wasn't until Monday. Calves would be unloaded into pens that evening and left for Hank to oversee, as he had already gone up for the Friday bull sale.

Across the dashboard, Butch laid a thick crease in the dust with his finger. "You know there's about an inch of mud on the floor?"

"What about it?" Steve said.

"You ever think about cleaning your truck?" Butch asked.

"What for?" Steve scoffed.

"If you clean your truck, you might get a girlfriend."

17

WALTER JENNINGS—A BLACK MAN IN SACRAMENTO—
was blessed with skin of the smoothest perfection, which is
precisely how Pansy thought of him. From the South Sacramento congregation, he had never married. He wished to marry,
someday, he said.

A pleasure, the desire for charm, took Pansy's thoughts.
"I've not married, either," she said. "The need is great for more
of Jehovah's servants in Siskiyou. Perhaps you might visit us?"
She clasped her hands together and looked to Walter for a reply
that didn't come.

At the end of the convention, Pansy asked Butch to pass their
telephone number to the man. Remind Brother Jennings that
the need is great in Siskiyou, but not when she was near, she
said. "Don't want him to think I'm being too forward."

Butch delivered the note.

Walter read it, then shoved it into his pocket. "Tell me, any
women of color in the Farnsworth congregation? Black
women?"

Butch coughed loudly. "Not in Siskiyou County. We're as

White as can be. If you come visit, you'll be the only Black person. Probably ever."

Walter nodded in slow appreciation of this honesty. "Well, I'm looking for companionship, if you understand what I mean."

Butch laughed. "There is my mother, of course. She might want some companionship."

"Ahh, yes. There is your mother."

Aroused at the hint of romance, Pansy was buoyant on their drive home. "Perhaps Brother Jennings will call. One never knows."

"Perhaps," Butch repeated. "One never knows." Pansy did not recognize that this may have been the only occasion in which her son had ever spoken that way. Perhaps.

How should he refer to Brother Jennings, Butch wondered aloud. "Would I call him Brother Jennings . . . or Daddy?" He threw his head back in a loud giggle. "Never thought you'd try to give me a Black daddy!"

Pleased at his humor, a smile came to Pansy. "He seems like a very nice man."

"Yes, he does," Butch agreed.

Their thoughts went to themselves for a long stretch of Interstate 5. In time, Butch broke the silence.

He asked, "Why won't you talk about my real father?"

Pansy turned cold. "Why would you ask that?"

"Why wouldn't I? Everyone has a father. Why won't you talk about mine?"

"You can ask when I am on my deathbed. Until then, I won't discuss him. Not ever."

The following weekend, at the B-Bar-Seven, Steve was roping the dummy steer out by the Pippin apple—the repetitious practice of the perfect head loop. Butch occasionally joined but often lost interest when Steve got too technical in evaluation. "Need to turn your elbow up . . . nope, nope. You're side-swinging. Don't do that. Swing it flat." Perfection was not what Butch was looking for, so he retreated to the fence line, watching Steve's replication of a flawless head catch.

"I asked my mom about my dad the other day," Butch said.

"How'd that go?" Steve asked.

"She thinks he was a piece of shit." Butch chuckled. "She'd never use that word, of course."

"And you?"

"Shit?"

"No. You think your father's a piece of shit?"

"That's what my mom thinks," Butch replied.

"Well, you might want to come to your own decision about things," Steve countered. "If you don't know the guy, you can't really think about him, one way or the other. You don't know his side of the story."

"I've never seen him. Not even a picture. Just up and disappeared, apparently. Sounds like a piece of crap to me."

"Don't know why you would put that on yourself. You think less of the man, you're gonna think less of yourself, too." Steve said.

Butch fumbled with his rope, moving coils from one hand to the other.

"He made you. There must have been somethin' good about him," Steve offered.

"My mother doesn't see it that way."

"She's got her own axe to grind. Sometimes, things happen that we have no control over. Sometimes people won't let go of it . . . they just carry the anger. Poisons 'em," Steve said. "There's no reason for you to drink her poison."

Butch nodded. "Maybe."

"Someday, you might hunt him down. Ask for his side of the story."

"Would be tough to find a guy I don't even have a name for," Butch pointed out.

"Maybe. Well, here's something that'll piss off your mother," Steve said.

Butch tossed his rope flat to the ground.

"You watch Bonanza on TV. You like that show, you said."

"I do," Butch confirmed.

"So, of the three boys, which is your favorite? Hoss, Adam, and Little Joe. Which one?"

"That's easy. Hoss. I look just like him," Butch said.

"Exactly. Hoss Cartwright might be yer daddy."

Pansy's own father, Lick, often came into her mind. She struggled to recall the specifics of his features. Was his hair attended to? Combed neatly? She believed him to have been thin, unusually so. Was he clean-shaven? Tired? Yes, he was always tired.

Butch was sprawled across the couch with a *Field and Stream* magazine. He resembled his own father in no way that was obvious to her. He hadn't chosen to cut his hair into the style of the day. Hippies, they were called. Butch, and the men of Siskiyou County, kept their hair closely shorn, in the way of cowboys. Neat and well-mannered. A pleasant smile swept her face.

18

DICK HAD TAKEN TO DRIVING TO MEDFORD ONCE each month, always on the second Friday, early in the afternoon, returning late Saturday. He checked in to the South Medford Residence Inn each Friday afternoon at 3 p.m. They knew him there, now. His routine was to eat early at the diner downstairs, then bathe in an enthusiastic hope for cleanliness perfection before going out for the evening. "People take vacations," he had said to Pansy. "Time I got one, too. Once a month. I'll give you a raise to $3.15 an hour, but only on Friday and Saturday, when you can mind the camp for me. Only on the second weekend of the month."

Pansy seemed, to Butch, hardened by dark thoughts, turning sour on things. Dick didn't pay enough. Her knees were bothering her. Jehovah was demanding. Butch was spending too much time fishing.

"Dick says you should be out in service to Jehovah more often. In these last days, you should be bringing others to The Truth," she lectured him, again.

"We've talked to every human being in Siskiyou County.

Every single one. Repeatedly. Except for the Indians. We've never once set foot on the reservation," Butch responded.

"Dick says the Indians are unlikely to be receptive to The Truth."

"Right," Butch replied. "So, we just let them go. Hell, Dick might have us out lookin' for Bigfoot someday, just so we can witness to him, too. Maybe Bigfoot won't be receptive, either. Seems to me, we should be able to call it quits."

"The scriptures say The End can't come until the good news of the Kingdom has been preached across the Earth. You know this," Pansy said.

"Matthew 24:14," Butch said flatly.

"We are so close to The End. So very, very close. The brothers tell us that The End will come before the generation of 1914 is gone. There are very few of them left. The new system could be days away. You should be more devoted to Jehovah in these last days. Brother Stinchfield has told us that, many times," Pansy said.

"Dick is too hung up on sixty hours a month. Unless you're an unemployed pioneer, who has sixty hours?" Frustrated, he raised his voice to his mother. Perhaps the first time Butch had ever done so. "We've talked to everyone in Siskiyou! Everyone! What's Dick gonna do? Send us back to do it again?"

"Maybe he will."

"Enough is never enough for him."

"Dick is concerned about your time with Steve. Perhaps you should spend less," Pansy snapped.

"Steve is my boss. Dick is not. Steve pays me to work for him. Dick does not."

"Steve's never going to leave the worldly life," Pansy said.

"No, he's not. But he's a good man. Been like a father."

"He's *not* your father," Pansy retorted.

"He might as well be. He's a good man. You've said so yourself."

"Steve is a worldly man. He will not be in the new system. You might want to think about that. The End is so close. You should spend more time with Dick. He doesn't have kids. Maybe he'll give you the campground someday, if you act right," Pansy said.

"You *just* said The End is too close to be thinking about things like that." Butch retorted.

At 842 Tenth Street, downtown Sacramento, the spire of a three-story home stretched heavenward. Built in 1878 by a wealthy gold miner, its turrets rose high. Shingled like icing on a cake—satisfying the miner's vain need for attention, it shamed adjacent homes, which had been built decades later. In town for the smaller circuit assembly, Butch and Pansy were staying three blocks over at the Perkins Motel on Eighth, walking distance to the Memorial Auditorium. At the end of the assembly, returning the same path to their hotel, Pansy fell under its spell.

"This will be my house," she uttered with absolute certainty. She turned her face to Butch. "This is going to be my house in the new system. This is where I'm going to live."

"Here? Why here? You could have one of the ranches in Farnsworth," Butch said.

"A ranch? I have no desire to live on a ranch!" Pansy practically shrieked in horror at the thought. "A ranch won't be a ranch in the new system! The Bible says lions will lie down with lambs in the new world. No one will give any thought to eating cows in the new system."

"I might. I can't imagine eating vegetarian forever," Butch retorted almost under his breath.

"What you can imagine is irrelevant," Pansy snapped. "It is of no consequence whether you want to follow Jehovah's rules and enjoy everlasting life in the way he intends. It is not your place to question them."

Butch sighed. "Why wouldn't we question things? It's not a sin to want things to make sense."

"We do not debate the intentions of Jehovah. The crux of the matter is this: if Jehovah wants us to have answers to our questions, he will provide them. If the answers have not been provided, Jehovah does not believe them necessary for us to be faithful. If he wants us to be vegetarian in the new system, that's what we'll be. We won't give meat a second thought in the new system. I doubt that Adam and Eve ever looked at the lions and contemplated eating them."

"We don't eat lions," Butch replied.

Pansy scowled. "Fine. Play that game. Adam and Eve never thought about eating lambs in the Garden of Eden. They were perfect, as Jehovah intended. When the new system comes, we'll be *perfect*. It will be the most wonderful thing you could imagine. The Earth will be restored to Jehovah's original plan, and we will live forever in this beautiful garden on Earth."

"You don't need to come down here to get a mansion. You could have the Mills Mansion," Butch suggested.

Pansy rejected the idea. "Perhaps Brother Stinchfield wants the Mills Mansion," she replied.

Butch laughed. "Yeah, I can see it now—nasty fights over who gets to live in the Mills Mansion. And a nasty fight with some other Witness who's already spoken for this one."

School would resume from its long summer break on Monday. The day was warm, the reek of fresh shit soiled the air, and

Butch was helping Steve unload the B-Bar-Seven's bulls at the Farnsworth Rodeo grounds. The bulls, sluggish in the warmth, pushed into a huddle in the far corner of the holding pens.

Both men walked to the bleachers. A few parents rested here and there. Steve nodded hello to everyone, had some brief words of blather with two, then sat at the top with Butch.

"Do you charge them for this?" Butch asked.

"Sure I do," Steve replied. "Fifty bucks, four bulls."

"Fifty bucks? No wonder you're poor. You should charge fifty bucks a head."

Steve grinned, meaning his mustache rode higher on his lip. "I'm just helpin' the local kids who need some practice time."

"The rodeo club could hire a stock contractor. There's one in Red Bluff," Butch said.

"They can't afford him. The kids need some practice. None of these bulls will be that hard to ride. No one will get killed. And these kids all live here, like me, so we just chalk this up to doin' a good deed." He pointed to the arena. "Watch Rooster Powell. He's gonna be good in another year or two."

"Rooster's a short little dude. Maybe I should be riding bulls," Butch suggested.

"You wantin' to be a bull rider?" Steve asked.

"Nah. Mom wouldn't let me," Butch replied.

"Nope. She wouldn't." Steve stuck his legs out on the bench in front, then leaned back, his arms folded behind his head. "You remember that conversation I had with her about football, right after you came here?"

Butch didn't remember.

"I told your mom that you'd make a good football player," Steve explained. "She wasn't havin' any of that. She gave me a lecture about how sports will get in the way of your Jehovah time, or something to that effect. Pissed me off, I can tell you.

Football could have gotten you to college. You'd be a beast on the football field."

Butch rose from the bench suddenly. "I'm not goin' to college. But I am going to take a leak."

From their vantage point, Steve could see the bathrooms on the backside of the snack bar. Just moments earlier, he had seen Tim Fedorcheck standing nearby. There were rumors in the county about Tim. Steve had heard them but shrugged off most as not being any of his business.

"Just watch what you're doin' in there," he advised.

"Watch what I'm doing?"

"There might be people in there who don't keep their eyes to themselves. Just tellin' you," Steve said.

Butch grimaced, but he left for the bathroom and returned minutes later.

"Any problems?" Steve asked.

Butch looked hard at the older man. "Why would there be problems?"

"Ahh . . . just wonderin'."

"Wonderin' *what*? Sometimes I think you're gettin' weird on me," Butch declared.

"Let's watch the bull riding," Steve said, changing the subject.

The dust rose, and the clang of bullrope bells filled the air. "Maybe I should be down there," Butch said. "I'm bigger than any of them guys."

"That's your problem," Steve replied. "You're too big to ride roughstock. Little guys, like Rooster, make good bull riders."

"Rooster just got bucked off."

"You're not gonna out-muscle a bull. When a bull throws all his power at you, you've got all your weight at the end of your arm, and you'll never win that battle. You've got too much weight up here, in your shoulders." Steve slapped Butch on the chest. "You're top-heavy. All that weight can't handle what a bull's gonna give you." He stood and took the first few steps down the bleachers. "But I'll tell you what. Let's put you on one."

Steve approached the bucking chutes. Rooster stood over top another bull, his feet on the chute. "Hey! Rooster! Do me a favor. Let Butch sit on that one."

Straddled over top, Butch took instruction from Steve: Don't tie your hand in the rope while you're standing. That's a good way to get hurt. Sit your ass down, on his back. Slide your hand in the rope.

Steve pulled the tail of Rooster's bullrope tight. Butch felt the energy of a half-ton animal run up his arm. "Don't you dare open that gate," he growled at Steve, then bolted straight and climbed out of the chute. "Not a chance in hell." He looked squarely at Rooster. "There's somethin' wrong with your head."

Back home, over dinner, he described the thing to Pansy. He'd made a thick stew of venison and barley for dinner. Pansy complained that deer meat stinks, so she busied herself with grilling a cheese sandwich as Butch described his visit to the bucking chute. Had about crapped his pants, he said to her, and she pounded the table at his vulgarity.

"Doesn't sound vulgar to me," Butch said. "It sounds real. Nothin' wrong with bein' real."

Each school year, starting in elementary, Yreka's student population began a slow drain in number. By its senior year, a graduating class was likely to have lost a quarter of its original enrollment. The Yreka High class of 1977 numbered forty-seven.

Melody Brunswick tiptoed onto campus as if convinced it would prevent her from being noticed, but she was wrong. Tiptoeing wouldn't hide a new face. A new student was a curiosity. Why would anyone move to Siskiyou County?

Melody was a damaged child of broken relationships and temporary homes. She harbored secrets. She hid what she wished from those who asked for personal information and disguised the difficulties that existed behind the closed doors of her life with an abusive father. Tight-lipped in response to questions, most students saw her as a nut too hard to crack. Why did you move here? No one moves here. Do you have a mother? No? Siblings? What does your dad do?

Melody was drawn to Butch's calming energy, for reasons he did not think to wonder. They shared a creative writing class, which was not an elective. Students who felt they had no creative bones in their bodies groused about it, Butch being one. A senior, the conclusion to a formalized education near, he felt no inclination to write. "Write about what?" he asked Mr. Balssey.

"Whatever spurs your creative juices."

"Good God. I don't have creative juices," Butch replied. He grimaced at the imagery of the crass statement.

"Will they be graded?" Melody asked.

"Of course," Mr. Balssey replied. "There are ten weeks in this semester, and you'll write one each week. Each will be graded."

Mr. Balssey hadn't taught anything about being creative, Melody pointed out, to which he replied that each essay would be critiqued by him.

"Critiquing isn't the same as teaching. Do you teach creative writing, or do you just judge it? If you tell me to be creative but don't teach me how to do it, you're just like all the other teachers," Melody said.

Mr. Balssey gasped at the boldness of her criticism. "*Which* other teachers?"

"You're all that way," she replied. "Teachers rarely teach. They just judge. No one has taught me to write creatively, and here I am, required to take your class, and you're telling me to do something you haven't taught."

Butch relayed the conversation at home.

"She sounds like a rebellious teenager," Pansy said.

"Sounded brilliant to me."

Three yellow school buses ferried students from rural roads to Yreka High each day. Three simple arrivals and departures—all short buses, each designed for ten passengers. Three years prior, as a freshman, Butch had immediately claimed the front seat. Now a senior, he still occupied that spot, and for the last two weeks, Melody sat directly behind him.

Dick Stinchfield advised caution of "worldly-girl" dangers. Pansy had warned, "Bad association will get you nowhere. First Corinthians 15:33."

On this day, Melody started toward her own home but then retreated and walked back to the little green house to join Butch. Music blared from Steve's truck out front. Booger was sprawled under the lilac tunnel, and Butch was singing along to Foreigner's "You're as Cold as Ice."

"You can't sing," Melody said. "In case no one's told you."

Butch thrust an imaginary dagger through his chest and writhed in exaggerated agony. He then climbed in the front seat of Steve's truck. "Jump in!" he yelled. "I gotta get Booger home."

At the B-Bar-Seven, Steve had hung a young steer upside down from a brace in a cottonwood tree. He'd cut the brisket, the gut pile still quivering in a wheelbarrow of blood.

Melody went queasy, but Butch came to her aid. "A steer that broke his leg. Wasn't gonna make it to the finish line."

"What's he doing to it?" Melody asked.

Steve submerged his skinning knife in a bucket of water laced with Clorox. "Gettin' ready to eat it. What else?" He nodded to Butch. "Hank will be over later. He's takin' most of it." Steve wiped the knife clean. "Grab that side . . . yeah, strip that down." He cut the fat as Butch ripped the steer's hide from its carcass. "I'll send you home with a slab off the hind quarter." He looked to Melody. "You want some?"

She shook her head, no.

"Suit yourself," Steve said.

Steve sent questions Melody's way, non-invasive as it wasn't in his nature to inquire into the business of others. Butch responded for her. "She called out Mr. Balssey, right there in front of everyone."

Steve carved wide lumps of fat from the steer's ribs and tossed them into the wheelbarrow. Not to be distracted from his butchering, he didn't look up to Melody when he offered a prediction of consequences. "You'll find out if you pissed him off when grades come out."

Butch shrugged. "Doesn't matter. When school's over, it's *over*! Graduation, then never set foot in school again!"

"Any plans for what happens afterwards?" Steve asked.

"Next year? Good God, that's next year."

"Your senior year will go by fast."

"I'll figure it out when I get there," Butch replied.

"Not headed to college?" Steve asked.

"Right." Butch rolled his eyes. "My mother is swimming in money and wants to send me to Harvard. I'll become a lawyer, most likely."

Steve shrugged. "There's plenty of work around here. The feedstore's always hiring."

Melody had wandered to the Pippin apple. When out of earshot, Steve nodded in her direction. "She's a pretty little thing. Might keep you busy."

"Yeah, she is. I like her."

"You want to keep the truck tonight?" Steve offered.

"What for?"

"You could take her out for a drive," Steve suggested.

"A drive? What for?"

"You might want to *show her around*," Steve said.

"Show her what?" Butch asked.

Melody returned a few minutes later, a half-dozen apples balanced in the crook of her arm. She asked permission to take them home.

"Sure, you can," Steve said jovially.

He opened the door of his truck. Butch hustled around to the back, then climbed over the tailgate and sprawled across the bed. To Melody, he nodded toward the front of the truck and said, "You can ride with Steve if you want. I'll ride in back with Booger."

On Saturday, Melody traveled early to the little green house. Butch offered breakfast. "I'm a good cook," he stated and cracked three eggs in a hot skillet. He lounged over coffee, enjoying the company of a girl who had the confidence to visit without invitation. Pansy strode heavily from her bedroom, announcing plans to clean house. Unexpected company would be in her way, she stated. "You'll need to find something else to do," she said to Butch.

Butch carried dirty plates to the sink, then pointed outside to the pasture. "That's my special place," he said to Melody. "We'll go hide out there."

She leaned her head to his bicep. "I have a place like that, too. A special place where no one bothers me. I'll take you there, and then you can take me to yours."

Miss Emily Walker was of an age where the number didn't matter, except that she was thankful for having reached it. Her home, built the year she was born, 1895, sat on a broad corner, a full acre in size, the property lines now pinched on two sides by non-descript houses.

Her front yard mirrored those of her neighbors—barren blankets of dirt. Grass out front was unintentional in spring, but in late summer, the heady smell of ripening fruit wafted west on the wind.

Melody led Butch through Miss Emily's back gate. He raised his nose in the air. "Something smells good."

The rusted collection of old farm implements was stacked in an orderly fashion against the rear wall. Shovels and rakes. Most wooden handles had long since rotted away. New sprouts of red Russian kale, bitter greens, and cabbage rose in lines of color through a long garden bed.

Miss Emily looked as if she might whirl her way through an impromptu garden tour. "Taste what you like. Let your nose guide you."

Butch stopped near a canopy of two trees, their limbs bent nearly to the ground with fruit. "It's these," he stated. He lifted one. Small, fuzzy, splotched with shades of green and purple.

"Looks like a peach." He turned to Miss Emily. "Why are they so ugly?"

"They are *different*. Different isn't ugly," Miss Emily corrected him.

"I could smell them out to the street." Butch ran his fingers over another—sickly yellow in spots. "Can I eat one?"

"Of course. There's a box I just picked, sittin' right over there, under the shade." Miss Emily pointed to it.

Butch went to where she had directed him. Melody sidled up to his shoulder as he sank his teeth into the soft flesh of a ripe peach. Red juice dripped from his fingers.

"It's a blood peach," she said.

"Blood?" Butch pulled back in horror.

Melody giggled. "Silly. The juice is red, like blood, so it's called a blood peach."

"Oh." He wiped his fingers, a sticky-sweet stain, on the backside of his pants. "I've never seen these in a store. My mom would buy them. How come no one else has these?"

Miss Emily walked to the table. "They were bred by the Cherokees who knew a lot more about farming than people give them credit for. Cherokee Indian blood peach. It's a late peach. Comes in after Labor Day. My father brought them from Oklahoma." She motioned to the grass nearby. "You can join me under the apple tree if you like." She made her way to a worn Adirondack chair and lowered herself to its seat. She moved slowly.

Butch sprawled across un-mowed grass nearby, which was not intended to be lawn. "People would never know you have paradise in your backyard," he said to her. He brightened. "You could do this in front, too!"

"Sometimes you need to create paradise where you want it," Miss Emily replied.

A bug fell from the limb above, landing on Butch's belly,

flicking its antennae left and right. He placed his index finger in its path. It climbed over, Butch brought it close to investigate, then swung his arm out to the grass and lowered the invader to the ground.

"You know anything about bugs?" Miss Emily asked.

He shook his head, no, he didn't know much about bugs.

"That was a soldier beetle. It would have hurt my feelings if you had squashed it," Miss Emily said.

"Squashed it? I didn't know what it was."

"No, but you were kind to it. That's important to know about you." Miss Emily rose. "You'll make a good man. Come with me. I'm going to send you home with some treats."

Later in the day, a block away, Butch hefted both sacks of treasure for Melody's appreciation. "She was sure a nice lady."

Melody smiled. "Yes, she is."

"So that's your special place?"

"It is. Miss Emily found me one day, out front by the chain-link fence in front of my house. It's just around the corner. I can sneak out to her garden when I need to get away from my dad," Melody said. "He doesn't even know."

"I've never seen her before."

"You probably have. You just weren't paying attention. How often do you look at old ladies?"

"Could be." Butch quickened his pace, and on the west side of town, Melody stopped at the marker commemorating the arrival of railroad service in 1886. She sat on its cool concrete. Butch again hefted both sacks upwards. "We'll never eat all of this." He sat next to her. "My mother is going to freak out when I tell her what these are. *Blood* peaches!"

"Like you did, back there?" Melody said playfully.

Butch denied her accusation. "I didn't freak out," he replied.

Melody giggled. "You did. You should have seen your face when you heard about the blood."

"The Bible says it's a sin to eat blood, that's all."

"You looked like you were gonna get beat for it when you got home," Melody said.

"Beat? People don't get beat in my house." A frown came over him. "Is that why you don't go home?"

Melody stood, not answering the question. "You still have to show me your special place. You promised."

They walked the remaining blocks in silence.

Thirty minutes later, in her kitchen, Pansy imagined the peaches packed in glass jars, sealed for winter storage. She rolled one under her hand, then walked to the back porch for an empty Clorox box to hold them. She decided that she would can peaches, just like her grandmomma.

At the edge of the slough, Butch flopped in the soft meadow grass at the water's edge. Melody kicked off her shoes, then waded into the mud, squishing the muck between her toes. "I have something to tell you." She looked up to him with a coy smile on her face. "It's not a secret. The Buffet sisters like you. Apparently, you haven't noticed."

"How would anyone know? They can't talk," Butch countered.

"I've seen them looking at you. Not hard to figure out what they're thinking."

"Which one?" Butch asked.

"Both of them.'"

"Both? Tell them to go see Rooster Powell. He likes them," Butch suggested.

"Rooster Powell? Not a chance. He's short."

"Short? Rooster's a good-looking guy. I like him. Steve says he's gonna be a good bull rider, someday."

Melody shook her head. "No girl wants to go out with a short guy. Not even the Buffet twins. They like you." She abandoned her play in the mud, then joined Butch in the grass. She sat close, leaning into his shoulder. "I like you, too."

"You know I'm not interested in you that way."

"Why not?"

Butch shrugged. "I don't know, but there's not a chance in hell that my mom would let me go out with a girl. Not unless you're ready to marry me."

Melody giggled. "I'm not ready to marry you."

"Yeah, well, I'm not allowed to date until I'm ready to get married. And my mom refers to you as the 'worldly girl.'" Butch wrapped his arms around his knees.

"She doesn't like me," Melody stated.

Butch laughed. "Nope. She doesn't. You're not a Witness, so you are definitely trouble. Hell, so are the Buffet sisters. You're all worldly girls."

"There's no Witness girls around here."

"Nope. There's not. Not unless you join," Butch suggested.

Melody rose. "I'm not joining your church. And you're going to be miserable if you can only go out with girls who are in your religion."

"Yeah, I am. If that day ever comes. But right now, I'm not interested in going out with anyone," Butch said.

Melody pulled Butch to his feet, then wrapped her arms around his midsection. "That's not normal. You should be interested in girls." She stretched high, grasped his face, then kissed him on the lips. She pulled back for his reaction. "How about now? You interested?"

Butch shrugged off her embrace, then nodded at the little green house in the distance. "My mom probably saw that. I'll hear about it later. The sin of kissing a worldly girl." He turned to the barn. "Come on. I'll show you what we came here for."

Upstairs, Butch leaned out the open loft door. He pointed south. "I can see the back of my house." He found humor in the thought. "My mom can see us here, too, if she leans over her sink to look, which is exactly what she's doing, if I was to bet on it." He then pointed in the direction of the river, a mile north. "I can almost see my favorite fishing hole on the Shasta. And more importantly, Dick Stinchfield wouldn't dare follow me here."

Melody then felt an appreciation for the place. "So, this is where you go when you need to hide from someone. Dick."

"I don't *hide* from Dick," Butch responded. "Sometimes I just don't want to be around him. This is the place that makes me happy. Away from school, away from Dick, and away from the Kingdom Hall."

Melody sat closer. "Why do you have such problems with Dick?"

Butch shrugged, as if exhausted by the thought. "There's no satisfying him. He's either irritated because I don't go out in service every weekend or because I haven't gotten baptized yet. There's always something."

"Why does he care if you're not baptized?" Melody asked.

"Because that's what you do if you are a Witness. When you're ready to devote your entire life to The Truth, you get baptized. I'm just not ready. Dick doesn't like that."

"If he's only chasing you for religion, you might get out of the religion. You have a choice," Melody said.

"Nah. I've been a Witness ever since I was born. Someday,

I'll live forever in paradise," Butch replied. "Dick won't be a problem in paradise. Everyone will be perfect."

"Perfect?"

"Yeah, perfect. As in, nobody sins. All part of God's original plan," Butch stated.

"You mean don't sin again? Or haven't ever sinned? Because once you've sinned, you can't call yourself perfect. If you've ever done something wrong, or been an asshole, you can't call yourself perfect." This analysis had come to Melody quickly.

"Well, you can in the new system. Everything will be new, and people will be perfect," Butch argued.

"Even Dick Stinchfield? Or my dad?"

"I don't know your dad," Butch said.

"You wouldn't want to live with him forever," Melody assured him.

"In the new system, I might. Anyone who makes it into the new system will be perfect, and the world will be different. We won't even remember things from the past or the people who don't survive Armageddon. The Bible says everything will be new," Butch informed her.

"The Bible doesn't say that."

"Sure, it does. Isaiah 65:17. 'For here I am creating new heavens and a new earth, and the former things shall not be called to mind.'"

"Holy shit," Melody whispered. "You can just pull scriptures out of your head from memory? Just like that?"

"All Witnesses do. We study the Bible," Butch explained.

"So then, in your new system, you won't be you," she concluded. "You'll be someone else."

"I'll still be me. I'll just be perfect," Butch countered.

"No, you won't. If you don't remember anything about this life, or if you don't miss people like me who don't get into Armageddon or whatever you call it, or if Dick Stinchfield is something different, then you aren't you, and he isn't him. You're all just different people. If you're a different person and don't remember who you are now, you're not you. And if I make it there with you, how would I even know if I like you? Maybe you'd be some new person who nobody likes? Maybe Dick Stinchfield will still be an asshole. You can call him perfect all you want in your new world, but an asshole is still an asshole."

Butch choked. "Funniest thing I've ever heard. An asshole is still an asshole."

"Have you ever convinced someone to join your church?" Melody asked.

"Not yet," Butch answered.

She moved away, a few feet further into the hay bales. "I wouldn't think so," she said. "None of what you just said makes any sense."

In the deep silence of that Farnsworth evening, Pansy watched the moonlight shadows fling their evening dance across her bedroom wall with usual randomness. She no longer saw them as comforting. Her window was in need of a thick curtain, she decided. The worldly girl's affection for her son lay heavy in her thoughts.

In his own bed, out in the back porch, Butch pondered Melody's rejection of his faith. What did living forever mean? And how could girls think so little of short men? Rooster Powell had a strut to his walk. A masculine confidence from a manly sport. Butch stroked himself in boredom, wondering if this would also cease to exist in the new system.

Pansy drove out to the lumber town of Etna with Dick, thirty miles southwest, for what he described as important JW business. She agreed to busy herself sightseeing the five Etna business blocks while Dick administered a private spanking to Sister Nellie Flimsee. Known to frequent the Lumberjack Bar next to the Etna Post Office, Nellie had been seen partaking in tobacco.

A quarter mile from the center of town, Dick drove by the Brickman Mansion, built and abandoned by a man who found wealth in lumber which, ironically, had taken him back to Sacramento. "A beautiful house," Pansy commented. A quarter mile further, she asked, "Would it be out of line to expect that some rules be put in place in regards to what happens to certain properties after Armageddon?"

Dick's brow furrowed. "Which properties?"

"Well," she pointed out the window. "That one we just passed, for example. What will happen if two of Jehovah's people wish to live in it, after this wicked system has been destroyed? Or the Mills Mansion in Farnsworth. What if you and I both desire to live there . . . not together, of course."

Dick frowned. "I can assure you that I have no desire to live in the Mill's mansion."

"Well, I don't either," Pansy replied. "Just hypothetically, I was asking. If I want a specific house in Sacramento, for example . . . what will happen if someone else wants it, too?"

"Jehovah has not given direction for that sort of situation, so we'll jump off that bridge when we get to it," Dick stated. "Shouldn't be long before we find out. The new system will be here soon."

Dick stopped the Town and Country where Highway 3 dead-ended at Sawyer's Bar Road, in the heart of Etna. He waved his arms, right and left. "Etna's only four blocks. You got an hour to shop, and I'll meet you back here at precisely noon."

"Someday, you might pay me enough to go shopping," Pansy

retorted. "I only have a dollar and fifty cents with me, which means I'm on a budget."

She climbed the two steps up to the Etna sidewalk, where buildings had been raised about four feet above street level.

A block away, where Pig Alley intersected Diggles Street, the Trash and Treasures consignment shop held its door ajar with a three-legged stool.

The disarray inside assaulted Pansy's sensibilities. Mold, she detected. Sweet wood smoke, even the acrid stench of tobacco. The store sold clothing, none new. Her eyes flicked from one outfit to another. Men's jeans, women's halter tops. She pulled two dresses from the rack and decided that Etna was full of very small people. Etna women were of the philosophy, kudos to them, that if one couldn't purchase the new fashion featured in the *Medford Tribune* Macy's ad, then one might as well buy that second-hand green polyester pantsuit that was hanging in the back corner of Trash and Treasures. The one that's a cool minty shade of green—the one that Fred Wedemeyer had told his wife, Idell, to go down and buy—I seen it on Florence Green last spring at the feed store, he said to her. You gotta go get a good look before someone sneaks in there and steals it. Yes, the one Florence wore, just before she died. Would look good on you, Idell, and b'sides, it cain't cost more than two bucks now, given that it's hangin' there at the Trash and Treasures. Florence sure as hell ain't gonna be wearin' it no more. Idell Wedemeyer said she could see the sense in that. Florence was dead, so she rushed on down to Diggles Street to get a look for herself. She was there now, competing with Pansy for clothing of larger size.

Idell was the sort of woman who busied herself with the business of church . . . less so with the righteous-get-to-know-Jesus side of it. She counted the quarters in the donation basket each Sunday at St. John the Baptist Church of the Brethren. Fred was not a believer. He said he wasn't raised that way, which wasn't a satisfactory explanation given that Idell wasn't either, raised that way. But she craved the social structure of the few but like-minded rural ladies who praised Jesus for every iota of goodness and tragedy that came their way. Sister Susan Baskin had lost her favorite peach tree after her husband ran his truck into it, but Sister Judith had plenty of extra to share from her garden, praise Jesus! Pastor Bludgins' wife, Cora, took sick with the cancer, so the whole congregation got together for special praise for her healing, and when she had the bad lung, blackened with disease, snipped out of her body, she snapped back to good health. When she returned to church, the congregation cried out, "Thank you, Jeeezzuzz!" Six months later, Cora took an accidental fall down the basement steps and broke her neck. Pastor Bludgins found her in a folded mess at the bottom ... the congregation then praised Jesus for calling her home.

Fred was a normal man of Siskiyou County who didn't believe in the whole twisted explanation of how Jesus works, but he was a good husband and believed he ought to make Idell happy, so he was always out there on Sunday, sittin' in his truck during church services, ready to load his wife in the front seat and drive her home after she was done wailin' and prayin'.

Pansy paid for her purchases at the front counter of the Trash and Treasures. Thirty minutes later, she laid a crimson red polyester Western shirt across the dash of Dick's Chrysler. "Look at this," she said to him. "It will fit Butch just perfectly."

Dick raised his eyebrows. "You'll see him comin' from a mile away."

Pansy pulled from her bag a neon green blouse and shoes that she had already tried on both feet, back at the store. "The place was a bargain. Two dollars and seventy cents. For everything."

Dick grunted. Just an hour earlier, Pansy had told him she only had a dollar fifty, which he stated.

"I wrote a check," she replied.

Dick rubbed his hands over the steering wheel, looking as if to buff it to the shiny gloss of gold leaf. Looking left, out the window, he muttered something about not seeing a check with Pansy's name on it in the contribution box at the Kingdom Hall. "Didn't know you had a checking account."

Pansy said she didn't care to write checks to the Kingdom Hall. She preferred giving cash.

"Well, that's not gonna happen," Steve grunted. The red polyester shirt laid across the hood of his truck in full glory.

"I said the same thing," Butch agreed.

"A man who puts himself in that shirt is gonna look like a fuckin' tomato. With tits," Steve said.

Butch collapsed on the hood in giggles. "It does," he gasped. "Wished I'd explained it that way to Mom. But I wouldn't have said 'fuck.'"

"You're old enough to use the word 'fuck' if you want. Maybe some other things that men think about." He lifted the shirt and flung it to Butch. "Don't know what you're doin' with this, but it ain't goin' home with me."

Butch stuffed it back in a paper sack. "I don't think my mom's ever used a cuss word in her life."

"That's too bad. Would loosen her up a little bit. The way I see it, people should use the word fuck every now and then," Steve said.

"*Every now and then?*" Butch repeated.

"Sure. Your mom's not thinkin' right. The word 'fuck'

doesn't know it's bad. What's bad is using it in a place where it don't belong," Steve stated.

"Like?"

"Let's say I forget to put sugar in my coffee. I would sound like an idiot if I said, 'Fuck, I forgot to put sugar in my coffee.' Fuck doesn't add anything to that. It's not the end of the world to walk back to the kitchen. Using it stupidly just makes you sound like trailer park trash. If you're using cuss words because you think they make you sound grown up, as you younger guys seem to think, they don't."

Butch nodded. "Like Rocky Bale. Rocky thinks a sentence isn't a complete sentence without a 'fuck' in it. Two 'fucks' is even better."

"Exactly," Steve agreed. "And I don't know what your mom was thinking, but clothes like that aren't goin' in my closet. Jeezuzz . . . can you imagine showing up at the auction in that thing?"

"Mom thought I'd look like John Travolta in it. She thinks he's a great cowboy." Butch laughed at the silliness of the thought. "We've been here for ten years, and she still doesn't know much about cowboys."

"She bought the shirt for *you?*" Steve asked.

"Well, yeah, but I wasn't supposed to tell you that. I said heck no, so she asked me to pass it on to you. You won't look like John Travolta in it either."

The blood peaches had erupted in mold inside their Clorox box. Red syrup had just begun to seep across the green tiles on Pansy's kitchen counter that morning. Butch wiped up the mess, then placed the box in the sink. He walked to the Weaver barn and moved a dozen bales of alfalfa from outside to the protection of the barn. The forecast called for strong winds and rain to roll through the valley the next day. The pasture was grazed down to a brittle stubble, the valley would soon turn to winter sluggishness, and Steve had left a dozen cows at the Weaver barn. The horse troughs needed filling, which Steve was doing. He asked Butch to ferry a pitcher of ice water to the barn for the work to be done the next day.

"Load it up with ice," he said. "Miles will be here in the morning. And it would be great if you stick around and help unload."

"Is Miles being paid?" Butch asked.

"The hay is forty bucks a ton," Steve answered.

"Why would I do the work if he's being paid?"

"The right thing to do when someone shows up at your place is to give 'em some help. And when you find yourself in that position, they'll do the same for you. You should know that."

About seventeen miles north of Yreka, in Hornbrook, Miles Knickerbocker, the younger son of rancher Austin Knicker-bocker, drove over to the pasture with eight tons of decent quality alfalfa hay and pulled into the pasture just after eight in the morning. The rear of his gooseneck trailer rode so low it scraped steel across the cattle guard at Steve's gate coming off of Farnsworth Road. He circled around to the south side of the barn on a darkly wet morning, a poor choice of timing for when one might move hay. The sun hadn't yet shared its cheer and wouldn't until the following week when the rain would cease. Three days earlier, the creeks had run beyond their banks, and people in town talked about how much they needed it, except they didn't need it today. But it was unusually dry the previous year, and people did what they were supposed to when water fell from the sky in such abundance that they could stop grousing about it being sent to the southern end of the state where rich people poured it out onto lush miles of lawn.

The rain left the air cool; the alfalfa was sweet in fragrance. "Son of a bitch, it's wet," Miles grumbled. He grabbed a steel cheater bar from the bed, then pried the cargo straps loose. He pulled a plastic tarp from the top. "Hey," he nodded to Steve.

Age twenty-seven and of Portuguese descent on his mother's side, Miles was a spectacularly handsome man. Beauty ran in his maternal line—dark-haired, wide and thick-shouldered with strong masculine features. His eyes were dark, nose broad, and he smiled easily, unaware of the gazes that came his way for longer than most would find comfortable.

He put his hand out in greeting and clasped Butch's big palm in his own. "Who are you?"

"Uhh . . . Butch."

"You givin' me a hand?" Miles asked.

"Uhh . . . Yeah." Butch stalled in confusion. He held up an Igloo. "I have some water," he stammered.

"Ahh. Great. Brought my own," Miles said.

Steve looked sideways at the clumsiness of the introduction, then turned to leave. "All righty. You two can handle this without me. I'm gonna go pull the shoes off of Speckles."

Miles climbed to the top of his delivery, then threw the sharp spike of a hay hook into a bale. "Everything gets wound up in these goddamn three-wires these days," he groused. "Pisses me off. They could just as easily put 'em in two-wire bales like they used to. It's a helluva lot easier to move the two wires."

"Yeah," Butch replied.

The two men silently transferred the load, bale by bale,

stacked it tight inside the barn, rising six high in a very particular, professional manner.

"Bales fall over if you don't stack 'em right," Miles said. When finished, he stripped off his shirt, then pulled a dry replacement from inside the truck. His back rippled. Shoulders —a proverbial barn door. Embraced by thick deltoid bookends, he drew stares to the splendor of his masculine perfection. When Miles turned around in an unintended show of manhood, Butch caught his breath and looked to the ground.

Steve, who had been sitting just outside the tack room, rose and walked to his truck.

Tim Fedorcheck was a man of Siskiyou who dragged rumors through his path. He was an ordinary sort, friendly when he wanted to be. Opportunistic, when circumstances provided. He took jobs as they came his way. A chimney sweep. Handyman. Little old ladies paid him to clear debris from their gutters. Two days before the turn of spring, Steve had brought him over to the B-Bar-Seven to inspect a chimney he never used.

Tim was on his hands and knees, looking up the bottom end of the flue. He shone his flashlight through the interior, then said, "Doesn't look like you ever use it."

Steve had retreated to his couch. "Nah, I don't." He picked at his thumbnail, inspecting it.

"But you want me to clean it?" Tim asked.

"Nah, it's fine. I don't use it." Steve seemed distracted by the condition of his fingernails but asked, "Can I ask you a question? Not related to chimneys."

Tim stood straight, then clicked off his flashlight. "Sure. What do you want to know?"

"Ahh . . . just wantin' to understand some things," Steve explained. "Things that don't come up around here, much. But people talk sometimes. Rumors maybe, about people. No judgment here, but people talk."

Tim didn't respond.

"I've heard stories. No names, except for yours. Just stories." Steve looked at Tim, who was still standing across the room. "Any of 'em true?"

The air turned heavy. This is the way opportunities sometimes presented themselves. "There might be some truth to what you've heard," Tim replied.

Steve raised his hands upwards, disclaiming any presumption of condemnation. "Again, no judgment here, but some people say you might be a guy who doesn't like women."

"I like women just fine. I just prefer some activities to be with men, if that's what you've heard," Tim said.

Steve nodded. "Yup, that's what I hear. There are people around here who don't care for that."

Tim tightened his grip on his flashlight like a man might grasp a weapon. "You one of them?"

Steve grunted. "Nah. Not me. It's none of my business. I'm just figurin' out if there's any truth to what I hear."

Tim's grip softened. "Let's just say there are men who will bend the rules on what they might do in private."

Steve nodded, accepting this reply.

"You thinkin' you might want to be one of them?" Tim asked.

Steve burst into a spontaneous roar, and the conversation immediately turned casual. "Oh, hell no! That's not where I was goin'. Not askin' to be on that list."

"Oh. That's too bad," Tim said.

"Too bad?" Steve questioned.

"You're a handsome man," Tim stated.

Steve gave a loud snort. "Good to know, but I'm not playin' on your side of the barn."

Tim shrugged. "Some men around here might visit the other side, once in a while. Out of frustration, maybe."

"Like who?" Steve asked.

"There's a few."

"Like?" Steve pressed.

Tim tilted his head in thought. "Well, there's an older guy in Yreka. Apparently, women have a limit on how many times they'll have sex before getting something in return, he says."

Steve again laughed. "Ain't that the truth."

"Some guys can't get what they need at home," Tim explained. "Blow jobs," he suggested.

Steve grunted.

"There's a guy in town who hangs out at the tranny bar in Medford," Tim added.

"What the hell's a tranny bar?"

"A bar full of men who dress like women. Transexuals. Or transvestites. I don't really know, same difference, I think, but they have dicks. So, this guy goes to Medford, just to get what he wants, which is a woman who can fuck him. It's a conundrum, really."

"I don't know what a conundrum is," Steve admitted.

"A fuckin' shitty place to be, if you ask me. It makes me feel for the guy, you know. He's a straight man who needs sex with a penis. On a woman. He likes getting fucked but can't do it with a man. An impossible place to be, which is where a tranny comes in."

"How many trannies are in Medford?" Steve asked.

"Enough for the bar to turn tranny once a month, apparently. Two or three? I don't know. The straight men keep them busy," Tim said.

"Do I know the guy?"

"Is there anyone around here you don't know?"

"Probably not. You gonna tell me?"

"Of course not. His business isn't my business. Or yours."

"Good answer," Steve said.

"He won't let a guy do him. He'll only take it from a guy who *looks* like a girl. It makes them both happy, I guess." Tim shrugged. "Sometimes you gotta do what makes you happy."

"Yeah," Steve replied. "Sometimes you gotta be happy. I like that." He was no longer distracted by the state of his fingernails. "One more question. How do you know when someone's interested? How do you know when someone is thinking like you?"

"It's a look. I can usually tell by the look," Tim answered.

Steve shot a quick glance at his jeans. Wranglers, relatively new. He'd worn a hole in the sole of one boot months earlier.

"What look?" Steve wondered.

"Not *how* you look," Tim corrected him. "It's a look someone gives. The air suddenly changes."

Steve leaned forward.

"It feels tense, sexual. It might be something you've never thought of before, but there it is, right in front of you, and you can't hide that when you think it."

Steve nodded. "I've noticed that. Just recently, in fact."

"With who?" Tim asked.

"None of your business," Steve replied.

"Sometimes I'm in a place to help a man indulge his curiosities," Tim offered.

"I don't have curiosities," Steve said.

"Maybe you do," Tim suggested.

Abruptly, Steve picked himself up off the couch and walked to the door. He declared his head to be near to exploding. "You do realize that if I hear you've told anyone about this, I will come lookin' for you?"

A week later, Steve stepped from the shower, pondering the unthinkable. He sprawled across his bed and grabbed himself until he'd pulled it into an erection. He reached down with an index finger, touching his sphincter, then pulled back in disgust. *Not gonna happen,* he said to himself. Not with his own finger.

Booger was on his way out at the age of twelve. Steve said he would take care of the business himself. He offered the task to Butch, who declined and walked home. When Butch woke the next day, the weather had turned hot, Booger was dead, and Melody was nowhere to be found. "Moved out in the middle of the night," Miss Emily told him.

The following day, Clark's Grocery lit itself on fire. Nothin' Edith could have done about it, she said.

Thirteen people stood with Edith east of the railroad tracks, across from Clark's, watching its roof collapse through her first floor. Roger Dodger, the insurance man, drove out from Yreka, then stood with the rest. "That's burnin' awfully hot!" He looked to her. "What the hell you got inside to burn so hot?"

People meandered about, talking of fires, wayward cattle, hopes for a letup in the rain, and girls who might have gotten pregnant and left town. Not the first time that's happened, some said.

Pansy had driven home from the campground, then stood at the corner of Eleventh and Spiers with others who had been drawn by the smoke. Heat radiated out to the onlookers. A shame to see Clark's destroyed, some said. That girl, Melody, had moved out in the middle of the night, someone gossiped.

She'd gotten pregnant, was the rumor. Butch was the daddy, someone had heard. Pansy walked home and called Dick.

The accusation had already found its way to him.

Nothing was more important to Dick than public displays of devotion to the Great Jehovah. He was remarkably honorable, in that way.

Phone calls had already flown back and forth with the elders in Medford to discuss the rules for judicial council protocol. Dick must first form a two-elder investigative committee, which must then meet with the accused to determine if the wrongdoing would necessitate the forming of a three-elder judicial committee. In his haste to deal with the situation, Dick chose to dispense with the formality of the investigative committee. He had enough evidence, he said, in a further call to Elder John Jennings in Medford, to leap directly to the judicial council meeting.

The two ambushed Butch with Pansy's assistance in the little green house two days after the fire. Sitting at the head of his parents' old kitchen table, Dick prayed in earnest, then opened the secret pamphlet of guidelines for shepherding the congregation. The average JW did not know of this book, a testament to the seriousness in which elders took their duties. Jehovah was a lover of justice, the book read, which was precisely how Dick initiated the interrogation.

Pansy had gone to her bedroom and closed the door but could eavesdrop on the entire proceedings. A mistake, she thought of Dick. To allow a woman to listen in on the elders' private conversations with Jehovah.

There were multiple prayers in that kitchen. One requested that Jehovah direct their steps in this matter of wrongdoing. A second during deliberations, after Butch had been sent outside. A third near the conclusion, when Butch clung to denial of his sin, but asserted his loyalty to The Truth. Dick said he felt Jehovah's Holy Spirit upon them and ultimately determined that a public reproof in the Kingdom Hall was sufficient punishment.

Butch was released from the interrogation, then stomped through the pasture to the Weaver barn on a search for solace. He momentarily imagined the Kingdom Hall destroyed by fire, then unloaded his frustrations on Steve. "Dick thinks I got Melody pregnant!" Butch blared. "Fuckin' pregnant! What the hell is he thinking?"

"Can't help you there," Steve said.

"I was only pretending to want to stay in," Butch replied. "Dick can kiss my ass. The Truth is sounding like bullshit to me."

"You don't want to be part of it anymore?" Steve asked.

Butch pulled a stream of air into his lungs. "I believe in Jehovah, but I'd be happier about it if I lived somewhere else. In this little town, Dick reproves people for things they might not have done. And then we pretend they're invisible. They sit in the back of the Kingdom Hall, by themselves, until they repent and get reinstated, and then we're all buddies again. I never thought there was anything wrong with it, until now, when it's happening to me."

"Jeezuzz. There's special seats in back?"

"They know where they have to sit. They come in late. No one turns around to look. Then they leave early, like in the middle of the last song, just so no one is tempted to say hello." Butch kicked at the dirt. "Now I'm going to be sitting there, too."

"And that feels right to you?" Steve questioned.

"Not *now*. It's gonna happen to me, now."

"If you don't want to be part of it, you can tell Dick to go pound sand," Steve suggested.

"I almost did. Almost told Dick to shove his Truth up his ass. I don't want to be part of the bullshit anymore. I didn't do anything wrong, but Dick said I was lying. What the hell? I don't lie," Butch said.

"But you did there, right? You told him you wanted to stay in, but you really wanted out? That's a lie, sounds to me."

Butch shook his head in rejection of the accusation. "That's different. But I swear to God, if I find out who told him I got Melody pregnant, I'm gonna kick his ass. Dick said someone called him and told him it was me. And then he wanted to know everything, and I mean everything. Things that never even happened, he wanted to know about."

"Like?" Steve asked.

"He asked why I'd kissed her. I told him it wasn't my idea. She just grabbed my face and planted one on me. What the hell was I supposed to do? Dick didn't believe me. My mom must have told him. She saw it, but he said people don't kiss just once."

"Nope, they usually don't. Dick's right about that." Steve stroked his mustache in thought. "I didn't know you'd kissed her. And you haven't kissed her again? She's a pretty girl."

"*Was* a pretty girl. She's gone. Got pregnant, apparently. I never thought of her that way. But that's not the point. The point is that it wasn't my idea to kiss her, which I told Dick, but then he wanted to know if I think about her when I jerk off, although he called it 'masturbation.' Who the hell uses the word masturbation? I told him it's none of his fucking business when I jerk off. And then he went down this hell hole of questions, like, did we have oral sex? Or anal sex, but he couldn't say that word, so he asked if we had sex in front or from behind, and when I asked him what the hell he meant by that, he finally coughed out the word anal. Did we have anal sex? Jeezuzz Christ, what a fuckin' retard! For God's sake, what the hell is anyone gonna do down there? Jesus."

"Jeezuzz," Steve whispered.

"So I'm just sittin' there, tellin' the truth, and he keeps looking in some book I've never seen that must have been tellin' him what to do, maybe that's where he learned about anal sex, and then they're telling me how I'm not really showing a repentant attitude. And then I just lost it and asked how the fuck could I have a repentant attitude for something I didn't do? And I used the word fuck about seven times, which is not okay, and then it all went downhill."

"What happened?"

"They kicked me out of the room. When they brought me back in, they said Jehovah's decision was to let me stay in The Truth. But they took my privileges away, so I can't comment at the meetings anymore, or go door to door, until they see a repentant attitude."

"You don't like going door to door," Steve pointed out.

"I fuckin' hate it, but having my privileges revoked means everyone in the congregation will assume that what they heard about Melody getting pregnant was true. They'll announce it from the podium next week. Brother Stinchfield will stand up there and announce, 'Butch Blackwell is no longer an unbaptized publisher of the congregation.' Or he'll say, 'Butch Blackwell has been counseled for his actions.'"

"What happens after that? Does everyone applaud?" Steve asked.

Butch's eyes narrowed. "Of course not!"

"So, you're not called a publisher anymore? Sounds like you work at a bookstore. Selling magazines," Steve said.

"We don't sell magazines. We offer them to people who are interested in The Truth in exchange for a contribution."

"Right. You exchange magazines for money."

Steve reached out to Butch and pulled him close. Butch breathed the musty scent of alfalfa and cologne.

Steve drew back but left one hand on Butch's shoulder. He

looked the younger man in the eye. "You're old enough to start thinkin' for yourself, but the two most important things in life are this: One, be a good man. Your word should matter, and people should believe what you tell them. And second, you only get one shot at life. There's no goin' back and doin' it over. When you get that one chance at life, you damn sure better live it in the way that makes you happy. It's okay to be happy."

19

THE SENIOR YEAR AT YREKA HIGH BLEW BY. BUTCH had graduated, it was now the peak of summer, temperatures were high, and Dick Stinchfield had so much crap scattered about the campground that his decorative taste appeared to revolve around abandoned furniture. He'd hired Butch to move it, clean it, and periodically sort through the rubble, moving piles from one end of camp to another in a repetitive shuffle. Pansy had once sorted through the chaos and determined that her cleaning responsibilities did not extend to rotting furniture.

Once a week, sometimes twice, Butch showed up at the campground for hourly work. Pruning trees, moving furniture. Re-shaping stone firepits. Still on restriction and released from religious duties, he had stayed on the minimal B-Bar-Seven payroll and was awash in summer apathy, turning sluggish, even setting his fishing poles aside.

In conversation with Steve, Butch lamented Dick's shortcomings. "He's frickin' crazy. He sticks a couch under every damn tree!" Butch brightened. "Hey, you got an old couch you need to get rid of? Dick will take it."

The vast majority of American cowboys were poor. There wasn't the slightest chance that one would hit it big on beef. The lower rung of cowboy life was crowded by men who scraped by on the certainty that ranch work would never go dry. It kept them employed, but none would find wealth. Most often, the few men of money got it elsewhere, usually through land or business dealings, then made themselves scarce when the work turned dirty. Those at the top of the heap engaged in the horse and cattle world for pleasure. To throw money on great cutting horses, then pay others to ride them. To fish, purely for fun. The Dan Baldwins of Placer County, for example, who were now in town for the Siskiyou Cutting Horse Show.

The Baldwins had pulled into Dick Stinchfield's Pine Cone Resort on the morning of September 1st with a thirty-foot fifth-wheel trailer attached to one truck. A four-horse trailer clung to the back of another. Dan Baldwin drove one; his son Rusty was behind the wheel of the other. It only took a few seconds for Rusty to catch a hard stare from Butch.

Rusty stepped out of his truck in the same manner that he rolled out of bed each morning. A stocky redhead, he appeared unaware that one could travel through life in any way other than with a grin and eagerness to see the day. Confident, perhaps entitled by his family's intimacy with money—he wasn't aware of either. Unintimidated by sexual desire, he met Butch's stare.

Intrigue on the part of men was unwelcome, perhaps feared, in Siskiyou. Butch looked to the ground. Rusty would have none of it. "Hey!" he said, then strode to the trees where Butch had retreated. "I'm Rusty. What's your name?"

Butch accepted a handshake, mumbled his name, and felt panic rise in his throat.

Rusty motioned at the firepit Butch was re-building.

Concrete blocks were stacked aside, a wire grate rested on its end. "You work here?"

Butch nodded. "Sometimes. Just helpin' out today."

Rusty again nodded to the blocks and suggested he could help if Butch needed assistance with moving the heavy stuff. He looked directly at the biceps bulging from Butch's T-shirt. "Doesn't look like you need help. Not with arms like that."

Butch stood straight.

An hour later, Dan had gone to Farnsworth to get an early look at the competition. Pansy was knee-deep in dirty toilets, Dick stalked the campground in the manner of someone in charge, and Butch was standing inside the Baldwin's fifth-wheel, his shirt removed by Rusty. The redhead had wrapped one arm around Butch's shoulders and pulled him close.

"I've never kissed a man," Butch began, but Rusty made the statement untrue.

"Now you have," he said.

They whispered . . . Butch mentioned his fears, and their exploration began, above the waist only.

The trailer door flew open, and Dick leaned inside. He jabbed his stubby finger at Butch.

"This is exactly what happens when you go down the path of being sexually immoral! You got that girl pregnant, and now you've turned to homosexual activity! The Youth Book even warned us about this, how you would get tired of masturbating and engage in homosexual practices!"

Later that evening, Pansy sat in her kitchen, her Bible on the table, prepared for much reading and page-turning. In her hand was a long strand of twine, and she had wrapped it tight around the tip of her index finger. When the string broke, she doubled both pieces together and twisted it into one.

Dick came through the front door. He carried a leather brief-case and pulled notes from inside. He laid them in front of himself, where he again took what he thought to be the head of the table, then spoke to Butch, who was seated at the other end.

"You are eighteen," Dick stated. Dispensing with the rules, as printed in the elder's handbook, he leaned toward Butch. "You have to take responsibility for your actions."

To Pansy, he suggested they share a scripture. "The second book of John, verses 9 through 11." She opened her Bible, but Dick read it aloud from his own. "He that does not remain in the teaching of Christ does not have God. If anyone comes to you and does not bring this teaching, do not receive him into your home or say a greeting to him, for he that says a greeting to him shares in his wicked works."

"I will not share in your wicked works," Pansy said to her son.

Dick opened a bound volume of older *Watchtower* publica-tions. He again read a chosen passage aloud.

"A disfellowshipped person, even a family member, should be made to appreciate that his status has changed and he is no longer welcome in the home," he quoted to Pansy.

"You are no longer welcome in this home," Pansy said to Butch. She set her back straight against her chair.

Butch awoke in the middle of the night, rushed to the door, and threw up outside the barn. He rose the next morning, angry, crawling out from his sleeping cubby in the hay. Hungry. He walked into the rising sun, then threw alfalfa flakes to the horses. The stalls needed shoveling. He did that, moving manure by wheelbarrow out to the south side.

Steve pulled in, and Butch went to the truck before Steve had turned it off.

He waited for Steve to open the driver's door. "I did something yesterday that you're going to hear about," Butch said to him. "I'd rather you hear it from me."

Steve stepped from the cab and walked to the front. He leaned against it.

"You'll find this out soon enough, but I want you to hear it from me," Butch again said.

A few moments went by with neither man speaking.

Eventually, Butch broke the silence. "I met someone at the camp yesterday. A guy who's here for the cutting horse show. Dick Stinchfield caught us together. Me and the other guy. Together."

Steve removed his hat, turning it over a few times. He sorted his thoughts, then asked, "Some sort of private thing that you wouldn't want people to know about?"

Butch nodded. "We didn't do anything. But Dick thinks otherwise. You're going to hear about it from him."

"So, let me ask you something," Steve said. "You don't have to answer if you don't want to, but there's something I'd like to know. You said you didn't do anything with the guy?"

Butch nodded. Yes, that is what he had said.

"But did you want to?"

"Yes."

Steve placed his hat back on his head. "Well, I'd say that settles it. You'll know soon enough if you really are that way. If it's who you are, you don't need to go around announcing it to everyone, but you don't need to beat yourself up over it, either. Everyone deserves to be happy."

Butch frowned. "It doesn't feel like that."

"It will, someday. If it's true, you can't bash yourself over something you didn't have a say in. But it won't take long before Dick lets everyone in town know. He's evil, that way."

"They kicked me out of the house."

"For the day?" Steve asked.

"Forever."

Steve snorted, then pulled the truck door open and climbed back into the driver's seat. "Get in," he said.

"Where we goin'?" Butch asked.

"To your house."

"I can't go there."

Steve motioned to the passenger seat. "Get in," he repeated. "I'm gonna take care of this for you."

"How?" Butch asked.

"I don't know yet."

Butch turned, looking back at the green house. He'd made that walk a thousand times over the last decade. He squinted at Steve. "We're driving?"

"Driving," Steve said. "I need some time to figure out what I'm gonna do when I get there."

Dick and Pansy were seated at the kitchen table, again locked in discussion of sin from the previous day. The gravity of the situation, Pansy had said.

"I can't let him stay in the congregation," Dick was saying.

"Of course not," Pansy agreed. "The congregation must be kept clean."

Steve blew through the front door, failing to knock. Pansy rose to meet him in the living room.

"Oh, fuck off," Steve said. He pushed his way into the kitchen.

Dick stood.

"Sit the fuck down," Steve ordered.

"I own this house . . . " Dick began, but sat, as he was told.

Steve looked back to Butch. "Grab that tarp in the back of the truck. Throw all of your things inside, and I'll help you carry it out." He then leaned to Dick.

"You make things difficult for him, and I'll make life miserable for every Jehovah's Witness in this county. I can do that," Steve warned.

Butch heaved clothes into the tarp and took two cowboy hats out to Steve's truck. One went on his head; the other no longer fit there, being a gift from ten years earlier. He returned for his shotgun and deer rifle.

When Steve's truck roared away, Dick gathered his authority for another prayer. He bowed his head and thanked Jehovah for protection from the cowboy who had gone crazy. He prayed that Butch would turn from the evilness of sexual perversion, but Pansy did not mutter amen.

Butch retreated into his own thoughts in the truck; an introspection of mistakes and desires as they entered the B-Bar-Seven. The morning sun was high on the eastern horizon, the day becoming brighter. Apples lay rotting under the old, gnarled tree.

"When I woke up this morning, I thought of all the things you might say." He turned to the older man. "None of it was this."

"You didn't trust I would be there for you?" Steve asked.

"That's not what I'm saying. You've always been there for me," Butch said.

"Damn right, I have," Steve replied.

"What I'm saying is that I didn't know if you would look at me differently, afterwards." He took a deep breath. "I'm gay," he said, hearing the acknowledgment out loud. "A fuckin' homosexual. Telling someone you're gay isn't the kind of thing you get all confident about, you know? I didn't know if you would respect me afterwards, if I told you the truth."

"You always tell the truth. It's something that makes you a good man. I've never had reason to doubt your word. Ever," Steve said.

"Thanks," Butch said softly.

"And I've had my suspicions for a while. How long have you known?" Steve asked.

"Known what?"

"That you aren't chasing girls," Steve answered.

"Every time I went over to Trixie's house for eggs and she pushed up against me, like she was tryin' to get my pants off." Butch grimaced at the memories.

"Trixie hit on you?"

"Oh, hell yeah. It was gross."

"Most men don't find Trixie gross," Steve replied.

Butch shrugged. "And then when Melody thought we needed to get busy kissing. I couldn't get excited about that, you know? But I get fired up around Rooster. There's somethin' about him that I can't put my finger on, but I just decided to not think about it. Yesterday, that guy Rusty made me think about it. Took about two seconds to think about it with him. Like he stepped out of the truck and lit some fire under me." Butch exited the passenger side, closed his door, then leaned over the hood.

Steve leaned next to him. "You got kicked out of the Jahoovers."

"Jahoovers?" Butch repeated.

"They're like Hoover vacuums. Suck the life right out of you," Steve said.

"Yesterday I wouldn't have thought that was funny," Butch replied.

Steve laughed. "That religion is so damn focused on a future in heaven, that your life ain't worth shit today. That's no way to live."

"We don't believe in going to heaven."

"It ain't 'we.' *They* just kicked you out. You don't belong to them anymore." He poked Butch in the shoulder. "So, what happens next? Do you have to sign something, you know, tear up the contract or somethin'?"

"I'm already announced as not being a publisher after that whole Melody thing, and I'm not baptized, so they can't disfellowship me."

"What's the difference?"

"None, really. Both are bad. It's just a matter of degree, in terms of how bad. Publicly reproved, which is what I was, is a warning to the congregation that I'm a danger to everyone, so they should avoid me, which just about everyone already has. After Melody," Butch said.

"All six of them? That's all there is in your church, right?"

"There's about a dozen, depending on who gets the urge to drive in from Happy Camp, or tourists coming through town. But I've been sitting in the back ever since I got Melody pregnant." Butch laughed, loudly—a surprise to both. "I didn't get her pregnant, but Dick doesn't believe me, so I was punished for something I didn't do. I'm already invisible. I could bump into them tomorrow at the Food-Rite, and they would pretend I wasn't there."

"Even your mother?"

"Oh, hell yeah. She gave me that whole lecture yesterday. The Witnesses won't tell her to shun me, I don't think, given that I was never baptized, but I am now dead to her. Same way she thinks of my father," Butch said.

Both walked to the house. Steve pushed through his collection of rubble at the back door, then went to his bedroom. He tossed a pillow and blanket through the open door, landing in the living room. "That there couch is gonna be your friend for the next few nights. Give me some time, and we'll put things right. I got a couple ideas I'm workin' on." He returned to the living room. "If you're hungry, help yourself to whatever's in the fridge. There's Cornflakes in the cabinet. You know where it is." Steve pulled a pile of *Western Horseman* magazines off the couch and threw them on the floor. "And if you get cold on the couch, just let me know."

"What are you gonna do if I get cold?" Butch asked.

"I'll throw you another blanket."

20

Young guys often walked away from the Medford Livestock Auction for better pay at the Tastee-Freeze. The position most frequently abandoned could be referred to as an auction-yard-attendant. Butch, who had taken that job, was simply known as the guy who shoveled shit. During auction hours, Thursday through Sunday, he filled water troughs, chased livestock up and down return lanes, and wouldn't be recognized by name until six months in.

Steve had made three phone calls the day after Butch was banished from home. The first to Trixie Bleaker. With $643 in savings he had stashed in the Weaver barn, Butch bought her 1957 Ford pickup for $500.

A second call was to the Medford auction yard. It required no favors to procure a position for Butch.

The third went to Rex Pullman. A man from Siskiyou, Rex was an Oregon Fish and Game officer, living alone in Medford but married, having a wife and home in Farnsworth. Fifty-two, gray hair spiked short in a crew cut, Rex was an affable man who made a good friend—unless you broke the law. Fit, mature, and serious, Rex was an ordinary sort of handsome.

On the day Butch moved into Rex's spare bedroom, he felt a tension, perhaps discomfort, in the air. He wondered if Rex was aware of his secret. Steve had shared the details, Butch assumed.

Rex's home, a two-bedroom rental just outside of town, was far enough from neighbors to allow for solitude and reflection. When Rex was away enforcing wildlife regulations, Butch kept to himself, mostly killing time at the auction yard. He often ate at the coffee shop there but shared meals at home with Rex, sometimes. Rex was warm and comfortable, Butch eventually decided. If aware of Butch's flaws, the man didn't let on. Over the Thanksgiving and Christmas holidays, Rex traveled to Farnsworth to be with his wife, but on New Year's Eve, back in Medford, he cracked the seal on a fifth of whiskey and handed it to Butch. Drinking straight from the bottle, Butch felt the smooth burn roll down his throat.

Rex stopped him after the second gulp. "Need to know how it's gonna play you," he said. "Go easy, if this is your first time."

Butch turned the bottle back to Rex. Eventually, he laid his head back, relaxed, boldened. "I'm guessing that Steve told you why I had to get out of Farnsworth," he said.

"He didn't," Rex answered.

Butch licked his lips for a taste of alcohol. "Ahh. I thought you knew."

"Nope. Didn't think it was any of my business. He just said you'd had a falling-out with your mother, or her church, or something like that."

Butch looked across the room. "I did something with another guy once, something private. We got caught."

Rex set the whiskey bottle back on the table.

"A sexual thing," Butch said.

Rex sat up straight. "Those things happen to me too, sometimes." And that was enough.

Butch soon reached for Rex, pulling him close.

"You're a beautiful man," Rex said.

"Thanks."

"I'm old enough to be your dad," Rex added.

"So?"

"Exactly."

Rex gave in to a kiss that Butch then fumbled for. Urgent. Exploratory.

Butch was first to shed his clothes. "Son of a bitch," Rex exhaled.

They stumbled to the bedroom—Rex's bedroom—Butch pulled the older man to the mattress.

Afterwards, saturated in liquor and guilt, Rex slurred a demand to Butch. "Promise that you will NEVER do this again unless your dick is wrapped in a condom. Promise me. Not unless you want to end up dead."

Spring came to Medford, soft and gentle in arrival. Butch had taken to his tasks at the auction yard, relishing the limited hours that allowed him to fish on days off. Rex, as a condition of his occupation, was a fountain of information for prime, but secret, fishing holes. In times of need, Butch went to Rex's bedroom for pleasure and most often slept through the night there, under a soft green and ivory quilt patterned with vertical lines of acorns and quail, hand-stitched by Rex's wife, Joyce.

"She's a good woman," Rex often said. "Married her right out of high school. Before I knew anything about what I wanted or thought I had a choice."

When Rex brought Joyce to Medford that spring, her condition of decay from cerebral palsy drove long spikes of guilt through Butch's conscience. Kind and motherly, she looked to Butch with the glassy-eyed innocence of a woman who didn't know the poison of suspicion.

Butch moved to his own apartment the following month, rebuffing hints from Rex for intimacy.

"I can't," he explained. "Not now. I know Joyce."

21

A MAN AT SIX FOOT FIVE, TWO HUNDRED EIGHTY pounds, has reason to be secure in his existence without awareness of what makes him so. Butch looked capable of lifting small trucks and sometimes found sexual release with strangers at the rest stop south of town. Names and identities were never shared there. Anonymity was de rigueur. Wait for the stranger who meets your desires, then retreat to a dark corner and get the task done.

Seven years into his employment at the auction yard, he led horses from the show arena, exiting down the return lane at the Medford Gelding Sale. Up in the bleachers, in the third row, on this particular day when Butch led a young gelding into the show ring, Rusty Baldwin's head snapped so hard that it might have flown off. Rusty then stalked Butch for an hour.

Out in front, the auction had closed, and the blood drained from Butch's face at recognition of the man who pursued him.

In the cab of Butch's truck, the two men inquired into each other's pasts, feeling the power of their earlier attraction.

"Did your dad find out what happened?" Butch asked.

"Oh, yeah. That little shit who owned the campground . . . what was his name?" Rusty asked.

"Dick," Butch answered.

"Right. Dick. The next day, when we were checking out, that little fucker told my dad that he'd caught two queers in our trailer, me being one of them. My dad punched him in the face. About knocked him out," Rusty said laughing.

Butch's jaw could have dropped to the floor.

"My dad's no fool. He's always known I'm gay. Won't take shit from anyone about that. My dad doesn't put up with stupid," Rusty said.

"Damn," Butch said.

"Damn right." Rusty leaned over to Butch. "And we need to finish what we started."

"Seven years ago," Butch answered.

They drove both trucks to the South Medford Inn.

A decade ground by.

Butch and Rex fished the Oregon rivers often. Hunted deer together. Sometimes drove out to the coast. Butch occasionally drove down to Placer County, just east of Sacramento, for a visit with the redhead but wouldn't allow Rusty to return the favor, unless for the Medford Gelding Sale in January. He likened any other suggestions for Medford visitations to shitting in his backyard. "Last thing I need is to get caught fuckin' a man in southern Oregon. Good way to get shot."

Three times in those ten years, when dating someone else, Rusty retracted the welcome mat for Butch. When unattached, the pull on both to visit was strong but fraught with fears and limitations for Butch. Intimacy between men didn't belong in daylight, for him. Rusty's suggestions for social time in a Sacramento gay bar were smacked down hard. "Not a chance in hell," Butch had growled. An open expression of affection in the Baldwin's horse barn brought revulsion. "What the hell is wrong with you?"

Rusty had plenty of money. A man with money was a better man, Butch concluded. He asked where it had come from.

"From rental property, of course." Rusty answered simply, as if everyone had rental property. "The ranch is for fun."

"Maybe I need to get me some rental property," Butch mused.

"It's a lot easier to make money when you already have some. My dad's been sayin' that for years. He buys every parcel that comes up for sale. Every rancher who wants to sell comes to my dad, and then he complains the property taxes are killing him."

Butch turned thirty-five and drove down to Placer, consenting to Rusty taking him to dinner for his birthday. He would accept the gift without complaint, he promised. The restaurant in downtown Sacramento, frequented by men of business and money, was stunning. Intimate.

Butch chose the farthest seat, across the table.

"You can't sit next to me?" Rusty asked, which wasn't really a question to answer. He raised his glass in appreciation of an old-vine zinfandel.

"A Budweiser would have been fine," Butch said.

Two slabs of the finest prime rib came to their table, and Butch felt the burn of acid in his belly at the price tag. When the check arrived, he agreed that it had been a very good meal. A side dish of creamed spinach was something he'd never before tasted. "A beer would have made it better."

Rusty gazed up at the vaulted, wood-beamed ceiling. "It's a beautiful place, isn't it?"

Butch shrugged. "Sure, if you like that kind of thing." He ran his finger across the condensation on his water goblet. "Kinda fancy glass for water."

Rusty emptied the last of the zinfandel into his wine glass, then looked to Butch. "You ever think you might settle down with someone?"

"In southern Oregon? Shit, I'd get shot," Butch said.

"You could get out of Oregon. You could come down here," Rusty suggested.

"And do what? My job's in Medford. The auction yards are all closing down, except for the one in Shasta County. I'd get shot there, too." Butch leaned into the table and spoke, nearly in a whisper. "If you're wondering if I've ever fantasized about moving in with another cowboy, the answer is no."

"Good to know," Rusty replied.

"Sorry. Don't mean to offend you."

"But you do. It's like you've got this chain around your neck, wallowing in the world of rednecks."

Butch laid his fork on his plate.

"It doesn't have to be that way," Rusty said.

The following January, when the Medford Gelding Sale opened, there was no phone call from Rusty.

22

THE PINE CONE RESORT WAS NEARING DESOLATION, suffering from neglect. The Siskiyou Manor had offered a full fifty-cent raise over Dick's hourly rate and threw in a small one-room apartment to bring Pansy to their twenty-bedroom motel. On the first floor, her unit was next to the laundry facilities. Still obsessive about order and cleanliness, Pansy began work each morning by walking ten steps to the laundry room for clean linens.

Butch had moved up at the Medford auction. He had a title now: a ring man, or bid catcher, during the auction. A record keeper afterwards.

Joyce Pullman succumbed to her illness in the summer of 1996, and Butch returned to Farnsworth for the service. He spent the night on Steve Bultemeyer's couch. Nearing his seventy-first birthday, Steve's facial lines had deepened. He smacked at his mustache less often with his razor. They drove to the Weaver barn that morning, Sunday, doing nothing more than reminiscing of old times. Steve no longer brought cattle to the pasture.

They made their way to the barn. The tack room had been emptied.

"You gonna see your mother while you're in town?" Steve asked.

"Not a chance," Butch said.

"That's too bad."

Butch shrugged. "Nah. Wouldn't accomplish anything. She will live and die as a Jehovah's Witness. Ain't a chance in hell that she would talk to me if I'm not coming back to the Kingdom Hall. And straight."

"You know what I think about religion," Steve said.

"Yup. I think the same. You're supposed to believe what they tell you, don't ask questions, and wait for Armageddon to arrive. They'll kick you aside, otherwise, especially if you're gay," Butch said.

"You believe in God?" Steve asked.

"Not anymore," Butch answered.

"Good man." Steve removed his hat, pushing his fingers through hair that had gone white. "Most people I know who are all hung up on God don't really care much for people like you." Steve grinned. "And while we're at it, I got somethin' I need to tell you. It's a confession. You remember that time when you got that girl pregnant? Or when people thought you did?"

Butch nodded. "Of course."

"I should have told you this long ago. That was me. I started that rumor," Steve said.

"You! Why?" Butch demanded.

"Because I'd figured out who you were," Steve answered.

"You'd figured it out?" Butch asked.

"Sure, I did. People like you exist. That's the way it is. Some people around here don't like that kind of stuff, so I gave you an alibi, I think it's called."

"Sonofabitch. I wouldn't have guessed," Butch said.

"Yup. Was just lookin' out for you. Some people are stupid . . . your mom, Dick Stinchfield, for example, who aren't bright enough to know you weren't ever gonna get a girl pregnant . . . what was her name? Monica?"

"Melody," Butch said.

"Right. Melody," Steve confirmed. He snorted. "She was a pretty little thing. You should have been all fired up about that, but you weren't . . . so that added up to you being something else. Wasn't hard to figure out. I gave my nephew Kenny a dollar to call Dick and spread the gossip. Didn't take nothin' more than that."

"That's evil," Butch stated.

"Nah. It woke you up . . . got you to thinkin' about things," Steve replied.

"Yeah, it did. Would never have guessed it was you."

"And there was that thing with Miles Knickerbocker. Am I right?" Steve asked.

"*What* thing?"

"That thing when you about stopped breathing." Steve doubled over in laughter. "Damn, that's funny now."

"I didn't know what to do with it then. Didn't believe it, then," Butch said.

"That's what I figured. I saw how you looked at him, and then when you couldn't get your act together with that cute little gal who was dyin' to kiss you, I figured I'd help you out. That Monica girl leaving made it easy to start a rumor."

"Melody," Butch corrected.

"Right, Melody. I didn't know it was all gonna blow up." He shrugged his shoulders in disgust, like shaking off a blanket of ignorance. "People are stupid. You don't choose what you like."

"You think Miles knew?" Butch asked.

"Nah. A guy that good-looking gets used to people staring," Steve answered.

"Haven't thought about him in a long time. How's he doing?"

"He moved down to Red Bluff. Don't know how many kids he's got now . . . maybe three. I talk to him on the phone every now and then. He doesn't have a clue what he looks like. He just thinks the rest of the world is especially friendly," Steve said.

"A really quick way for a good-looking man to turn ugly is to be aware of it, and that ain't Miles," Butch said.

"Nope, it ain't," Steve agreed.

"What else is happening around here?" Butch asked.

"Wally Barker went to prison for forgery. Not his first time doin' that." Steve winked. "People are who they are."

"Words of wisdom from Steve Bultemeyer."

"Rooster won the bull riding in Red Bluff last year. Told you he was gonna be good," Steve said.

Butch smiled. "Rooster was the first guy who got me to thinkin' about what I liked, way back then. There was somethin' special about him that I couldn't figure out."

Steve laughed. "Yeah, Rooster's a cocky little bastard, but that wouldn't look right. You're a monster. He's a little guy. You could stick him in your pocket."

"Nothin' wrong with little guys," Butch said.

"Let's talk about you. Found anyone special in Medford?" Steve asked.

"Nah. That's not gonna happen up there."

"Yeah, not much different than Farnsworth, I s'pose. People like you move. San Francisco is where they go, I think. You might move there," Steve suggested.

"What the hell would I do in San Francisco? Not a chance," Butch said. "But I did meet that guy who got me kicked out of the Witnesses. His name is Rusty."

"No foolin'?"

"Yup. Bumped into him at the auction, almost ten years ago. You would have liked him. He's got good horses. Horses I can't even dream of being able to afford. He lives down near Sacramento," Butch said. He paused for a moment. "I haven't talked to him in a while. Missed out on something good there . . . he has some other guy now, I think. Oh well. You can't go back and fix spilled milk."

"Sure, you can. When you mess something up, you suck it up and go fix it."

"Too late for that."

23

On a stormy afternoon in November 1996, Steve Bultemeyer fell over dead. Never knew what hit him, people said.

Friends crowded into a wet pasture to offer their respects. Some said kind things, reflecting on their grief. Others blathered about themselves, but the dead don't mind. It had rained the evening before. Visitors said their words, memories and friendships brought tears and laughter, deep discussions of heaven and a few prayers to God. Most felt Steve had died too soon. None expected a religious man to preside over his passing.

Butch brought an old cowboy hat with him—a gift from Steve twenty-eight years earlier. Just outside the tack room, he momentarily laid it on the memorial table, then walked it back to his truck. He returned to the Weaver barn, scuffing hay in his path. *Don't kick Speckles in the belly,* he remembered. From the upper loft, emptied now, he gazed out to the Shasta. In the opposite direction, a few hundred yards to the south, stood the little green house. He wondered if anyone was living there now.

Some trees had been taken down. There was no hint of the plum thicket. He went downstairs.

Bales of hay had been laid about the first floor of the barn. People sat on them, as intended. Most trucks eventually filed out to Farnsworth Road. Young blades of pasture grass shimmered in the light; tire tracks lay deep scars in the mud.

Miles Knickerbocker had come to the service. He stood near Steve's brother, Max, conversing of younger times.

Max wanted to get things wrapped up. He'd turned old. Gray as Ebeneezer, Max lifted Steve's ashes from the memorial table, still packaged in a cardboard box. Steve wanted to be scattered in the Siskiyous, Max said. "Don't remember where, but we'll find a spot for him. Somewhere in the mountains. Don't really matter. Don't think Steve's gonna know where he's scattered, at this point."

"You mind if I take care of that for you?" Butch offered. There was a spot he knew of. A special place in the mountains that Steve had taken him to, many years ago. "Would mean a lot, if you'd let me do that."

Max shrugged. "Sure enough," then turned the box over to Butch. "Appreciate the help." When he left the barn, Butch wondered if Max would go home to a trailer.

Hank's oldest son, Rumford, had cleared the contents of the memorial table into a couple of Food-Rite Grocery sacks. Hank had died a couple of years back. Now that Uncle Steve was out of the way, which was precisely how Rumford described it, the pasture would be sold to the county. The people at the County Planning Department would rip up the pasture, grade it flat, and pave wide strips of black asphalt into a landing strip for a new airport.

"What will they do with the Weaver barn?" Butch asked.

"Doesn't matter a damn bit to us, once we've cashed their

check," Rumford replied. He carried the ephemera of Steve's death out to his truck, then made his way out of the pasture.

Miles hadn't yet gone home. He and Butch stood together inside the barn, appreciating the sudden solitude, talking of the man who had been their friend. "Don't know that Farnsworth will ever be the same," Miles said. He reached out to Butch, grasping him in a long embrace. "That man thought of you like a son." He sighed, his arms wrapped tight around Butch's shoulders, then kissed him on the cheek and turned to leave.

A storm skulked across the Shasta Valley. The rain came slow, but would later drive hard, pushing the Shasta River to overrun its bank, muddied, until one could no longer see to its bottom. In the seclusion of his own vehicle, Butch cried for the man who had shepherded him through childhood. He turned to Farnsworth Road.

24

BUTCH RANG RUSTY THE NEXT MORNING.

"I've thought about calling you many times," Butch said.

"Maybe you should have," Rusty replied curtly.

"You still seein' that same guy?" Butch asked.

"Which guy? Chuck? Nah. That didn't last long."

"Would be nice to see you." Steve had died, Butch said.

"Sorry," Rusty said sincerely.

"He was like a father to me," Butch said.

"I know," Rusty said.

"They're selling the place. The Bultemeyer family. The barn, everything. They're gonna bulldoze the barn, I hear."

"We could move it to the Baldwin Ranch," Rusty suggested. "They'd probably let you have it for free. If not, I could buy it for you."

Butch went quiet for a moment. "Would be nice to see you. Really soon, if that's okay."

The landscape was changing along the Highway 80 corridor. Development sprawled across the Sacramento foothills. Ranches had been leveled. The Baldwins were responsible for much of the destruction. Butch drove down on a Saturday morning, and by evening, the two had settled on going out to dinner.

"McDonald's," Butch suggested.

"Cattleman's Steakhouse," Rusty countered.

"Nope. I can't afford that," Butch said.

"You don't need to. I'll buy dinner," Rusty offered.

"Nah . . . I'm not takin' money from you. I didn't come down here for that. Don't like how it makes me feel."

"Some things never change," Rusty mumbled.

They drove to the Taco Bell in Rocklin, a few miles from the Baldwin Ranch.

After dinner, they retreated to Rusty's home at the far end of the ranch. Butch rambled in conversation. He'd met a man at the truck stop north of Medford the previous year, he said.

"Good lookin' guy," Butch described. "Couldn't get him to do anything with me, though. Not even in the truck. The man was scared to death."

"Like you?" Rusty asked.

"I'm not scared. Not thinkin' I'm gonna get caught when it's dark," Butch replied.

"It's too bad that anyone chooses to live that way. In the dark," Rusty said.

Butch shrugged. "Where I live, you keep your business to yourself. You do what you need to do, if you want to stay alive or keep your job. That guy was so scared he wouldn't even tell me his name. What's a guy like him gonna do? Sell the ranch and move to San Francisco? Some guys just get stuck where they live, you know?"

Rusty rose. "Don't know why you needed to know the man's

name, if you couldn't get off anywhere other than inside your truck. In the dark." He walked to the kitchen.

"It's different, where I live," Butch said when Rusty returned to the front room.

"Then you should move," Rusty retorted.

"Can't afford to. The truck stop will take care of things when I need it." He laughed aloud. "Most of the time. You don't ever see the same people at the truck stop, mostly. Except for one guy who is there all the time and only chases Black men—the younger, the better. He's a good-lookin' man, but he won't look at me."

"Right. You want to hook up with a man who chases dark meat," Rusty said.

"Jeezuzz Christ, that's an ugly thing to say."

Rusty shrugged. "Yeah, it is. I'm in an ugly mood."

"You're a man who likes men. You know how it feels to worry about getting caught bein' who you are," Butch argued.

"I don't spend my life worrying about getting shot for being gay. The world is changing," Rusty replied.

"For Black people, too?" Butch asked.

"Don't know. When I was a kid, the Blacks stayed in Sacramento. Wouldn't have dared to come out here to the ranch land."

Butch threw his fingers up in mock quotes. "The *Coloreds* is how people referred to Blacks when I was growing up. Like they're people we should think less of. It was ugly then and ugly now. My mother was about the only person I knew who didn't think that way. I should thank her for that."

"I don't think less of Black people," Rusty said.

"Sounds like you do."

"Things are changing," Rusty again asserted. He leaned across the couch and poked Butch in the leg. "Gay cowboys do shack up together these days and don't worry about getting shot."

"And maybe Black people get to live these days, too, without getting shot," Butch said.

"Touché. Changing the subject. I hear there's another gay bar in Medford. Two of them, now."

"Sure, there is. I'm never gonna set foot in either one. It's not like here. Not like that bar in Sacramento . . . what's that one called?"

"Faces. The one I tried to get you to go to," Rusty said.

"That was ten years ago. You remember that?" Butch asked.

"Of course, I remember. You couldn't get over your problem that someone might see you. Three hundred miles from home. Like that made a lot of sense," Rusty teased.

"I'm not driving all the way to Sacramento to go to a gay bar."

"Then go to one in Medford," Rusty said.

"Nope. Not goin' there, either. Not in my backyard."

Rusty shrugged. "Doesn't matter. You're not gonna find anything you like. Closeted cowboys don't go to gay bars where they live."

"Nope. We just stay in that closet, as you say. Not joinin' the guys who don't have anything to lose. Campy, you call it, right? The campy guys who are fruity as a box of Froot Loops. I'm bettin' the Medford bar is full of 'em."

Rusty agreed with the wager.

"Those people have nothing to lose," Butch stated. "They're so obvious that most people just think of them as being some other sort of creature . . . you know, they're not the typical man, or woman for that matter. Maybe they're normal in San Francisco, but in Oregon, they're so different that people just think of them as being different and let it go. But people like me . . ."

"Closeted," Rusty finished the thought.

"Sure. Closeted. Like the guy at the truck stop. It doesn't make sense, you know? How guys that rope cows and kill deer can prefer other guys. Guys like you."

"I'm not closeted. Never have been," Rusty said.

Butch shrugged. "It's easier to put the girly guys in a box, you know? People see a guy swish down the street and get all flashy with his hands, and they just say to themselves, that guy's a homo. They might not like it, but it makes sense to them. But then there's guys like me . . . how would I meet someone like me? Other than you, of course, and it took me four hours to get down here. But up in Medford, where is he hiding? And for that matter, even if I met him, we'd never get beyond occasional hookups in the truck. Men like me don't have a place in this world. Not where I live."

Later, in bed, the lights on bright, Rusty renewed the conversation. "Does it bother you, being gay?"

"Of course not. I like men. Would be stupid to get all bothered by something I didn't ask for. Just don't call me a queer. I met a guy once, a couple of years ago, who called me a queer. I about punched him," Butch said.

Rusty rolled his eyes upwards.

"Damn right. Some people's heads are twisted on backwards," Butch insisted.

Rusty laughed aloud. "Maybe the one who's fucked up is you."

"Maybe." Butch went vacant in thought for a moment. "I went up to Portland once to get a new horse trailer for Steve and went to that bookstore south of town. Bought a gay magazine. Took a lot of nerve to carry that out to my truck. It had pictures of guys, I think they were bikers, like Hell's Angels or some-thin,' in leather vests, chaps, stuff like that. They were all pulled over alongside the road, hangin' out naked in the irrigation ditch. Couldn't figure it out. Couldn't understand why a bunch of bikers would take their clothes off for a gay magazine."

"They weren't bikers!" Rusty laughed. "You picked up a magazine for men in leather. Gay men."

"Leather? Why?" Butch asked.

"Some gay men like to dress up. Some in dresses, others in leather."

"No foolin? Christ. Well, that doesn't explain what they were doin' in the irrigation ditch. Well, that won't be me, but anyway, I saw an ad for some bar in town, I forget what it was called. The Roughside? Something like that. Anyway, it had an ad about how this bar was a place for big, bearded guys. They said it was Bears Night on Thursdays. Holy shit. Apparently, I am a bear, which I didn't know then," Butch said.

Rusty reached out and pinched Butch's nipple. "You can be my bear."

Butch snorted in disgust. "Gawd."

"What? You know how I feel about you," Rusty said.

"I don't know what to do with that word," Butch explained.

"Accept it, maybe?"

Butch shook his head. "No, no. It doesn't make sense. It was the first time I'd ever heard about bears. I didn't know what to do, so I just hung out in a corner and nursed a beer. But guys came up to talk to me, which made me feel good, but goddamn, it's just freaky to be talkin' to a big, bearded dude, looks like he drives truck or works for the power company or some such thing, and every time he opens his mouth it's like there's a big girl in there, tryin' to get out. Couldn't make any sense of that, you know?"

Butch rolled to his back, looking to the ceiling.

"One came over, and the first thing out of his mouth was, 'How big are your arms?'" Butch recounted.

A soft smirk came to Rusty.

"I asked him what he meant, and he said they looked like maybe sixteen inches? And I thought, what the hell? How would I know how big my arms are? What kind of dunce measures his own arms, for Chrissakes?"

Rusty again chuckled.

"And then I met this other guy, a handsome dude, beard, blue eyes, sexy as fuck. All he wanted to do was talk about bears. I got tired of hearing about it, but I went back to his place, anyway. I thought he'd shut the fuck up after I got his clothes off."

"Did he?" Rusty asked.

"Oh, hell no. I was in the middle of plowing him and he started wailin', 'Oh yeah, Daddy, fuck my man pussy!'" Butch rolled to his side in hysterics. "I about lost my lunch. The guy was built like a tank, and he calls himself a man pussy. And apparently, he thought I was his daddy. I couldn't stand it. I was laughin' so hard, I couldn't keep a hard-on."

Rusty about lost himself in laughter. "What'd you do?"

"I packed up my dick and went home," Butch said.

Both chuckled.

Rusty suggested that some people might think Butch was homophobic.

"Homo what?" Butch asked.

"Phobic. Someone who doesn't like gay people."

"Holy crap. There's a word for that? Good Lord." Butch laughed. "How the hell could I be homophobic about gay people? I'm a gay people. You're a gay people, for Chrissakes."

"You can be gay and still be homophobic," Rusty said.

"Well, I'm not," Butch replied.

"I'm just telling you that if you talk about certain gay guys in the way you do, someone might think you're judgmental. That's how it might sound."

Butch lurched forward, sitting up. "You know, I've never once met a man in a dress. Or in leather clothes. Not once. I know there are guys from the city who do it," he nudged Rusty, "and hopefully, you're not one of them, but I've never seen one. Not one. That is so not gonna happen out in the ranch country where I live."

Rusty crossed one leg over the other, raised his right hand near to his head, and flicked his fingers across his hair, splayed out in a delicate flourish. "And what would you do if I met you at the door in some hot little cocktail dress?"

"I will slap you on the ass and congratulate you for being who you want to be, but I won't get naked with you again. If you turn into a woman, I'll still love you, but nothin' more than that. If I was interested in having sex with a woman, I'd go find a real one," Butch said.

"Wait, wait . . . back up." Rusty climbed over top of Butch, pressing their lips together. "You love me? That's the first time you've said that."

"Yup. I said it. Remember it, because I might not say it again."

"I love you too," Rusty replied.

Morning eased its way through the bedroom window. Horses needed to be fed at the stables, but there were other men there for that. Rusty lounged late over coffee each morning, and on this day, he was still under the blankets with Butch, who, deep in thought, had worked to refine his feelings. A distant memory of an afternoon with Steve Bultemeyer clawed at his thoughts. "People need to be happy," Steve had said at a time when philosophies of that sort made a difference.

Butch rose. He looked sideways to Rusty. "You know, I got something to say. If it makes a guy happy to dress up in leather and wave his hands around like he's Donna Summer, then that's what he should do. People should live in the way that makes them happy. I'm just sayin' that if a guy is really happy bein' that way and thinks he needs to get naked with me to be even more happy, that's just not gonna happen. What makes him happy is not gonna make me happy."

"Yes, I get it," Rusty said.

"No, no, there's more. I've been thinking about this all night while you've been snoring. Guys like that are just foreign to me, you know? I mean, seriously. What would you think if you hooked up with some guy and he told you that his greatest fantasy was to do it with an Eskimo? And the hottest thing he can imagine is to take the little Eskimo man back to his igloo and strip him out of his walrus pants in the back corner, and no one takes a shower because there are no showers in an igloo, but it would just be the hottest thing if the Eskimo dude would start wailin' about Eskimo pussy."

"You've lost your mind," Rusty declared.

"No, I haven't. You'd think the man was in need of therapy. It's such a foreign thing. Maybe that sort of thing happens in the city, but it doesn't happen where I live. Some things aren't part of my world and aren't gonna give me a boner. And that doesn't make me homophobic. Or Eskimobic. I don't think less of them. I just don't want to get naked with them," Butch said.

Rusty rolled to his belly. "There's more to it than wanting to get naked. For some people, it's about companionship. Having something in common and spending life together."

"That kind of life doesn't really happen where I live," Butch said.

"Not even with me?" Rusty spoke into his pillow.

"Not even you. Sorry. But I do spend a lot of time thinkin' about you, if that helps."

"It doesn't."

25

PANSY, IN HER ROOM AT THE SISKIYOU MANOR ON A Saturday, picked up the phone on the fourth ring, as was her habit, speaking to a man from New York City whom she did not know. The caller had spoken with kindness, relaying information she might wish to hear.

The next day, she phoned the Medford auction yard. Butch was called to the office, and she laid a single sentence across the telephone line. "Your father's dead."

The calves in the holding pens bawled for their mothers. The blowflies droned everywhere one wouldn't want them, and for a brief moment, Butch thought he might heave.

"Are you okay?" he asked.

"Of course, I'm okay," Pansy replied. "He is dead to me and dead to Jehovah, as are you if you don't correct your ways." Butch could hear her breath on the line, heavy, ponderous. "I promised to tell you about your father when I was on my deathbed. I didn't know that his would come first, but here it is. He's dead, so I'll tell you what you want to know. You turned out to be just like him."

"In what way?" Butch asked.

"Your father was a queer."

"Holy shit." Butch lowered himself to a chair, unaware he was doing so. "That's why you hated him?"

"Ace was a homosexual. You know what Jehovah thinks of homosexuals," Pansy said.

"So that's his name. Ace. I never even knew his name. You never told me."

"No, I didn't. I wasn't to speak of him again, after what he did to me. But now he's dead. His name was Ace Sharkey. His roommate called yesterday. I'll give you his address."

"Thank you." Butch reached across the desk for pen and paper.

"You should see if he had any money. He might have had something, I don't know. Write this down. Are you ready?" Pansy asked.

"Yeah."

"His address is 351 East Eighty-Fifth Street, New York City," Pansy recited.

"New York City? How the hell did *that* happen?" Butch asked.

"I haven't any idea, but I've lived up to my promise. Your question has been answered."

Butch sighed. "Are you still working for Dick?"

"Dick died a few weeks ago. The same day as your father, coincidentally," Pansy said.

"Dick's dead? How?" Butch asked.

"How? I wouldn't know how. But he had the promise of eternal life, and I'll see him soon in the new system. Unfortunately, I won't see you, unless you wake up. Turning from Jehovah the way you have. The End is so close. That's all we hear from Bethel these days, about how close we are to the end of this wicked system, and you need to wake up."

"It's nice to hear from you," Butch replied gently.

Pansy's tone went cold. "You know I can't talk to you. I've already done more than you deserve with this call." The line went dead.

For a few long moments, Butch held the receiver to his ear. The tone of an abruptly ended connection echoed.

There was only one man in New York City who went by the name Ace Sharkey, and he was dead. His friend and roommate, Brad, short in stature, long and angular in features, soft in belly and demeanor, was a psychologist. Brad opened his front door to Butch's knock.

"You could scare people," he said.

Butch exhaled, and a great smile cracked his face. "Yeah, I'm a big bastard. No one fucks with me, I can tell you that." He shoved both hands in his pockets. "You called my mother, I think? I am Ace Sharkey's son."

Brad recoiled. "Are you sure?" He leaned against the door jamb. "I don't see the resemblance."

"I'm not completely sure, given that I've never met him." Butch sighed. "It's a long story. But my mother gave me his name and this address. She said you called."

"I did. She did not mention that you would visit," Brad said.

"Nah, she wouldn't talk to me long enough to even ask how I felt, or know what I would do," Butch said.

"No?" Brad looked sharply across the threshold. "Ace left documentation of a conversation with your mother. His notes mentioned your name, which is . . . ?"

"William would be the name on my driver's license. I can show you if you want . . . but I go by Butch. Butch Blackwell."

Brad nodded. "Yes, William is the name Ace had written in his notes. Did you come to get your inheritance?"

"Inheritance? Good God, of course not."

"Your father didn't have a nickel to his name. What do you know about him?" Brad asked.

"Nothing," Butch said.

"Nothing?" Brad asked, still suspicious.

"Well, I know his name, but I just learned that last week, thanks to you. My mother wouldn't talk about him. I know nothing about him except for his name, and this address. And that he was gay," Butch said.

"Well, that's a start. I'm gay, just so you know," Brad said. "I hope that is not a problem for you."

"Oh, hell no," Butch said. "I'm gay, too. That's kind of why I came, I think."

"You're gay?" Brad asked.

"Well, I am this year. But I might join the Jehovah's Witnesses next year. They could probably turn me straight," Butch said casually.

Stunned silence.

"That's a joke. It's supposed to be funny," Butch said.

A soft harrumph coughed from Brad's throat. "Thanks for letting me know." He suggested that Ace might have pushed harder to meet his son, had he known. "Your father might have wished to know. It appeared to me, from his notes, that your mother wouldn't allow him to see you. Would she have done that?"

"Most likely. My mother hated him," Butch answered.

"Well, I didn't know anything until I came across the letter he had written—similar to a will, except your dad didn't need a will," Brad said.

Brad looked Butch up and down, then said, "His voice was deep, similar to yours." He sighed, then said, "No one ever knew that Ace Sharkey had a son . . . and the kid is gay." He murmured, "Unbelievable," under his breath, then opened his door wide. "Come on in," he said. "I've got some pictures if you'd like them, perhaps my final gift to Ace."

Butch took a step inside. "Were you more than friends? You know what I mean?"

"'More than friends?'" Brad repeated. He looked askance; his brow furrowed. "How old are you?"

"Thirty-six. Why?" Butch asked.

"The word I think you're looking for is 'partners,'" Brad stated. "Or 'lovers', for those who prefer that. But no, we weren't lovers. Ace was my best friend. We met thirty years ago, but that's all. But it's unusual for a gay man of your age to have difficulty with that concept."

"Yeah," Butch chuckled. "I've heard that before, but it's not where I come from, you know? There's not a lot of homosexual lovers where I come from."

"Point taken." Brad again looked at Butch, inspecting his cowboy boots and Wranglers. "You don't look anything like your father."

"No?" Butch answered, "Well, I guess that's something to know about him."

"Your dad was tall like you, but rail thin."

"I look like my mother. I'd be fuckin' ugly if I was a woman. Just like my mother," Butch said.

Brad raised his chin ever so slightly. Butch was not his patient, he recognized. "That's not a kind thing to say about your mother."

"No? Well, she's not a kind woman," Butch replied. He softened. "She's big and blocky, like me."

"Why don't we just say that she would make an ugly drag queen if we dressed her up? As would you. That might be a little

261

less offensive to your mother. I take it you have unresolved issues with her," Brad stated.

Butch laughed. "That's puttin' it mildly, but I like that drag queen comment. I'd make one ugly drag queen. Gotta remember that."

Brad pointed to a chair. "Have a seat if you like." Butch did. For minutes after, there was some slight shifting in the room. His eyes roamed the interior. Oil paintings hung on walls. Contemporary art. White gauzy curtains were hung long, their ends pooling on the floor.

"How did you find my mom?" Butch asked.

"Ace had tracked you down at some point. He took notes of it, of all things. I'll give them to you. There was an address in Fresno, and then another in Farnsworth. It only took a minute to call the operator and ask for a phone number."

"How did he die?" Butch asked.

"He got run over at the corner of Seventh and Christopher. Or Fourth and Christopher. It's a cluster fuck of corners there . . . someone was bound to get killed. We scattered his ashes out by Staten Island, three days after. My father is still angry about that. We're Jewish," Brad explained.

"Jewish? Like the guys walkin' around in black with the funny hair? I saw some today. With hats. They're Jews, right?" He pulled back, puzzled. "How come you don't look like them?"

"There are different kinds of Jews. I'm not Orthodox," Brad answered.

"Sorry. Didn't mean to be rude," Butch said.

"You weren't rude. Just uneducated, perhaps."

"But how can there be different kinds of Jews? If a religion is the truth, you'd think there would only be one version of it," Butch reasoned.

"Well, that, perhaps, is the most honest question to ask of religion," Brad replied in the crisp enunciation of an educated man. "But you'll have to ask it of someone else. I am not an apologist for faith."

"Sorry. Was there a service?" Butch asked.

"No. Your father was a quiet man. Didn't have many close friends. He lived quietly. Minimally. I don't think he ever had expectations for anything bigger or different than who he was." Brad rose and led the way to the other side of the room. At an elaborate bookcase built into the wall on both sides of the fire-place, he opened a drawer. "I have a few things you might like."

He handed over a small piece of silver jewelry, tarnished with age, a turquoise chip mounted in the center. "That's your dad's ring. Said he got it in San Francisco, back in the '60s, I think. You can have it, if you like."

Butch set it on the tip of his pinky. "Well, I guess that tells me something about my dad's hands. This is never gonna make it on my finger."

"And he had this." Brad lifted a porcelain ornament from the mantle and handed it to Butch. "Ace always referred to it as a God doll. It came from someone he once knew, but he never said who that was. It was important to him, though he never said why."

"Son of a bitch," Butch mused. He turned it over, rubbed his hand over the glassy finish, and inhaled deeply. "This belonged to my mother. It came from her mother."

"Well, there it is. An answer to where the God doll came from. Maybe you should send it back to her," Brad suggested.

Butch shook his head. "Nah, we had two of them when I was a kid. She bashed 'em to pieces in the kitchen with a skillet. Scared the hell out of me. She carried the mess outside after she killed them. Had to get Satan out of her house, she said."

"Satan?" Brad asked.

"The Jehovah's Witnesses told her they were from Satan. One of the elders told her she had to destroy everything that was Catholic, so that's what she did. We did what we were told as Witnesses."

Brad raised his brow. "You're a Jehovie? Goodness . . . I chase them off my doorstep all the time. Can't understand their insistence that they must convert me."

"No, no. Good Lord. I'm not a Witness. I grew up that way, but they kicked me out for," he raised his fingers in mock quotes, "conduct unbecoming of a Jehovah's Witness."

Brad squinted; one eyebrow remained upwards.

"They caught me making out with someone," Butch explained.

"They kicked you out for *kissing?*"

Butch nodded. "Yup."

"Boy or girl?" Brad asked.

"Boy. Obviously," Butch answered.

Brad's belly rolled in laughter. "Right. *Obviously*. That's the word I would have used, too." Waves of giggling consumed him. "Maybe you should take a look at yourself in the mirror. There's one, right over there." He gestured behind Butch. "Obviously," he repeated. "That's the funniest thing I've heard all day. And as for the God dolls, your mother sounds as if she may have some deep-seated neurosis of some kind."

"I think it was the Jahoovers. They gave her some craziness," Butch said.

"Perhaps, but I've found that people who embrace those sorts of callings usually choose one that fits who they are." Brad went into his therapist role, which he knew well. "Rarely does one become mentally unstable because of religion. More often they choose one that gives confirmation for how they wish to be. But that's not really my concern. She is not here to account for how she feels, but here's what I am most intrigued by."

"What's that?" Butch asked.

"Murdering the things in the kitchen sounds a little superfluous, don't you think?" They broke out in laughter.

"My mom turned into a nutcase from that religion. Or maybe she was a nutcase before, as you say. I don't really know," Butch said.

"Perhaps you should discuss that with her," Brad suggested.

"Nope. Not gonna happen. She disowned me when I was eighteen."

"It sounds as if your mother failed as a parent."

"Nah, I think my mother was a decent mother. Hell, a good mother, maybe, when I was growing up."

Butch again turned the God doll in his hands, rolling it around his thick fingers, pondering the holiness of a fragile object. "I remember the day she smashed them. Calm, she was. Like it was the most normal thing to beat the shit out of some Catholic dolls in your kitchen. Funny that my dad would keep this, something that came from my grandmother who he never knew. I never knew her, either. I guess this will be the only thing I have from her."

"She's dead now, I would imagine?" Brad asked.

"Oh, yeah. My grandfather pushed her off the balcony when my mom was a kid."

"Oy! Well, that's a story to tell." Brad nodded to the God doll. "Well at least you have it now, and you know where it came from. That's a good thing." He moved to the hallway. "Follow me."

They walked to a small bedroom at the back. "Do you know anything about Catholicism?"

"The Witnesses think the Catholics are about as close to the devil as you can get," Butch replied.

"Is that so? Well, I know a little about the Catholics, so I'm guessing that little doll is a saint of some sort. She most certainly has a name. If you knew her name, it might tell you why he kept her," Brad said.

"A name? God, I wouldn't have a clue. Wouldn't have occurred to me that it would have a name."

"Well, not in the way you might think. Not Veronica, for example. But she's most likely a replica of a person who was canonized as a saint. I don't know that for a fact, given that I'm a Jewish man from Queens, but I think that's how those things work. Might be useful to know who that doll represents. It might explain why your father kept her."

Butch again turned it over, almost caressing the coldness of its garment, then looked to Brad, a smile on his face. "Or maybe she just got caught up in my dad's luggage, and he never thought to throw her out."

Brad's eyes went distant. "The whole thing is remarkably sad, isn't it? Life is an extraordinary gift, and your father's history and experiences have been lost forever. He had a journey that he kept secret, and now he's dead, and you will never know why he kept that silly God doll. Why did she matter to him, I wonder?"

Butch sat on the bed, then set the figurine on the table next to him. "You know, I'm a simple man. I don't believe in God, so I can't imagine it means a thing if she has a name. But it's meaningful to know that this came from my grandmother, who I never met. That's important, and I'm happy to have it. Thank you for that."

"You are welcome," Brad nodded.

"Did he ever have someone? A 'lover,' as you call it?" Butch asked.

"No. It was kind of sad, really, at least from the perspective that most people might describe their circumstances. But I don't believe he was saddened by it. He certainly didn't exhibit any mental health issues that caused me concern for his well-being."

Butch retreated to his own thoughts, and silence consumed the room. A minute of silence is a long time, from the perspective of two people who have just met. He settled into a contemplation of his feelings and the connection to a man he'd never met.

"I think I'm like him," he eventually said.

"In what way?"

"Ever since I was a teenager, I've known who I am, but never felt like I needed anyone to share it. I've always known what gives me a hard-on, but it's not all that often when I need someone else to take care of it. I've never thought seriously about spending my life with anyone. I think I'm happier by myself," Butch said.

"If the right person were to come along, that philosophy might prevent you from recognizing it," Brad suggested.

"Some people are better off single. You're single . . . must be a reason for that," Butch countered.

Brad raised his head. "I spent twenty-two years with a wonderful man. Lost him five years ago."

"Oh. Sorry," Butch said.

"Those were the best years of my life."

"Sorry."

"Have you ever been with a woman?" Brad asked, changing the subject. "Sexually?"

"Nah. I know who I am. And I have met someone. He's been after me for years. The same guy who got me kicked out of the Jehovah's Witnesses for kissing twenty years ago. I should probably thank him for that. God only knows how shitty it'd be if I still belonged to them," Butch admitted.

"What's he like?"

"He's a good man. Anyone would be lucky to have him, but he's stuck on owning me for some reason," Butch answered.

"Why won't you let him?"

"I've messed that up more times than I can count. He usually ends up with someone else, but they never last long. He's got money, came from his parents, but you wouldn't know that if you met him. But he does, and you know, what's he gonna do with me? I'm too broke to fit into his world."

"That probably doesn't matter to him, if he's what you say," Brad suggested.

"I can barely afford the gas to go visit, and when I get there, I'm so broke that I can't afford dinner," Butch explained. "I'm poor. I sold my best deer rifle to a friend just to pay for the airline ticket for this trip. I have no clue how I'm going to buy it back from him, and then the hotel, which is frickin' outrageous, is going on my credit card that I have no idea how I'm going to pay. I found the cheapest hotel I could find, and it's a fuckin' dump. Shocked the shit out of me when I got in there this morning."

"Welcome to New York," Brad said consolingly.

"I'll figure it out when I get home," Butch replied.

"Where are you staying?"

"Staten Suites, in a shitty part of town, I think. It was the third hotel I stopped in to ask for rates—blew my mind how much a damn hotel cost here. Fifty bucks a night!"

"Well, perhaps I can assist you with that. You are welcome to spend the night in your father's room. That should be an experience for you," Brad predicted.

Butch blinked at the unfathomable gift.

"You're sitting on his bed," Brad said.

"Seriously?" Butch turned to the headboard. He ran his hand over the bedding, as if searching for the warmth of a departed soul.

"How many nights are you here for?"

"Three, counting tonight. But I've already checked into the hotel for today."

"But you can check out in the morning. You can stay for both nights, if you wish."

"You know, not a lot of people open their doors to strangers and say, 'Come on in.' Thank you for that." Butch smiled at the man who had been his father's best friend.

"You're very welcome," Brad replied. A soft wave of gratitude came over him, in remembrance of his friend. "I'm pleased to be of assistance to Ace Sharkey's son. I don't believe you're anything like what he might have imagined, but he would be pleased at who you are, I think. You seem like a good man."

Butch lowered his head slightly.

"All right," Brad continued. "Why don't you go explore the city. I'll see you here in the morning. If you show up any time after 8 a.m., I'll be presentable enough to entertain properly."

Butch entered a long, dark tunnel on his first subway ride, then leaned against the light post for a half hour at the corner of Seventh and Christopher. There was nothing to mark the spot for a life that was extinguished there. He imagined strangers reaching out to him in conversation, in compassion, to engage in his story. His father's story, but none did. He moved on. There was nothing there to see.

In Washington Square, he sat to rest on a park bench. Marooned there by the NYU alumni club's kilted bagpipers, their wailing filled his ears, and he pondered the words of his father's friend. *Life is an extraordinary gift,* Brad had said. A silly idea, Butch concluded. The bagpipe band moved on through the park. Life was not a gift, he was certain. Bagpipes. Now there was a gift.

Back on a Christopher Street corner, Butch wondered how

his father could have found himself at home here. The over-whelming crush of humanity swept by, unstoppable.

A younger man, a beautiful man, perhaps thirty, strode across Christopher to the Hot Video porn store. Butch followed, then shadowed him through the maze of arcade stalls in its basement.

The pervasive stench of sweat and cum could knock a man to the floor. Dark-haired, somber, and with smoldering eyes, the man was flawless. *A larger reflection of Miles Knickerbocker,* Butch thought. Other men, cloaked in anonymity, squeaked their shoes across sticky linoleum in search of activity behind locked stall doors. The big Italian had stopped and leaned into a dark corner. The arcade hunters paid him no attention.

How could a man of this sort be ignored? Butch made his way to that corner, then leaned against the wall.

"Two hundred fifty," the man said.

The next morning, Butch returned to Brad's apartment and joined him for coffee. Brad had laid some photos across his dining room table.

The long scream of sirens raged through an open window. Three police cars flew down the street. Butch leaned back in his chair. "Don't know how a man can live in a place like this. You'd never feel a moment of peace."

Brad assured him that people could get used to it.

"I'm still trying to figure out how my mom, who grew up in Denver, met my dad, who lived here. Did he ever say anything about that?" Butch inquired.

"Your father grew up in Salt Lake City. He left, he said, to get away from the Mormons. That's all I know," Brad said.

"Salt Lake City? Jesus. How did the two of them get together to make me? My mother was never in Salt Lake City. She grew up in Denver," Butch said.

"I can't help you there," Brad conceded.

"You know, I always thought that people who are trying to figure out where they're going have an easier time if they know where they came from. I don't know that I'll ever know where I came from," Butch said somberly.

"It may not have been a place where you, or them, had wanted to be," Brad mused.

Butch nodded. "True." He sighed and set his empty coffee cup on Brad's table. "I suppose I could say that I came from the man who raised me. Steve Bultemeyer. He was a good man. A good cowboy. It wouldn't be so bad to think that I came from him."

Brad nodded. "Sounds like a healthy resolution." Ever the therapist, he then asked, "Have you ever read up on Maslow's Hierarchy?"

"Maslow's *what?*"

"Maslow was a psychologist who theorized that we have certain needs, and some of those needs take precedence over others. Self-actualization can only come after the fulfillment of the most basic needs. Love and belonging can only be achieved after those basic needs have been met." Brad then pointed out that some reading on the subject might be helpful.

26

THE DEATH NOTICE ARRIVED ON A FRIDAY IN A PLAIN white envelope, hand addressed in a woman's flowing penmanship, blue ink, with "PRYOR HASLIP—ATTORNEY AT LAW" professionally printed in cold block type in the upper left corner. Inside, a short paragraph offered simple condolences for the death of Rex Pullman. A second paragraph requested that Butch pay a visit to the Yreka office for the review of the dispositive provisions of the Pullman estate.

It was too late to call, Butch thought. *Law firms are not open on Friday evenings, are they?* No, they aren't, he confirmed by dialing the number.

On Monday, Butch walked in the front door of Pryor Haslip's legal office.

Ever arrogant, Pryor dispensed the details of Rex's death. A temporary space heater inside his camper had drowned Rex in carbon monoxide, he said.

"Poisoned," Pryor stated. "And the man left everything he owns to you."

"Holy shit!" Butch muttered. "Seriously? Why?"

"Precisely." Pryor laid paperwork across his desk in the manner that suited his philosophies of wealth. "It's a simple estate. Rex had a retirement plan at Yreka Savings, which can be closed out today. You're the direct beneficiary, so you only need to deliver the death certificate and ask the bank to cash the account out for you. It's as simple as that."

Butch's mind went blank.

"The balance is over seventy thousand, if you're wondering," Pryor said.

"Okay," Butch whispered.

"Rex held the house in trust, so there's no probate or court involvement. You're the only beneficiary, so the house will belong to you." He pushed an envelope across the table. "The keys are in there. We'll be going through everything next week."

"Why are you going through everything, if it belongs to me?" Butch asked.

Pryor laid his pen on the desk. "I am the trustee. I have the authority to carry out the provisions of the trust. You are the beneficiary, which means I am responsible for carrying out the intentions of the trust in a manner that is in your best interest. Rex gifted all the household contents to Goodwill, anything that you do not wish to have, so they'll send a truck next week to clear it out. You're welcome to take anything you wish before then. I don't imagine you would want his socks, but I have no reason to tell you that you can't have them."

"Rex had a few guns I wouldn't mind having. I sold one to him last year when I was broke. Was my best gun. I hope he still has it."

Pryor nodded at the envelope on the table. "You have the keys. Feel free to take what you like." He leaned back in his chair. His tone became inquisitive, suspicious. "Rex came to my office to draft the trust after Joyce had passed. He said there was a kid he wanted to leave everything to, but you're not a kid." He leaned forward. "You've known Rex for a while, I'm guessing?"

Butch propped a boot up on one knee, reminiscing about the man who was now dead. "Yeah. I met him when I was eighteen," Butch answered.

"It's unusual, wouldn't you think?" Pryor asked.

"Unusual, how?" Butch replied.

"For a man to leave such a gift to someone who wasn't family."

"He didn't have family," Butch stated.

The attorney had folded his hands together, resting them at his chin.

"Rex was a good man. His wife was a good lady, too. They were very kind to me," Butch explained.

"Ahh. Well, I guess that explains things. They never had children of their own. Rex has left you a very significant gift. You will appreciate it, I hope. It will take a few weeks for the county to process the transfer to your name, but once the deed has been recorded, the property will officially be yours. I assume you'll move into it?" Pryor inquired.

"Not a chance. I grew up in Dick Stinchfield's little green house, his parents' house, in Farnsworth. I drove by it last year when I was in town. It's pink. My mother worked at Stinchfield's campground. Not interested in coming back to any of that," Butch stated.

Pryor nodded.

"Can I sell the house? Rex's house?" Butch asked.

"Of course. As trustee, I can list it for sale anytime you like if that is your intention. It would save some time, to avoid re-titling it into your name. The house will probably sell for fifty thousand. My granddaughter, Stephanie, is a realtor. You might know her," Pryor said.

"Her name doesn't sound familiar," Butch replied. "But if you can ask her to help me with this, I'd just as soon get it done."

"I'll get Stephanie over there in the next couple of days to take pictures and draw up the paperwork. In the meantime, the retirement plan is out of my hands. You'll have to take care of that at the bank. You can walk over there with this copy of the death certificate." He slid the single page, a description of the vitals on a legal green background, across the desk.

Butch pulled it to himself.

Pryor placed the cap on his pen, then clipped it into the front pocket of his shirt. He pulled his tie straight, laying the tail flat in his lap. "If you worked at Dick's campground, you might want to know that he left the property to the Jehovah's Witnesses when he died. Stephanie's been after them ever since, trying to get the listing. She's even sent letters back to the headquarters in New York, but they won't sell."

"I drove by it this morning. It's a mess. Can't imagine why they would pay property taxes on vacant property they could sell," Butch said.

"Taxes? A church doesn't pay taxes," Pryor replied.

"Not even property taxes?"

"Of course not. God doesn't pay taxes, of any sort," Pryor explained.

Butch snorted. "The Jehovah's Witnesses don't have anything to do with God. It's all a crock of shit, if you ask me."

"I didn't ask, but I share your opinion," Pryor said.

"I used to be one of them. That's how we knew Dick. We all went to the Kingdom Hall, here in Yreka," Butch said.

"That shut down a few years ago."

"No kidding? Where'd they move to?" Butch asked.

"Couldn't tell you. The place just fizzled out. There aren't a lot of people around here willing to buy into that bullshit. Live forever in paradise, my ass," Pryor said.

"Ahh, you must have read their magazines."

Pryor rose from his desk, then strode to the window that overlooked Miner Street. "Dick tried to convert my mother. Started dumpin' literature in her lap. I told Dick I would put a bullet in his fuckin' head if he ever came back. And now his old Kingdom Hall is a Blockbuster Video. Stephanie sold that for them a few years ago, but they won't sell the campground."

"So, what's the story with Dick's house in Farnsworth? The damn thing is pink. I can't see the Witnesses painting anything pink. Pink isn't really their color," Butch stated.

"The Jehovah's Witnesses don't own it. Dick gave it to a couple of women from Oregon. He lived with them for the last few months before he died, is what I understand. They moved into it after he'd been buried. They didn't like green, I guess." He turned from the window. "They told everyone they were sisters."

"Well, that's a nice thing," Butch said.

"They didn't look like sisters."

Pryor returned to his desk but remained standing. "They didn't last long. Moved out, a couple months after the house turned pink. They still own the place, but it's been vacant ever since."

He leaned into his hands, splaying them flat on the edge of his desk. "I can tell you though, it would have been big news in town if I'd told anyone how Dick died. You know anything about that?"

"About what?" Butch asked.

"Dick's death. You know anything about that?" Pryor pressed.

Butch shook his head, no.

The lawyer's eyes narrowed into the maddening fury of a

man who believes he has been wronged. "When the bastard got sick, he walked away from the campground and went to Medford. He died up there."

"He died in Medford? Well, hell, that's too bad. I would have gone to see him, if I'd known," Butch said.

"You would have visited him?" Pryor's eyebrows arched.

"Of course. Dick brought me and my mother to Farnsworth when I was a kid. I didn't like that man, but I would have gone to see him if I'd known he was sick." Butch paused and looked out through the north-facing window. "The older I get, the more it seems that the most terrible thing a man can go through is to die alone."

Pryor spat. "Well, of course he died alone! Wouldn't expect anything else. That's why he kept it a big damn secret. People around here wouldn't stand for that kind of trouble in this community."

"What kind of trouble?" Butch asked.

"You didn't know?" Pryor asked.

Butch shook his head.

"Dick Stinchfield died of AIDS." Pryor again spat.

A cold fear fell over Butch.

Pryor nodded toward a room on the other side of a closed door. "I handled the probate for his estate. Got a copy of his death certificate right over there in my files. The son of a bitch went up to Medford and hid with those two women. Just goes to show, you never know what kind of secrets a man might have." He returned to his chair, leaned into its back, and again peaked his hands at the fingertips. "Seems to me, to your point, that the most terrible thing that can happen to a man is to die alone from a dirty secret. The good people around here won't put up with any of those in this town. Dick was the only one, as far as we know, and good riddance to him." Pryor leaned forward, looking as if he might rise. "You want to see the death certificate?"

"No," Butch said. He wouldn't. He stood to leave and looked at Pryor, searching hard as if looking for the back of the old man's eyes. "I would have gone to see him," he stated. "Or someone else should have gone to see him. *You* could have gone to see him. No one deserves to die alone."

Rex Pullman's house smelled of manly things. Tobacco smoke. Old Spice cologne. Tanned deer hide. Gone were the extravagances of a woman's taste. Wooden replicas of chickens, decorated pink and blue, swaddled in red ribbon with short shafts of wheat, no longer hung on walls. A simple man, Rex had never been afflicted with desires to collect or hoard. His possessions had been whittled down to the needs of a man who believes he has enough.

Butch had stopped at Yreka Savings that afternoon, then went to Rex's house and sorted through the living room and kitchen, twice sitting on the couch to absorb the loss of a man he had loved but wouldn't have uttered those words to. He imagined Joyce there, the kind woman who had once called this home her own—but couldn't see her mark anywhere. It was the home of a single man, in its entirety.

He entered the only bedroom. Joyce's acorn quilt lay across the bed.

He bundled it into his arms and closed his eyes for a moment, recalling earlier times.

An Oregon Fish and Game jacket lay on the floor. In the closet, a collection of ball caps, stained with sweat, hung on the backside of the door. A twelve-gauge shotgun, three deer rifles, and a couple small-bore guns leaned in the corner. A note tied to the trigger guard of one: "For Butch. Saved it for you."

He folded the quilt into a square, then laid it on the passenger side of his truck. He pointed the guns muzzle-down, their stocks cradled against the quilt, then took a slower investigation of the house, finding no other items that he wanted. He locked its doors.

Standing out front, looking west to the dimming Siskiyous as the sun settled over top, he abruptly turned and walked to Ms. Walker's home, two blocks south. The heady scent of a blood peach filled his nose, but only in remembrance. There were no hints of fruit trees in back. A bedroom addition now sprawled across the former expanse of her garden. The graciousness of a kind woman, long gone, only existed in his memory. He smiled at what once was.

There was a new convenience store on Ball Mountain Road, at the corner of Sixth. He backed his truck into the southern corner and fingered his inheritance check, watching visitors come and go. A battered blue Toyota pulled in and parked opposite the entrance. His mother got out and then walked inside. She was not as tall as he remembered.

Pansy was gray. Hunched, perhaps. Heavier, maybe. Dressed in the style he remembered her to favor, which was bulky. Loose.

Butch left his truck, then stood in front, thinking she might notice when she returned to her car. Pansy returned with a diet soda in hand and, for what felt an excruciatingly long moment to her, gazed at him, stiffened in recognition. She gave thought to the promises of her faith.

Pansy climbed into her car and grasped its steering wheel, then looked to Butch in her rearview mirror, still leaning against the grill guard of his Ford. She turned the key in the ignition.

Ugly words came to mind. Words she had uttered in the past. When she pulled from the parking lot, her jaw clenched tight.

Butch folded the check and pushed it into his wallet. Sometimes, you gotta let things go. He looked down at his watch: 7:45 p.m. Medford was an hour away. Placer County was possible before midnight.

Chances were, a good man was waiting for him at the Baldwin Ranch.

THANK YOU!

Thank you for reading! If you enjoyed this book, please leave a review on Amazon, Goodreads, BookBub, The Story Graph, or anywhere else you like to track your recent reads. Alternatively, you could post online or tell a friend about it. This helps our authors more than you may know.

- The Team at Torchflame Books

ABOUT THE AUTHOR

Scott Terry was raised as a Jehovah's Witness, and spent his childhood praying for God and Armageddon to heal him of his homosexual thoughts. At the age of sixteen, he escaped from the Witness religion and was riding bulls in the rodeo as a gay cowboy.

Scott's memoir, (*Cowboys, Armageddon, and The Truth*) was named one of the Top 20 Must Read Books of 2013 by *Advocate* magazine. It was named one of the best LGBT releases of 2012 by Out In Print and Band of Thebes book lists, and was a double-award winner of the Rainbow Book Awards (Best Gay Debut, and Best LGBT Non-Fiction, 2013). Scott has written often for the *San Francisco Chronicle*, and his essays have been featured in the *Huffington Post, Gay & Lesbian Review*, and *Alternet Magazine*, amongst others.

Scott's rodeo gear, clothing, and championship buckles are in the permanent collection of the Autry Museum of the American West (Los Angeles), and are currently on display in the museum's *Imagined Wests* exhibit. He and his husband operate an organic farm in the San Francisco Bay Area.

REFERENCES

EVIL SPIRITS IN HOUSES AND OBJECTS:

"Repelling the Attack of Wicked Spirits: Investigating House and Household Objects," *Watchtower*, Dec 15, 1966.

MALE AUTHORITY OVER WOMEN:

"I Do Not Permit a Woman . . . to Exercise Authority over a Man—Why?" *Awake!*, August 22, 1967.

PREDICTING THE END OF THE WICKED SYSTEM:

"Is It Later than You Think? Is Time Running Out for This Generation? What will the 1970s Bring?" *Awake!*, October 8, 1968.

WICKED WORKS:

"Remain Healthy in Faith: Your Faith and Works," *Watchtower*, Jun 1, 1970.

SELLING HOMES BEFORE ARMAGEDDON:

"How Are You Using Your Life?" *Kingdom Ministry*, May 1974.

MORE FROM SCOTT TERRY

COWBOYS, ARMAGEDDON, AND THE TRUTH

An illuminating glimpse into a child's sequestered world of abuse, homophobia, and religious extremism. Terry's memoir is a compelling, poignant and occasionally humorous look into the Jehovah's Witness faith—a religion that refers to itself as The Truth—and a brave account of Terry's successful escape from a troubled past. He eventually left the Witness faith to become a cowboy, riding bulls in the rodeo.